"Monsieur Secre-
tary General of the U.N. was on the line. "I am sure by
now you have heard of the events which have transpired
over the past twelve hours."

"What do you mean?"

"My men have in each of the locations dozens of small
packages of plutonium attached to high-explosive
charges. These bombs, which are arranged so as to do
maximal damage to the oil fields, will be set off if anyone tries to attack or otherwise interfere with my men."

"But . . . but that is insane!" Chapelle argued. "That
would ruin most of the world's oil supply for generations."

"I am glad you understand," El Farrar said, all hint of
civility gone from his voice.

"All right, it seems we are at an impasse. What are
your demands?"

"Not now, Chapelle. First, I am going to airlift in some
more troops to each location, just to be sure you don't
try anything stupid. Would you be so kind as to instruct
all of the nations involved not to attempt any interference
with the planes delivering my troops?"

"You know I cannot tell sovereign nations what to do
with their airspace," Chapelle reasoned.

"Then, just inform them that if they do interfere with
any of my transports, I will explode my bombs and render their oil fields useless to them."

"But that would mean killing your own men."

"My men are perfectly willing to martyr themselves
in a good cause. I will contact you once again when my
men are in place. And Chapelle . . ."

"Yes?"

"I would advise you to keep the General Assembly in
close attendance. You will soon have some momentous
decisions to make."

BOOK YOUR PLACE ON OUR WEBSITE AND MAKE THE READING CONNECTION!

We've created a customized website just for our very special readers, where you can get the inside scoop on everything that's going on with Zebra, Pinnacle and Kensington books.

When you come online, you'll have the exciting opportunity to:

- View covers of upcoming books
- Read sample chapters
- Learn about our future publishing schedule (listed by publication month *and author*)
- Find out when your favorite authors will be visiting a city near you
- Search for and order backlist books from our online catalog
- Check out author bios and background information
- Send e-mail to your favorite authors
- Meet the Kensington staff online
- Join us in weekly chats with authors, readers and other guests
- Get writing guidelines
- AND MUCH MORE!

**Visit our website at
http://www.kensingtonbooks.com**

ENEMY IN THE ASHES

WILLIAM W. JOHNSTONE

PINNACLE BOOKS
Kensington Publishing Corp.
http://www.kensingtonbooks.com

ZEBRA BOOKS are published by

Kensington Publishing Corp.
850 Third Avenue
New York, NY 10022

Copyright © 2002 by William W. Johnstone

All rights reserved. No part of this book may be reproduced in any form or by any means without the prior written consent of the Publisher, excepting brief quotes used in reviews.

If you purchased this book without a cover you should be aware that this book is stolen property. It was reported as "unsold and destroyed" to the Publisher and neither the Author nor the Publisher has received any payment for this "stripped book."

All Kensington Titles, Imprints, and Distributed Lines are available at special quantity discounts for bulk purchases for sales promotions, premiums, fund raising, educational, or institutional use.

Special book excerpts or customized printings can also be created to fit specific needs. For details, write or phone the office of the Kensington Special Sales Manager: Kensington Publishing Corp., 850 Third Avenue, New York, NY 10022. Attn. Special Sales Department. Phone: 1-800-221-2647.

Pinnacle and the P logo Reg. U.S. Pat. & TM Off.

First Printing: September 2002
10 9 8 7 6 5 4 3 2 1

Printed in the United States of America

To Angus, a loyal friend and a gentle companion.

ONE

Claire Osterman drummed her fingers on her desk as her cold eyes roamed over the men sitting in her office. She'd called a meeting of her cabinet officers to discuss their current situation, and she wasn't happy with the news they'd been giving her.

Herb Knoff, her bodyguard and sometime lover, sat on her left, as usual. He was a large man with broad shoulders, coal-black hair, and a boyish face that belied his violent and unforgiving nature. The other men serving under Claire knew he was mean as a snake when riled, so they tried their best never to make him angry.

Claire glanced at Herb, a scornful expression on her face. "Herb," she asked in a low, dangerous voice, "can you believe this shit they're giving me?"

Herb smirked, shaking his head. "No, ma'am," he answered, his eyes narrow and flat.

Harley Millard, Claire's official second in command in the government, even though he was a weak, mild-mannered man who was completely under Claire's thumb, held up his hand. "Now, Claire," he protested in his usual whining voice, "you asked us how things were. It's not our fault the situation is so bad."

Wallace W. Cox, Claire's Minister of Finance, cleared his throat and added, "That's right, Claire. Things could be a lot worse. If Ben Raines and the troops from the SUSA hadn't intervened and helped us defeat those Middle Eastern terrorists, we could all be speaking Arabic now."

Claire fixed him with a steely glare. "How could things be worse, Wally? We may have won the war, but now you assholes sit here and tell me we're dead broke."

She stared at the other ministers in the room. "Hell, what good is it to win the war if we aren't left with enough money in the treasury to run the country?"

Clifford Ainsworth, Minister of Propaganda, nodded his head. "It's true that the treasury is at very low levels, Claire, but we weren't in good shape even before the invasion by El Farrar's men. I'm afraid if we don't do something soon, the people are not going to stand for more restrictions in governmental services."

"Cliff's right," Gerald Boykin, Minister of Defense, agreed. "My troops haven't received a paycheck in over a month. I don't know how much longer we'll be able to keep the soldiers in uniform if we don't come up with some way to pay them what we owe them."

Claire turned back to Cox. "I thought the United Nations had agreed to a loan package, Wally. Won't that help to bail us out until we can get the economy moving again?"

"It'll help some, Claire, but with half the country on welfare, the money they've promised us won't last six months."

"What the hell's wrong with everybody?" Claire asked, rolling her eyes. "Doesn't anyone want to work anymore?"

Ainsworth smirked. "Why should they, Claire, when welfare pays them more for sitting home on their butts than they can make with a job?"

Claire stared hard at Ainsworth for a moment, and then she slammed her hand down on her desk. "Damn it, I'm tired of being told there's no money in the treasury and the government has to cut back while these layabouts are living off the government's tit. Cliff, I want you to announce immediately that due to the current emergency, all welfare checks will be cut by twenty percent."

Ainsworth's eyes opened wide. "But, Claire, that'll cause riots in the streets."

She smiled grimly. "Good, then stopping them will give Boykin's troops something to do to earn their paychecks."

She got to her feet and leaned forward, her hands on her desk. "Now, get out of here and find me some way to get more money into our coffers—raise taxes or levy fines or something. The government cannot function without money!"

Her cabinet members rose from their chairs, casting worried looks at one another as they filed out of her office.

Claire took a deep breath and stretched her arms out over her head. "Damn, these meetings always make me tense," she said, glancing at Herb Knoff, still sitting next to her. She gave him a half smile. "How about a massage for your boss?" she asked with a lascivious grin.

He returned the look. "Anytime is a good time for a full-body rubdown, Claire."

She moved from behind the desk, took his hand, and led him into her living quarters adjacent to the office. As she went through the door, she began to unbutton her blouse.

Suddenly, a man dressed all in soldier's fatigues stepped from behind the door and whipped his left arm around Herb's forehead, stretching his head back while he put a long, curved knife to his neck.

"Holy shit!" Herb grunted, standing still as the razor-sharp blade drew a few drops of blood from his neck.

Claire whirled around, her hands going to her face. "What the hell's the meaning of this?" she almost shouted.

"My name is Muhammad Atwa," the man said in a heavy accent. "I have a proposition for you, but I first need your assurance you will not summon help."

"How did you get in here?" Claire asked, her eyes flicking toward the phone on her bedside table.

Atwa moved the knife suggestively. "Please do not attempt to call for help," he said. "I am not afraid to die, and I most surely will kill you both before your guards arrive."

"I asked you how you got in here."

He shrugged, his lips curled in a cruel smirk. "Your soldiers are very lazy. Anyone in a uniform is allowed to pass almost without questions."

Claire sighed and sat on the edge of her bed. "What is it exactly you want?"

Atwa reached around Herb's chest, took the pistol from his shoulder holster under his coat, and motioned for him to join Claire on the bed. Once Herb was sitting next to her, Atwa sat on a chair across the room and leaned back, crossing his legs with the pistol resting on his knee, the barrel pointed at them.

"I represent an organization called Al Qa'eda, based in Afghanistan."

"Al-Qa'eda?" Claire asked, her brow furrowed. "I thought we got rid of them back in the early part of the century."

Atwa smiled again, though without the slightest bit of

ENEMY IN THE ASHES

humor in his eyes. "Yes, that is what you thought. You did manage to kill our leader, Osama bin Laden, but we had others ready to take his place."

"And what proposition does Al Qa'eda have for the United States?" Claire asked.

"A friend of our organization, Abdullah El Farrar, has come to us with a plan to bring the world to its knees."

"El Farrar?" Herb asked. "Wasn't he the crazy bastard who led the terrorist attack against us this year?"

Atwa shrugged. "A misguided effort, as it turned out. He had neither the troops nor the matériel to complete his mission, though I think he would have succeeded had it not been for Ben Raines and the SUSA's intervention."

"I doubt it," Claire said. "We would have beaten him even without Raines and his troops. It would just have taken a little longer."

Atwa smiled again, showing he didn't believe her. "At any rate, the SUSA and the U.N. have frozen all of El Farrar's family's assets, and he is angry. He has come up with a very intriguing scheme to make them pay for what they did to him."

"Yeah? And just what does he have in mind?" Claire asked.

"To take control of the world's oil supply," Atwa answered simply.

"Oh, is that all?" Herb asked scornfully.

"Let me explain," Atwa said, moving the pistol so it no longer pointed at them. "As you know, almost all of the working oil fields are in Saudi Arabia and Kuwait since your country destroyed most of the others in Iran and Iraq during your hunt for Osama bin Laden years ago."

"You're forgetting our fields in Alaska," Claire said.

Atwa waved a dismissive hand. "Yes, you have enormous reserves, but your environmentalists have so far blocked you from exploiting them to any degree."

Claire nodded grimly. The tree-huggers were the bane of her existence. She'd been trying for years to get the Congress to let her open up the fields to full production, but so far they'd resisted.

"So, how does El Farrar plan to take control of those oil fields?" Claire asked. "They are under the protection of the U.N."

"My organization is prepared to put fifty thousand of our best troops at his disposal. He will use them to gain control of the oil fields and oust the U.N. troops, which are very poorly disciplined."

"So, and then what?" Claire asked. "Ben Raines and his SUSA troops would take them back in less time than it takes to tell it."

Atwa shook his head. "Not if you agree to help us."

"In what way could we help you?" Claire asked. "As much as I hate to admit it, our troops have never been a match for the SUSA's."

"We don't need your troops," Atwa said. "We merely need fifty pounds or so of the plutonium you have in storage."

"Plutonium?" Claire asked, puzzled. "You want to make an atom bomb?"

"No. We intend to place small amounts of the plutonium near all of the oil wells, rigged to explode if our demands are not met. As you know, plutonium is one of the dirtiest of all radioactive materials. If we set the bombs off, it will contaminate the oil reserves for thousands of years and make them unusable."

"But," Claire said, horrified, "that would throw the world back into the Dark Ages."

"That is how we have been living in Afghanistan for

decades," Atwa said, shrugging. "But I doubt it will come to that. Once the U.N. sees that we have the means and the will to destroy the world's oil supply, I think they will accede to our demands."

"And what will the United States get for our help?" Claire asked, a thoughtful look on her face.

Atwa spread his hands, a wide-toothed grin on his face. "Why, you'd get to be our partners in ruling the world, of course." He hesitated a moment, and then he added, "And Ben Raines would have to come crawling to you to get the oil his country needs to maintain their style of life."

The thought of Ben Raines having to beg her for anything persuaded Claire. She'd hated him for as long as she could remember, and now was her chance to get back at him for all he'd done to make her life miserable.

She stood up and stuck out her hand. "We'll do it!"

TWO

As Ben Raines ran, his breath came in short, gasping bursts and his chest felt like a giant hand was squeezing it. Sweat poured from his brow and ran down into his eyes. Finally, he stopped and bent over, his hands on his knees as he glanced at his malamute dog, Jody, who'd been running effortlessly at his side. She wasn't even breathing heavily, and was looking back at him as if to say, "Come on, let's run some more."

"Jesus, Jody," he managed to gasp between breaths, "give your master a break." They'd just jogged five miles, a trip he used to make without even breaking a sweat. He looked at his watch. They'd averaged six-minute miles, a feat most men would have been proud of. But not General Ben Raines, leader of the Southern United States of America Armed Forces.

He bent down, rubbed the back of Jody's neck, and ruffled her ears, something she loved. "It's hell to get old, Jody old girl," he murmured to her as she looked up at him with adoring eyes, her lips curled in a smile of delight.

Maybe it's finally time to step down and give someone younger a chance, he thought to himself. His adopted son Buddy had been champing at the bit lately, wanting more responsibility. Perhaps now was the time to give it to him,

Ben thought as he finally managed to slow his breathing down to normal levels.

He glanced back down the road running along the periphery of his base, and figured he had about another mile to go to get home. With a deep sigh, he began to jog toward his quarters, hoping he wouldn't have a massive coronary before he made it back. Jody barked with happiness as she ran alongside him, keeping a sharp lookout for a squirrel or rabbit just in case one happened to show itself alongside the road.

After a shower and a lunch with his troops in the mess hall, Ben met with his team of advisers in his office. As he sat at his desk, he looked around at the men and women in the room, his heart swelling with pride at the excellence of the team he'd formed so many years ago.

Mike Post, his Chief of Intelligence, sat smoking his pipe as usual, filling the room with the aromatic smell of fine tobacco.

Jersey, his bodyguard, who was half Apache, sat on a chair near his desk, her hand resting on the hilt of the K-Bar assault knife that was her favorite weapon. Her long dark hair was tied in a braid at the back of her neck and hung down almost to her waist.

Cooper, called Coop by most everyone, was his driver and sat next to Jersey, where he could whisper insults to her as the occasion arose. Their constant bantering was legendary and a source of constant amusement to the other members of the team.

Anna, Ben's adopted daughter, sat on the couch next to Harley Reno, also part Indian, with the characteristic red hair and blue eyes of the band of aborigines who were his ancestors.

Beth, the team statistician, sat next to Carrie, who was in charge of communications for the team. They were quietly talking to Scott "Hammer" Hammerick, Harley's closest friend and fellow commando.

On an adjacent couch sat Buddy Raines, Ben's son, who'd led the special-ops battalion until the previous year, when Ben had asked him to join the team as second in command.

The final member of the group was Dr. Larry Buck, who'd recently taken over from Dr. Lamar Chase, who'd semiretired to play golf and lie about his handicap.

It was a fine team, one that had fought together over many campaigns.

Ben took a sip of his coffee and then cleared his throat. "Okay, boys and girls," he said with a slight grin. "How about a status report on our current situation?"

Mike Post took his pipe out of his mouth and glanced down at a sheaf of papers, resting on his ever-present briefcase on his lap. The team often joked that if they ever wanted to separate Mike from his briefcase, it would have to be surgically removed.

"Well, to begin with, the good news is it seems all of the terrorists who invaded the United States have either been killed or captured. Other than a few stragglers who shouldn't be any problem to round up, the threat of any overthrow of Claire Osterman's government is over," Mike said.

"What of the leader, Abdullah El Farrar?" Ben asked. "Any news of him?"

Mike's lips curled in a sardonic grin. "The last intel I have says he returned to the Middle East, either Iran or Iraq, in disgrace for his failure. I'm also told his family is none too happy with his aborted attempt to destabilize the U.S. since it resulted in all of the family's assets being frozen."

"Oh, darn," Coop interjected sarcastically, "now they'll have to live like all the other poor people they've been robbing for the past twenty years."

Mike laughed. "Well, not really. They still have relatively substantial funds available from bank accounts the U.N. wasn't able to find, but their standard of living has definitely gone down."

"How about the governments that supported him in his takeover bid?" Ben asked. "Are they still behind him?"

Mike shook his head. "Don't know, since our intel is limited over there, but I would think not. They're not exactly fond of failure in that culture."

"So you think we can forget about El Farrar as a threat?" Buddy asked, leaning forward, his head cocked to the side in a characteristic mannerism.

"I wouldn't go that far," Mike answered. "But I doubt we'll be hearing anything from him for quite a while. After all, he lost almost twenty-five thousand of their best troops. It should take him some time to reestablish a force we'd need to be concerned with."

"I wouldn't be too sure of that," Harley Reno said.

"Oh?" Buddy asked.

Harley nodded. "Yeah. As you know, I spent some time over there a few years back. There's no shortage of crazy young Muslims who are willing to take a short ride to meet Allah by blowing themselves and any followers of the Great Satan in the West up with them. If El Farrar survives his return and isn't killed or disavowed by the leaders over there, he could rearm and have another twenty-five thousand fanatical followers before you know it."

"That's a good point, Mike," Ben said, his brow furrowed in thought. "Tell your sources to keep a sharp lookout for any news El Farrar is trying to raise another army."

"Roger," Mike said, making a note on his legal pad.

"Now," Ben continued, "what of the U.S.? How are the conditions up there?"

Mike shook his head. "Simply terrible. There are shortages of everything, from food to gasoline to heating oil. The country is in the worst depression since Claire took office. I'm told half her army is not being paid, and the government is so short of funds they've actually cut their welfare payments by twenty percent."

Ben snorted. "Damn! That means the poor folks up there might actually have to go to work and do something useful to help their country's economy."

"Hah," Jersey said. Her feelings about people refusing to work and accepting welfare were well known. "That'll be the day. Expect a revolt anytime if the layabouts are cut off from the government tit."

"Actually, Jersey's not far wrong," Mike said. "My sources tell me there have actually been food riots in most of the major cities, and the university students have been so vocal in opposition to the cutting of welfare that Claire has actually gone so far as to suspend classes until the situation clears up."

"That won't hurt the country much," Cooper said with a sneer. "From what I hear, about all they teach in those colleges are blatant socialism and other liberal bleeding-heart nonsense."

"How did the schools up there get so bad?" Beth asked.

"You know the old saw? 'Those that can, do; those that can't, teach'?" Ben asked. "Well, after the initial wars that decimated the world and caused us to split off from the U.S., men and women with skills found themselves much in demand. Others, mainly those who spent most of their time on the sidelines carping about peace and love and sharing the bounty, went into teaching. Those were the only jobs whose only requirement was a loud mouth and lots of opinions, none of which had to be realistic."

"That's why in the SUSA, all of our teachers are volunteers who have to support themselves at an honest job, huh?" Carrie asked.

Ben nodded. "Yeah. We saw right away that teaching should arise out of a skill, not just an opinion. All of our universities teach skills that are necessary in the real world to make a living or to be useful to society. All of the so-called liberal-arts curriculum they love so much in the U.S. is still taught here, but only to produce well-rounded people and only as an adjunct to useful subjects. Here, no one takes philosophy or art appreciation unless they're also enrolled in medicine or engineering or something they can make a living at."

"You left out the most important job of all," Hammer said, putting his hand on the butt of his Beretta 9mm pistol. "Soldiering."

Ben laughed. "A prejudiced point of view, but one with which I heartily agree. Only, soldiering is not taught at universities, but here in the armed forces," he added.

"And there's nothing like on-the-job training," Coop said, glancing at Jersey. "Why, just look at Jersey here," he said, smiling. "If she had to earn her living cooking or taking care of a man, she'd starve to death."

In a flash, Jersey drew her K-Bar and put the point under Coop's jaw. "I know how to 'take care of a man,' " she said archly. "Want me to show you how it's done?"

Coop gulped and leaned back, moving the knife from his throat. "Umm, I think I'll pass, dear."

Jersey grinned and put the knife back in its scabbard. "I thought you might, sweetie," she said.

Ben cleared his throat and hid his smile behind a hand as he said, "Now that our intel briefing is over, I have some news I want to share with you all."

The group settled down and gave him their full attention, wondering what was going on.

"I have decided that it is time for this old warhorse to step down," he continued, his face now serious.

As the group began to speak up, voicing their objections to this pronouncement, Ben held up a hand. "Now, hold on," he said, looking each of his friends in the eye as he spoke. "Leading an army is a young man's job, and I have recently come to the conclusion that it would be better left to someone younger and stronger than me." He inclined his head toward Buddy, sitting across the room. "After extensive consultations with my fellow officers and the joint chiefs of all the commands, as well as with the various battalion commanders, we all agreed that Buddy Raines should take over . . . effective immediately."

"Wait just a minute, Ben," Buddy objected, jumping to his feet. "No one, least of all me, can take your place!"

Ben shook his head. "You are possibly the only one who feels that way, Buddy," Ben said. "You've served an admirable apprenticeship, if that's what it's called, over the past couple of years, and you won't be exactly taking my place. I plan to stay on board as a sort of advisor, if you agree, but the ultimate responsibility of the day-to-day leadership of the armed forces of the SUSA will fall on your shoulders."

Coop got to his feet and placed his hand on Buddy's

shoulders as he spoke. "I think I can speak for all of us, Ben, when I say we don't think you're quite over the hill yet, but I can also say if you've made up your mind, then Buddy will make a fine leader."

"Hear, hear!" the other members of the team all shouted, getting to their feet to crowd around Buddy and shake his hand and pat him on the back.

Ben smiled broadly and also got to his feet. He indicated Buddy should take his chair behind the desk, and stepped to the side.

Shaking his head, Buddy moved to take the commander's chair, standing for a moment with his hands on the desk. Everyone could see the shiny film of tears in his eyes at the honor. He glanced at Ben. "I still think this is unnecessary," he said, his voice hoarse with emotion.

"Of course, as the new commander in chief, you'll be able to pick your own personal team," Ben said.

Buddy looked around the room. "If it's agreeable to them, I can think of no better team to help me lead than the one you've used in the past," he said.

Ben laughed and spread his arms. "I can't either," he agreed. "And I'm sure they'll give you the same loyalty and fine service they've given me over the years."

Every man and woman in the room nodded, and there wasn't a dry eye in the crowd.

THREE

Muhammad Atwa turned and shook hands with Herb Knoff at the Indianapolis International Airport. He'd just checked three suitcases onto the commercial aircraft he was taking to Mexico City. Two of them appeared to be aluminum cases, but were in fact lined with lead on the inside, and each contained twenty-five pounds of weapons-grade plutonium in an inner casing. The third suitcase was more conventional in appearance, being made of leather, though it too had a lead-foil coating inside to hide its contents from any airport scanners. In it were various assorted weapons arrayed for easy access once he reached his destination.

"Are you sure you wouldn't rather use one of our military aircraft to take you home?" Knoff asked as they grasped hands.

Atwa smiled grimly. "Would you also have me paint my forehead with a sign saying I am on important business with the U.S.?" he asked gently, so as not to give any disrespect to his new ally and friend.

"But will the . . . cargo be safe flying commercially?" Knoff persisted as he glanced at the bags being loaded into the cargo section of the plane, along with dozens of others, by the baggage handlers.

Atwa shrugged. "If it is Allah's will, the bags and I will

all make it home safe and sound. If we do not, then I am sure the people I represent will send someone else to procure another supply of what we need to bring the U.N. to its knees."

"I hope it doesn't come to that," Herb said. "I'm looking forward to the operation you've planned. The U.N. and Ben Raines and the SUSA have been a thorn in our sides for many years. It will be good to see them begging for oil for a change."

"There will be many changes once we've gained control of the oil fields, my friend," Atwa said. "I will send you a coded message to let you know when I've arrived safely in our headquarters in Afghanistan."

"So long," Herb said, watching as Atwa walked toward the plane as if he hadn't a care in the world.

Atwa, though a devout Muslim, didn't wear the beard of the true fanatics, or the turban. He was dark-skinned and was fluent in many languages, Spanish among them. He'd made his own flight arrangements, flying under the alias Emilio Gonzales. Only he, El Farrar, and El Farrar's second in command, Farid Zamet, knew his travel plans. Once he arrived in Mexico City, he was to take another commercial flight to Abu Dhabi in the United Arab Emirates, where El Farrar had arranged for a private Lear jet to meet him and fly him the rest of the way to their base near the city of Kandahar in southern Afghanistan. He anticipated no problems.

On the plane, when the flight attendant asked if he needed anything, he ordered a double scotch on the rocks. No alcohol was allowed in their camp due to Muslim prohibitions against liquor of any kind. Though Muslim, Atwa was flexible in the parts of the Koran he chose to follow, and he did love his scotch.

* * *

When he deplaned in Mexico City, Atwa chose to pick up his luggage himself instead of trusting the baggage handlers to transfer it to the correct flight. It wouldn't do to have his luggage lost or misplaced and sent to some other destination.

As he walked through the rather dilapidated airport terminal, struggling with his three bags, Atwa glanced around to see if there was a bar somewhere nearby so he could partake of another drink or two before his next flight took off.

Always on the alert for trouble, he noticed two men standing nearby who averted their eyes when his passed over them. Atwa's heart began to beat faster and sweat pooled in his armpits. He knew the signs of surveillance, and he suspected his cover was blown.

He gave no sign he'd picked up on the men, and turned into the first rest room he passed after seeing them. He stepped into the last booth at the end of the room and hurriedly unlocked his leather bag. He took a Beretta nine-millimeter pistol from its compartment, attached a silencer to the barrel, and jacked a shell into the chamber.

Stripping his pants and shoes off, he arranged them over the end of the toilet so it looked as if he were sitting there. Once that was done, he peeked out of the door of the booth and saw the rest room was now empty of other people.

Running as quick as he could, he entered the first booth near the door, and got up on the toilet so his feet couldn't be seen. And then he waited; sweat dripped off his face and onto his two hands, clutching the Beretta tightly before him.

Minutes later, he heard footsteps enter the room and the room door being closed and locked.

Soft voices speaking Farsi whispered, but he couldn't

make out what they were saying. He raised his head and peered over the stall walls. The two men he'd seen watching him were standing in front of the booth where he'd left his pants.

They each held large pistols, also equipped with silencers in front of them. He saw them nod, and then they both fired into the booth through the door several times. The sound of their gunshots was no more than a low cough.

Atwa had seen enough. He took careful aim over the wall of his stall and put a bullet in each of their heads, grinning at the sight of their heads jerking under the impact.

He was out of his booth before their bodies hit the floor. He retrieved his pants and shoes, put them on, and stuck his pistol inside his belt at the small of his back. Then he hurriedly dragged the bodies into stalls and sat them up on the toilets, leaning them back against the wall. To anyone who bothered to look under the doors, they would simply appear to be sitting on the john.

Atwa moved to the sink and washed all traces of blood off his hands, retrieved his luggage, and casually strolled down the corridor toward his plane's gate. His eyes constantly flicked from side to side as he watched carefully for anyone else who might be working with the pair he'd dispatched.

Just before he got to the check-in area, he stepped close to a trash barrel and slipped the pistol into it. He doubted the two bodies would be found before his departure, but he didn't want to be searched and caught with a gun he'd used to kill them.

As he sat in the departure lounge waiting for his plane to be called, he read a newspaper. The only sign of stress on his placid face was a single drop of sweat that rolled slowly down his cheek.

Seven and a half hours later, he was stepping onto a Lear jet at the airport in the United Arab Emirates bound for Kandahar. He was looking forward to his meeting with Abdullah El Farrar, for blood was going to flow. Someone would be made to pay for the security lapse that had almost gotten him killed and his precious cargo stolen.

El Farrar, and his aide-de-camp, Farid Zamet, were standing on the tarmac in Kandahar when Atwa deplaned. The hot wind blowing off the desert hit him in the face with the power and heat of a blowtorch, causing him to reflect on how soon the heat of the desert is forgotten in cooler climes.

El Farrar's eyes focused on the aluminum cases Atwa carried from the plane, and his lips curled in a wide grin. He moved forward and embraced Atwa, growling in his ear, "I see you have accomplished your mission."

"Yes, though not without some difficulty," Atwa answered gravely.

El Farrar leaned back, his hands on Atwa's shoulders. "Difficulty?"

Atwa glanced around at the people milling about near the plane. "Let's wait until we are alone and I will give you the details."

Minutes later, in the armored limousine El Farrar used for his trips to the city, Atwa gratefully accepted the glass of fruit juice El Farrar offered him from the well-stocked bar of the car—though he wished El Farrar were not so fanatically Muslim so he could add a jolt of the scotch he carried in an inside pocket.

"So, now tell me," El Farrar said, leaning back against the fine leather of the seat. "What sort of difficulty were you speaking of?"

Atwa glanced at Farid, and then back at El Farrar. "Two assassins were waiting for me in the Mexico City airport."

"What?" El Farrar exclaimed, his brow knitting in surprise.

"Yes. It was only because they were amateurs that I was lucky enough to spot them before they could kill me and take the plutonium."

"But," Farid said, "that is impossible! Your travel plans were known to only a few of our closest and most loyal associates."

Atwa fixed him with a baleful stare. "Exactly how many knew of my trip?"

Farid thought for a moment. "There were Abdullah, me, and the pilot of the Lear jet that flew you here. That is all."

Atwa shook his head. "There must be at least one other. Were the traitor the pilot, I would never have made it here."

El Farrar snapped his fingers. "The only other one is the man who radioed the pilot when to expect you in the Emirates."

Atwa took a long sip of the cool fruit juice. "Then I would start my questioning with him, perhaps with his family present as an added incentive to tell the truth."

Bluent Ecevil was sitting in front of his radio, whispering into the microphone, when the two security guards

El Farrar sent burst through the door. Ecevil, sweat pouring from his face, jerked a small-caliber pistol from his waistband and stuck the barrel in his mouth. Before the guards could grab him, he pulled the trigger and blew the back of his head off, showering the radio with bits of skull and brain and blood.

El Farrar stepped into the room as the smoke cleared. He shook his head.

"He was speaking into the radio when we entered, my leader," the first guard said.

Atwa entered behind El Farrar. "He was probably telling his employers that I'd arrived safely with the plutonium," Atwa said.

El Farrar turned to the guards. "Go and get his family immediately. We will see if they know to whom this piece of camel dung sold his loyalty."

FOUR

Buddy Raines told his unit to meet him on the firing range of their home base just after the noon meal. As the group gathered, they were all wondering just what their new leader had in mind.

Coop looked around, yawning elaborately to show he wasn't concerned, no matter why they were there. "Buddy probably wants to check us out on the targets, to see if we've lost our edge," he said.

Jersey smirked and gave a low laugh. "In that case, you'd better be ready for a dressing-down, Coop. I seem to remember your hit ratio in our last firefight against those ragheads wasn't all that high."

Coop blushed. "Hell, you know I was under heavy fire that night. I was lucky I didn't get my head blown off, and you expect me to hit everything I aimed at?"

"Not everything," Jersey said, turning to watch Buddy as he walked toward them. "But one or two would have been nice."

"Hey . . ." Coop started to rejoin, but was interrupted by the arrival of Buddy, who was being followed by Hammer Hammerick and Harley Reno, who were wheeling a large wagon of what looked like weapons and other equipment.

Anna and Corrie glanced at each other. "You know

what's going on?" Corrie asked Anna, figuring she might know since she was constantly in Reno's company.

Anna shook her head, watching Harley to see if he would give her any clues.

"Hello, boys and girls," Buddy said, a wide grin on his face.

"What's all this about, Buddy?" Cooper asked, staring at the wagon between Harley and Hammer.

"I've brought us some new toys to play with," Buddy said. "I dearly love Ben, but he was somewhat old-fashioned about weapons. He tended to stay with those he grew up with, and didn't particularly like to experiment with new technology."

"Oh," Jersey exclaimed, picking up a couple of exotic-looking rifles. "Whoever said diamonds are a girl's best friend hadn't seen these babies!"

"Easy, girl," Coop said, also stepping close to the wagon. "Don't get your panties in a bunch."

"Harley and Hammer and I have just come from the armory, where they had these big boys in storage, just waiting for someone with the balls enough to requisition them," Buddy said. "Now, I'll step back and let our weapons experts give you the lowdown on our new toys."

Harley Reno moved close to the wagon, and began selecting weapons and laying them out on a table they'd set up for that purpose.

"Let's start with handguns first," he said. He picked up an automatic pistol in each hand. "Though revolvers are easier and safer to use, rarely jamming, I prefer automatics for the field because of their high magazine capacity and less frequent reloading." He held up a very large and lethal-looking one. "This here is the IMI Desert Eagle, made in the U.S.A. back in the eighties and nineties. The first automatic pistol to use heavy magnum loads, which made it a favorite of the Mossad back in the days before the big bang. It's a .50-caliber, and will stop an elephant in full charge. Two problems. It's got a hell of a recoil, and it only holds seven bullets in the clip. Not suitable for troops with small hands, though it is my favorite side arm."

"Let me see that," Jersey said, taking his warning as a personal challenge.

He handed her the gun and a clip, which she promptly stuck in the handle as she moved over to the firing station. She held it out with both hands and glanced back over her shoulder at Harley. "It's really heavy."

He grinned. "It needs to be. Wait until you fire it."

She took aim at a man-sized target fifty yards down the range and squeezed the trigger. The gun exploded with a sound like a grenade and Jersey's arms flew straight up in the air, her face screwed up in pain at the shock of the recoil. Nevertheless, a two-inch-diameter hole was punched in the chest of the target.

Harley nodded. "That's a good shot."

Jersey shrugged and walked over to hand him the gun back. "A little too noisy for my taste," she said, rubbing her hands to get the circulation back.

Hammer gave a short laugh. "I'm with you, Jersey." He pulled a particularly nasty-looking black pistol from the holster at his waist. "I prefer the Colt Python .357. It also holds seven rounds, and unless you're going up against King Kong, it'll jet the job done with a lot less damage to your ears and hands."

Harley glanced at him as he held up the other gun, muttering, "Sissy," under his breath. He was perhaps the only man alive who would dare to call Hammer Hammerick a sissy and live to tell about it. "This one you're already familiar with," Harley continued. "The Beretta

M93R. It fires 9mm parabellum shells, the magazine holds twenty shells, and it can fire three shots on full automatic each time you squeeze the trigger. It also has a small folding stock for your free hand to help steady your aim on automatic. This is the gun we're currently using, and I think most of you should stay with it. Not too heavy and virtually no recoil on single shots."

He stepped to the side. "I'll let Hammer fill you in on the long guns."

Hammer bent over the table and picked up a submachine gun they were all familiar with. "This, as you all know from previous experience, is the IMI Uzi. Thirty-round clip, 9mm, easy to control with the folding stock out, and a bitch to use like a pistol." He smiled. "Still, at over six hundred rounds a minute, it's very intimidating even if you don't hit anything with it," he added, glancing at Coop, who blushed and looked down at his feet.

"The new guy in town is the Heckler and Koch MP-10. The H&K MP-5 was the best on the market in its day, but the MP-10 is even better. Very reliable, uses 9mm shells in a thirty-round clip, and the recoil is not too bad. It's one of the favorites of terrorists and SWAT teams, not to mention Harley and me also."

"What's that big boy there next to the MP-10?" asked Anna.

Hammer grinned. "You mean this monster?" he asked, holding up a long-barreled gun with a large shoulder stock.

"Yeah," Coop said, "tell us about it."

"This is the Calico 45200. It only fires three-round bursts, but it comes with an integral holographic aimpoint sight, gun camera, electronic ignition, gas vents, and a small gyroscope system that helps dampen movements from recoil. It's extremely reliable and controllable, has a two-hundred-round magazine, and fires 4.5mm shells. Not a gun you'd want to carry around in the field, but a nice addition to have available when you need lots of firepower."

Harley moved to pick up a very intimidating shotgun from the table. "Now, for close-in firefights, this is the best in the business. This is the Franchi FAS."

"That looks a lot like the Franchi SPAS we used last year," Jersey said.

"Yeah, but with improvements," Harley said. "This one is made entirely of composite materials, and we've hacked the chip that controls the firing mechanism so it's now fully automatic. It fires flechette rounds from a helical magazine that enhances the shotgun's precision and effect greatly, and it can also fire normal buckshot or slugs. And unlike the SPAS that only holds eight rounds, this baby will hold twenty. We've shortened the barrel and added a leather strap so it's easy to carry over your shoulder along with your other weapons."

Anna fingered the gun and raised her eyebrows.

"Go on, give it a try," Harley offered.

Anna moved to the firing platform and aimed from the hip at the target Jersey had shot at earlier. When she fired, the target was literally shredded by hundreds of needlelike, razor-sharp, steel flechettes.

"Jesus," she whispered.

Jersey clapped her hands, laughing out loud. "Hell, Coop. That's the gun for you. Even you couldn't miss with that baby."

Coop didn't answer, but his eyes were on the shredded target and a small smile curled his lips.

"Impressive, but worthless in heavy brush or against men wearing flak jackets," Hammer observed.

"You wanna show them the assault rifles?" Harley asked.

"Sure," Hammer answered. He held one up. "This is the Vektor 5.56mm CR21. It has an integral Vektor reflex optical sight, and is so accurate it can even be used for a sniper rifle. It can also be fitted with the latest RAPTOR night-vision scope, which will let you see in total darkness. As you can see, all of the new assault rifles are of the bullpup design."

"Uh, what the hell's that?" Coop asked.

"That means the butt plate is attached directly to the receiver with the trigger in front of the magazine, and they're usually shorter so they're easier to maneuver in the field."

He pointed at the table. "We included a couple of AK-07's, the successor to the original Kalashnikov AK-47. The Finnish Valmet Corporation consulted with the Russians on the remake, and they did a good job. It, like the others, is a bullpup rifle, very short and easy to shoot, reliable in the worst conditions of sand or mud, and we'll probably be seeing it in use against us since the Russkies shipped them to every Third World country known to man in the old days."

"Show 'em my favorite," Harley said, his eyes excited.

"Yeah, mine too," Hammer said. He picked up an exotic-looking rifle. "This is the ECAI, made by the European Combined Arms Initiative. It is the most advanced assault rifle in the world. It's a binary propellant rifle, so it doesn't need gunpowder. Instead it relies on two volatile gases that explode when mixed. It used to need to be in wireless contact with a central computer, but our lads at Intel have gussied these up to use imbedded chips. It can designate targets; it can coordinate indirect squad fire. It comes with an integral holographic aim point sight, telescopic sight, infrared vision, gun camera, gas vents, and it also has a gyroscope to control recoil. It even has an integral grenade launcher that can control the grenade trajectory perfectly."

"Tell 'em the best part," Harley said.

"Oh, yeah. The user has his profile programmed into the gun, so when he, or she, grasps this rifle, it automatically formats to the individual soldier's preprogrammed settings. That means, if the gun is lost or confiscated, it can't be used by anyone else. It fires 4mm BP shells, has a four-hundred-round magazine, and its gas bottle holds enough gas for eight hundred shots."

"Holy shit," Coop said. "That sumbitch is like something outta Buck Rogers. A computer gun."

"That's why I like it so much," Harley said, laughing.

"I have a question," Beth said.

"Yeah?" Hammer replied.

"If these are programmed to individual troops, what if the user goes down and one of us needs to use the gun? Are you saying we won't be able to?"

"Not at all," Hammer said. "We plan to have several of these along, one in each assault vehicle, and all of them will be programmed to accept any of our group as a primary user."

Beth nodded. "Good, 'cause in a firefight, I don't want to pick up a weapon and have it tell me, 'Sorry, Charlie.' "

"Hey, what the heck is this?" Coop said. He was standing next to the table where Harley and Hammer had laid out all the weapons. "Don't tell me we're going back to using bows and arrows."

Harley stepped over and picked up the mini-crossbow Coop was talking about. It was pistol-size, and could be used with one hand. Next to it lay several different types of projectiles.

"This little baby has been included to be used when stealth is necessary. Quieter than a pistol or rifle with a silencer, and extremely deadly at up to a hundred yards. And even better, these new darts we're using will penetrate a Kevlar vest or a flak jacket better than a bullet will." He dropped it back on the table. "But of course, we'll probably never need it. It's really more for the scout teams than us front-line-type troopers."

Hammer looked at his watch. "There's more here to go over. We still haven't gotten to accessories and communications yet, but it looks to me like it's past the lunch hour. Why don't we meet back here later this afternoon and we'll finish up and let you guys have some fun on the range with the new guns?"

The group all agreed and moved toward the mess hall, with Coop muttering something about them finding his bones bleaching in the hot sun after he starved to death.

FIVE

After they'd finished eating, the group reassembled at the firing range, where another table of high-tech equipment was on display.

Harley and Hammer stepped up to the table. "Corrie," Hammer said, "this is mainly for you since you're our communications expert, but the rest of us need to get acquainted with the equipment too, just in case you get put out of action."

"Bite your tongue," Corrie said with a rueful grin.

"This is the AN/PRC 132 SOHFRAD," Hammer said, indicating a field radio equipped with a strap so it could be worn like a backpack. "That stands for Special Operations High Frequency Radio. It makes an uplink to any one of the special telecommunications satellites orbiting the earth and relays the signal back down to the headsets the troops wear, as well as anywhere in the world it's programmed to communicate with."

Corrie's eyebrows rose. "You mean that our field communications would be able to be monitored by headquarters during a firefight?"

"Exactly," Hammer answered. "Unfortunately, the signal doesn't have a scrambler on it, so in a worst-case scenario, our enemies might be able to listen too."

"The way around that is to change frequencies on a

preset schedule," Corrie said, a thoughtful look on her face.

"Yeah?" Hammer asked. "Well, I'll leave the details for you experts to work out with Intel and headquarters," Hammer said with a deprecating smile.

Corrie nodded as she ran her hands over the radio, obviously intrigued with her new toy.

Harley pointed at the table. "We also have some other goodies for you to get acquainted with. Those tubes over there are Stinger missile launchers, and next to them are the new JAVELIN antitank weapons—lightweight, portable, fire and forget, and they fire a 127mm-diameter missile. They'll take out just about anything in their range, from a ship to a helicopter or tank."

He moved a few feet to his left and indicated some grenades lying in a row. "Here we have some bang-bangs you've all used before: M-76 smoke grenades, M-25 CS riot grenades, and M-651 tear-gas grenades, along with the usual frag and stun grenades. We even have a couple of CPAD Tech rocket grenades for you to try." He looked up at the group. "I know you've all used these before, but Buddy wants us to do some practicing since it's been a while since we've been in action."

Hammer added, "There're a couple of new night-vision scopes there too. The best is the RAPTOR, though the BENS 9304 and the Jaguar ain't bad. Buddy wants us to get used to firing at night using all of them."

"I hope it's better than the old ones," Coop said. "I couldn't see shit through them."

"And your shooting showed it," Jersey muttered, causing Coop to grimace.

"This newer-generation scope doesn't have quite the greenish tinge the older models had, and some can also be used with thermal imaging so you can pick out your enemy by his body heat. Anyway, tonight after it gets dark, we'll all give them a try."

"Buddy's gonna join us," Harley said, grinning. "He says he's got a lot to live up to taking over from Ben an' he plans to make sure he'll hold up his end."

Coop looked around at the group. "I'm sure I speak for all of us when I say I've seen Buddy in action before and he doesn't have to take a backseat to anybody, Ben included."

The other members of the group all nodded their agreement, and they left to get some supper and get ready for the night's fun and games with the new toys.

In Kandahar, Farid Zamet walked into El Farrar's office, finding him in a discussion with Muhammad Atwa.

Farrar looked up, noticing Zamet's clothing still had specks of blood and tissue on it.

"How did the interrogation of Ecevil's family go?" he asked, his nostrils flaring a little at the stench of excrement and urine that entered with Zamet.

"Not well. Neither the wife nor the children knew of his treachery."

"Are you sure?" Atwa asked, clearly not convinced.

Zamet examined his hands and idly picked at the blood under his fingernails while he answered. "Believe me, I asked them real hard. If they did know anything, they took the information with them to their graves."

Atwa turned back in his chair to face Farrar. "We must assume at least part of our plan has been compromised. I suggest we move as rapidly as possible before significant opposition can be mounted."

"I agree," Farrar said. "In fact, the operation is already under way."

"Oh?"

"Yes." Farrar hesitated, wrinkling his nose, and then he looked at Zamet, still standing before him. "Farid, would you mind going to your quarters and taking a shower and changing your clothes? I find the continued olfactory remnants of Ecevil's family extremely annoying."

Zamet rapidly nodded, backing toward the door. "Of course, my leader."

"You were saying?" Atwa asked after Zamet had left the room.

"I have arranged for several teams of our most trusted and able troops to ship out of the port of Karachi in Pakistan today."

Atwa appeared surprised. "You're sending them by ship? I thought you would have them parachute into the oil fields."

Farrar shook his head. "No, they need far too much equipment to do that, and I don't want the plutonium put at risk that way."

"But how will they manage to take over the oil fields by ship?"

"At this moment, there are at least ten oil tankers returning to the Persian Gulf, empty after off-loading their cargoes of oil in various nations. The ship my men are on will intercept each of them and claim to be disabled. When they stop to help, squads of our troops will take over the ships. When they finally call at their home ports in Kuwait, Saudi Arabia, Iraq, and Iran, my men will take control of the ports and then proceed to the oil fields. By the time the UN can send in backup troops, the plutonium bombs will have been set."

Atwa inclined his head in admiration. "Ingenious plan, Abdullah."

Farrar glanced at his watch. "Within forty-eight hours, my men should be in control of the oil fields in all of the countries bordering the Persian Gulf." He stared at Atwa with the glittering eyes of a fanatic. "Then it will be time to present my demands to the U.N."

Atwa smiled and spread his arms. "And they will have no choice but to accede to them."

"If they do not, we will destroy eighty percent of the world's oil supply and drive the infidels back into the Dark Ages."

"Oh, my dear friend," Atwa said, frowning, "you are much too negative. Let us think only positive thoughts, about how the entire world will be at our knees in a fortnight."

"You are right, Muhammad," Farrar said. He raised his glass of juice. "To success," he said.

Atwa hid his grimace and returned the toast, choking down the juice and again wishing it were scotch.

SIX

Jason Briggs, captain of the oil tanker *Exxon Marquis,* was in his quarters going over satellite weather reports when his second in command, Peter Gallagher, entered the room.

Briggs looked up and saw the worried look on Gallagher's face. "What's up, Pete?" he asked, reaching automatically for his pipe, which he seldom lit but constantly chewed on, especially in times of stress. "The weather reports couldn't be better."

"There's something you oughta see out here, Cap'n," Gallagher answered.

Briggs sighed and got to his feet, wincing as his knees cracked. He was going on sixty years old, and planned to retire at the end of this year. His joints were shot after forty plus years of standing on bucking, jumping decks of ships.

He led the way from his cabin to the bridge, which was only about fifty yards away.

When they got to the bridge, Gallagher pointed through the huge Plexiglas front windshield and asked, "What do you think about that?"

Briggs leaned his head to the side, staring out from under bushy gray eyebrows. "Damned if I know. Has there been any radio contact? SOS or Mayday calls for help?"

"No, and that's what I can't understand," Gallagher replied.

Five hundred yards in front of the ship, a rusted-out freighter lay dead in the water, billows of smoke coming from her forward hold and sending black clouds over the water to lay there like a bank of fog.

"Has anyone appeared on the decks?" Briggs asked, reaching for the pair of ancient binoculars hanging next to the captain's chair.

Gallagher shook his head as he stared at the ship. "No, sir."

"Well," Briggs sighed. "There's nothing for it. We have to send a boat over. Take a few men with some fire extinguishers and the medical officer with you, and go and see what the hell's happened to the crew."

"Aye, sir," Gallagher said, and started to leave.

"And Pete," Briggs added.

"Yes, sir?"

"Be careful. I don't like the looks of this one bit."

"Don't worry, Cap'n," Gallagher answered. "I'll take my side arm and make sure a couple of the men are armed too."

"Good. And take a walkie-talkie with you and let me know what you find as soon as you can."

Gallagher went directly to the locked storage cabinet in the captain's cabin and dialed a combination to open the lock. He opened the double doors and took out three M16A assault rifles, a handful of clips, and a Colt Commander .45 automatic pistol in a leather holster. He clipped the holster onto his belt and carried the rifles out onto the deck.

"Johnny," he said to a junior officer standing there, "take these, find two other men and the medical officer, and come with me."

After Johnny picked the men and rounded up the medical officer, Gallagher led them to a thirty-foot tender hanging from davits on the side of the ship. They all climbed in, and Gallagher signaled to another crew member to lower them into the water.

As the boat touched the large swells next to the ship, smoke from the freighter began to swirl and roil around them until visibility was reduced to a dozen yards or less.

The officer named Johnny started the seventy-five-horsepower engine on the tender, and they began to make their way toward the stranded freighter, all under the watchful eyes of Captain Briggs.

The trip took almost twenty minutes, going slow in the reduced visibility, until they were next to the side of the freighter that rose from the waters like a great, rusted wall of iron.

Gallagher was surprised to find a boarding ladder had already been lowered.

"That was thoughtful of them," he said, a frown on his face.

"Probably lowered it when they abandoned ship, Mr. Gallagher," Johnny said from the helm of the tender.

"You're probably right," Gallagher said, "but keep those M-16s handy."

"Yes, sir," Johnny said as he cut the engine and made the tender fast to the ladder.

Gallagher, like all good officers, was first up the ladder, and he clambered over the rail of the ship with his .45 in his hand. He saw nothing but smoke, and gestured for the rest of his men to join him on deck.

"You men spread out and see if you can find anyone alive," he said. "I'll check the bridge and see if they left a log or anything to indicate what happened."

Gallagher climbed up a ladder to the bridge and entered the iron door on the side. He was surprised to find a man sitting in the captain's chair, calmly smoking a cigar.

"Good afternoon, sir," the man said, swiveling in his chair to stare at Gallagher.

"What the . . ." Gallagher began, until he felt the barrel of a pistol against his temple.

"Please be so kind as to hand your weapon to the gentleman behind you and you will live to see another day," the man with the cigar said.

Gallagher handed the Colt over his shoulder and said, "Just what the hell is this? We came to try and help you."

The captain spread his hands, a wide grin revealing brown-stained teeth. "As you can see, we are in no need of help. May I ask what your name is?"

"I am Peter Gallagher, second officer on the *Exxon Marquis*."

"Achmed," the man said, "would you please relieve Mr. Gallagher of that radio on his belt and hand it to me?"

As Achmed complied, the captain shrugged apologetically. "I wouldn't want you to attempt to make any inadvisable calls back to your ship. It would only result in more bloodshed."

"More bloodshed?"

"I am afraid the men with you who were carrying

weapons have been . . . dealt with in the only way possible."

"But I didn't hear any gunfire," Gallagher said, and then he noticed the pistol the man called Achmed was holding was equipped with a silencer.

Gallagher whirled back toward the captain. "You bastard!" he yelled, and moved toward him.

Achmed swung the barrel of his pistol in a high arc and slammed it down on the back of Gallagher's head, knocking him senseless to the floor.

When he came to, Gallagher noted from his wristwatch that only twenty minutes had passed. He shook his head and got up on wobbly feet. He looked around the bridge, and saw the medical officer standing with his hands tied and his head lowered, a baleful expression on his face.

"Where are the rest of my men?" he asked.

The medical officer looked up, and then he cut his eyes to the rear of the bridge. Gallagher followed the look, and saw Johnny and the other two men laid out in their underwear with bullet holes in their foreheads.

Standing next to them, dressed in their clothes, were three dark-skinned men, all carrying the M16As Gallagher's men had been carrying.

"Just what is the meaning of this?" Gallagher asked the captain. "If you're planning on hijacking the ship, I warn you, it is empty. We were returning to Kuwait to refill, so you won't be able to sell any cargo."

The smile vanished from the captain's face and he got to his feet. "My plans are of no concern to you, Mr. Gallagher. Right now, I need you to radio back to your captain that all is under control and that you will be returning to the ship with several casualties for proper medical treatment."

Gallagher sneered. "And if I refuse?"

The captain shrugged as he gave a signal with his eyes to Achmed. The man walked over to the medical officer and put the barrel of his gun against his head.

"Why, then I would have no choice but to tell Achmed to kill the officer and yourself," the captain answered.

"That's better than losing the entire crew," Gallagher replied through a tight throat.

"If that is what is worrying you, I will give you my word your crew will be safe," the captain said. "They will be taken as prisoners and held on board with no further loss of life, if you do exactly as I say."

"Why should I believe you?"

"Achmed, take Mr. Gallagher to the aft hold, show him what we have there, and then bring him back to me."

Achmed grabbed Gallagher by the shoulder and roughly led him along the deck until they came to a ladder leading down. They went down three flights, and then Achmed opened an iron door.

Gallagher's eyes opened wide when he saw the amount and types of armament stored in the hold. There was everything from Stinger antiaircraft missiles to mortars and heavy machine guns, along with crate upon crate of hand grenades.

Achmed smiled at the expression of horror on Gallagher's face, and took him straight back to the bridge.

When he entered, the captain smiled grimly. "As you can see, Mr. Gallagher, we are perfectly prepared to blow your ship out of the water with the resultant loss of all hands. However, if you do as I say, I will guarantee you no one else will be harmed."

Gallagher's shoulders slumped. He knew when he was beaten. "What is it you want me to do?"

The captain handed him the radio. "Here is what you must say. . . ."

Captain Briggs watched through his binoculars as the tender threaded its way through the soupy wall of smoke toward the oil tanker. He could see three men lying in the gunwales with bloody bandages over their heads and hands.

"Jesus," Briggs whispered to himself. "I wonder what they're carrying that could cause such a fire. Probably some sort of nitrite fertilizer."

Fifteen minutes later, he saw the tender being hauled aboard, and sat back down in his chair until Gallagher could give him his final report.

He jumped out of his chair when he heard the sound of gunfire, and was moving toward the door to the bridge when it burst open. Gallagher was shoved inside and followed immediately by two men.

"Captain, I'm sorry," Gallagher gasped as he fell against a chair.

"Good afternoon, Captain Briggs," one of the men said. "My name is Al Hazmi, and I am taking control of your ship."

"I'll be damned," Briggs cried, starting to protest.

Hazmi raised an automatic pistol and aimed it at Briggs's head. "Please, Captain. You have no choice. Even now my men are locking your men in one of the holds, and I assure you if you do not cooperate to the fullest, I will have them all summarily executed."

Briggs cast his eyes at Gallagher, who merely nodded. "He means it, Cap'n," Gallagher said, his voice almost a moan. "He's a stone killer."

"I will tell you what I told your first officer, Captain," Hazmi continued. "I mean you and your men no harm. I just have need of your ship to gain access to the port at Kuwait."

"They'll never let you dock," Briggs said.

Hazmi smiled grimly. "No, but they'll let you dock, Captain Briggs."

Briggs folded his arms across his chest. "I refuse to help you do anything."

"Do you really mean to say you are willing to forfeit the lives of all of your crew and yourself just to keep me from getting into the port at Kuwait?" Hazmi asked, his voice silky smooth.

Briggs sighed. "No, I guess not."

SEVEN

Buddy Raines was with the rest of his group at the firing range trying out the new weapons when the cell phone on his belt rang.

He put down the Vektor CR-21 he was firing and answered it. "Raines here," he said in a loud voice so he could be heard over the cacophony in the background.

"Buddy, this is Ben."

"Hey, Ben, why don't you come on over here to the firing range and try out these new goodies we're using?" Buddy asked, knowing Ben liked nothing better than to spend some quality time on the range.

"Love to, but can't right now. We've got a visitor from across the pond and I think you and the group oughta give a listen to what he has to say."

"Be there in fifteen," Buddy answered, knowing Ben wouldn't interrupt their training unless it was very important.

He signaled his team to put their weapons down and to follow him to Ben's office pronto.

"What's going on, boss?" Coop asked as he lowered the Franchi FAS shotgun he'd been firing at an already shredded target.

"Some brass from Europe here to talk to us. I don't

know what about, but Ben said to hotfoot it over to his office."

When they entered Ben's office, Buddy and his team found a man dressed in the combat fatigues of the British SAS sitting across from Ben's desk.

Buddy walked over and held out his hand. "Hi, I'm Buddy Raines."

The man stood up, and Buddy noted he must have been six and a half feet tall. "Hello General Raines," he said, "My name is Bartholomew Wiley-Smeyth."

Buddy grinned as they shook hands. "It's Buddy to my friends, and what do we call you? Major Wiley or Smeyth?" Buddy asked, noticing the major's insignia on his shirt.

The man grinned. "Bart will do nicely, thank you."

Ben explained. "Bart is here as part of SAS Intel, so I've asked Mike Post to join us."

Just as he finished speaking, Mike Post, Chief of Intel for the SUSA Army, walked in the door, his unlit pipe in his mouth and carrying his ever-present briefcase as usual.

"Hey, guys, sorry I'm late. Had to finish decoding some communiqués from the U.N."

"That's okay, Mike," Ben said. "We were just getting started. Why don't you grab some coffee from the pot and we'll let Major Wiley-Smeyth give us a sitrep."

"Sitrep?" Bart asked.

"Situation report," Ben said.

Bart smiled. "Oh, in England we call it an oprep for operations report."

"Like they say," Ben said, "two countries separated by a common language."

Once everyone had cups of coffee or juice from the

bar in the corner of Ben's office, Bart leaned back in his chair and crossed his legs as he spoke. "I've been sent here to give your people a heads-up on some recent happenings in Europe and the Middle East."

He paused to take a sip of the tea Ben had fixed him, trying to hide a grimace at the taste. "Our Intel had some information about a possible plan to smuggle some weapons-grade plutonium out of the U.S.A. and into Europe a couple of weeks ago."

"Plutonium?" Ben asked. "Does anyone over there besides Britain have the capability to use it to make a bomb?"

Bart shook his head. "No. That's what got our interest up in the first place. Why would any country risk transporting something so useless?"

"What did you find out?" Buddy asked.

"We had information the contraband was going to be flown from the U.S.A. to Mexico City and then to someplace in Europe, but we couldn't get any information on the final destination. We did, however, know the name of the man making the carry: Muhammad Atwa. So, I sent two of my best men to intercept him at the Mexico City Airport. They were Hispanics, but could speak Arabic and Farsi and pass for Middle Easterners, just in case they were spotted by the Mexican authorities."

"Did they make the intercept?" Mike Post asked as he fiddled with filling his pipe.

Bart's face sobered. "No. In fact, they were found shot to death in a rest room stall after Atwa's plane had taken off for Abu Dhabi in the United Arab Emirates."

"Do you think this Atwa killed them?" Ben asked.

Bart shrugged. "There's no other possibility. My men were extremely well trained, but he must have somehow spotted them and taken them out."

"From my experience, you SAS guys are pretty tough.

You think a mere courier could take out two SAS men that easily?" Coop asked.

"The only explanation is that Atwa is not a mere courier, as you say, but a trained terrorist operative," Bart said.

"Do you have any information on where he went in the Emirates or who he made contact with there?" Ben asked.

"No. By the time we found out where he'd gone, our operatives in the Emirates could find no trace of him."

Mike Post opened his briefcase and withdrew a sheaf of papers. "It's interesting that your man with the plutonium has Middle Eastern connections," he said. "The message I got from the U.N. may be connected to this plutonium transport."

"Oh?" Bart asked.

"Yeah. The U.N. has some intel that factions of the old Al Qa'eda, Hezbollah, and Al Nahda terrorist networks are reforming and joining forces for some as yet unknown mission."

"I thought all of those cells were destroyed years ago in the war in Afghanistan," Jersey said.

Bart shook his head. "Not all of them, just the leaders at the time. A lot of the terrorists merely joined in with the refugees and went back underground."

"As you know," Ben said, a thoughtful look on his face, "we had a problem last year in the U.S.A. with a man named Abdullah El Farrar. He tried to invade the U.S.A. and take over the government there. The U.S.A. asked us for help, and the invasion was thwarted and most of his soldiers killed or captured, but El Farrar managed to escape and return to the Middle East. Do you think this could have anything to do with him?"

Bart gave a harsh laugh. "Hell, Ben, in that region anything is possible. The radical Muslims have hated anyone non-Muslim for so long, there is no telling what they'd do if they got the chance."

"But," Mike Post said, "for the Middle Eastern terrorist organizations to try and procure plutonium makes even less sense than if another government did it. To our knowledge, they have had almost no technical ability with nuclear weapons since the U.S. took out Saddam Hussein after the war in Afghanistan back in the early years of the century."

"You're right, Mike," Bart said. "But if the terrorists went to all this trouble to get some plutonium, you can bet they have a plan for its use, and that plan will probably entail the deaths of a lot of non-Muslims somehow."

"Are you sure they got the plutonium from the U.S.A.?" Ben asked.

Bart nodded. "We have that on a very good source."

"If it was stolen, you'd think Claire Osterman would be yelling at the top of her lungs for something to be done about it," Ben mused, almost to himself.

"Unless she was ashamed that something so deadly could be stolen from her so easily," Mike Post said.

"Something doesn't smell right here," Ben said.

"Surely you don't think President Osterman could be cooperating with the same group that tried to take over her country and kill her, do you?" Bart asked.

Ben snorted. "Hell, if Claire thought it would do her some good, she'd make a deal with the devil himself." He got up from his desk and poured himself another cup of coffee, a thoughtful expression on his face.

When he sat back down, he glanced at Mike. "Mike, I want you to get your Intel men to work with our scientists to try and figure out what possible use plutonium could be to a group of men who are still living in the Dark Ages technically. See if they can come up with any scenario where the plutonium could be used to cause us harm."

Bart got to his feet. "I'll do the same back home," he said, preparing to leave.

"Bart," Ben said, "leave Mike here a contact person in your Intel group and we'll keep in touch. As soon as we know anything, we'll let you in on it."

"I appreciate that, Ben. We'll do the same."

After Bart left, Ben looked at Buddy. "Looks like you and your team had better start some desert and mountain training, son. I've got a feeling we may be sending some troops over to the Middle East sooner rather than later."

Buddy stood up. "You got it, Ben. I'll issue us some desert fatigues, and we'll head on over to the training field in west Texas at first light in the morning."

"Texas?" Coop asked.

"Yeah. Good old Texas has both desert and mountains where we can try out our new equipment to see how it stands up to those conditions," Buddy said.

"Are the mosquitoes as bad in Texas as they are here in Louisiana?" Jersey asked.

Ben laughed. "Hell, the mosquitoes in Texas don't bite you; they put you under their arms and take you home to eat later."

"It's not the mosquitoes that worry me," Coop said, a look of distaste on his face. "It's those damned rattlesnakes."

Jersey grinned. Coop's aversion to snakes was well known. "You know the difference between a rattlesnake and a pissed-off woman, Coop?" she asked as they headed out the door.

"No, what?" Coop asked.
"The rattlesnake warns you before he takes a bite outta your ass."

EIGHT

Al Hazmi put the *Exxon Marquis* crewmen under guard in the forward hold, finally agreeing to leave the top open to keep the men from dying from the accumulated vapors from the crude oil that had been stored there. He kept Captain Briggs on the bridge under close guard in case a radio message needed to be answered.

Once that was accomplished, he lowered the tender and sent it back to his freighter to load additional troops and weaponry for the eventual assault on the port at Kuwait. When all was in readiness and his men were in control of the ship, he turned command of the ship over to one of his lieutenants, Dinise Jabagh. Hazmi had known Jabagh since they were children playing together in the slums of Kandahar in Afghanistan and dreaming of the day when they'd bring all infidels to their knees.

"Dinise," Hazmi said as he bade his friend good-bye, "I am counting on you to take the port of Kuwait on my signal. Do not let me down, old friend."

Jabagh slammed his right fist against his chest over his heart. "I swear on my life, my leader, I will succeed."

With that, Hazmi smiled and said, "I know you will. Remember, this is something we've waited our entire lives for."

He climbed down the ladder on the side of the ship,

and got into a Magma Marine Patrol boat, a twenty-seven-foot-long boat capable of over sixty miles an hour, that he used for transportation from his freighter to other ships. He waved as the boat took off back toward the freighter. He had several more ships to invade before his day would be done.

When he again boarded his freighter, he set a course to intercept another tanker headed this time toward the port city of Dhahran in Saudi Arabia. His third target was a tanker en route to Bushehr in Iran. There, his men would have to travel a good distance by truck to get to the oil fields, so that tanker would be allowed to dock first to give his men time to get to their destination.

Three other freighters, all supplied by the United States and Claire Osterman, were in the process of intercepting other tankers bound for different targets. Before the next day was over, the terrorists hoped to have control of all of the major oil fields in the Middle East.

As he sailed to rendezvous with the second tanker, Hazmi sent a coded message to El Farrar that step one had been accomplished as planned.

In his headquarters in Kandahar, El Farrar read the message to Muhammad Atwa, and the two men grinned like schoolchildren at recess. Farrar turned to a large map on the wall, his eyes glittering with anticipation at the land that would soon be under his control, giving him a power no one man had held since the Caesars ruled the Roman Empire.

At the same time, a C-130 transport was landing at the Midland Airport in Texas. Inside were Buddy Raines and

ENEMY IN THE ASHES

his team, along with over a hundred scouts, under the command of Major Jackson Bean and his second in command, Willie Running Bear, a full-blooded Sioux Indian. Squad Leaders Samuel Clements and Sue Waters were also present. All had fought with Ben Raines and his team the previous year when they defeated Abdullah El Farrar in the U.S.A.

When the troops deplaned, the temperature was in triple digits and there was a thirty-knot wind blowing, and visibility was limited by the amount of sand being carried by the wind.

Coop wiped tearing eyes and observed to Jersey, standing next to him, "Jesus, what is this? A sandstorm in Texas? Christ, it feels like an oven out here."

"To paraphrase an old saying about the Mississippi River, the air here's too thick to breathe and too thin to plow," Jersey observed as she took a kerchief from around her neck and folded it into a triangle. Then she put it over her nose and mouth and tied it behind her head.

Coop stared at her and began to laugh. "You look like a bandit in the Old West," he said.

"Laugh all you want, pilgrim, but I can breathe now. How about you?"

Coop started to reply, and then had a coughing fit from the sand in his mouth. He turned red-rimmed eyes to Jersey. "You happen to have another one of those handy?" he rasped through a raw throat.

Her mask hid Jersey's grin. "Sure. Running Bear is giving them out back in the plane. He said he knew we'd need 'em sooner or later, him being from Texas originally."

The troops assembled in front of the aircraft while some of their heavier equipment—Bradley Attack Vehicles, light tanks, and HumVees specially equipped for traveling over sand—was unloaded and parked near the troops.

"All right, you guys, heads up," Major Bean called when the troops were assembled. "I'm gonna go over some of the heavy equipment we're gonna be usin' if we get deployed to the Middle East."

He stepped over to a long vehicle with tracks on it like a tank. "This here is the HEMTT, pronounced Hemit. It's a heavy-equipment, mobility-tracked truck. We use it for cargo-carryin', recovery, and it can also carry large amounts of fuel or water—things we're gonna need in the desert. Next to it is the Bradley Attack Vehicle, which carries a 120mm cannon and a fifty-caliber machine gun. We'll use it to move our attack teams into place. It has a five-man crew: two to run it and three to attack once it's in place."

He moved down the line. "Here is the M1 Abrams, a light tank which can move at forty to fifty miles per hour over sand and can target up to six targets simultaneously with its laser sighting. Next to it is the Sheridan tank, which, as you can see, is modified to have a low profile, just in case we come up against some LAWS or Stinger missiles. And these little babies are the Vulcans. They're small, but they carry a helluva punch with their 120mm cannon. We'll use these to protect our flanks if we go in on foot against a superior force."

He spread his legs and put his hands on his hips. "Any questions?"

Coop raised his hand.

"Yeah, Cooper?"

"Yes, sir. When do we eat?" Coop asked, to a general laugh from the rest of the troops.

Bean smiled an evil smile. "Why, Mr. Cooper, you'll

eat when I'm convinced you know how to drive and operate each and every one of these here vehicles."

The troops all groaned, until Bean held up his hand. "Listen to me! We're Scouts, not Regular Army. We go in when it's not possible to send in large forces, so we all have to be jacks of all trades. Now, Squad Leaders Clements and Waters will take you through the basics with this stuff. I don't expect you to be expert at it, but in case the driver or gunner is taken out, every one of you needs to be able to step in and take their place. Am I clear on that?"

"Yes, sir!" the troops all responded.

"Then get to it. The sooner you're all checked out, the sooner you can get some chow."

As they gathered around the equipment, Coop touched Samuel Clements on the shoulder. "Hey, Sam. How's the wound?"

Clements, who'd been wounded in the fight against the terrorists the previous year, grinned and spread his arms. "What wound?" he asked.

"That good, huh?" Coop asked, relieved that the friend he'd made last year was in good health.

"No problems, *compadre*. Now, why don't you climb up in that HEMTT and see if you can get it started. It only has eighteen forward gears."

"I didn't join the force to be a truck driver," Coop grumbled, but he climbed up in the driver's seat anyway.

Clements stepped up on the running board. "Coop, I know this baby ain't exactly pretty, and it sure as hell ain't as exciting as driving a tank, but when you're out in the middle of nowhere and dying of thirst with no gas for your HumVee, you'll kiss the driver that shows up in one of these."

Coop scowled. "Not unless it's Sue Waters," he said.

Clements laughed. "You try to kiss Sue, and she'll probably do no worse than break your arm, pal."

Coop shook his head. "Now, Sam, you just don't know how charming I can be when I try."

Clements nodded, a sarcastic look on his face. "Yeah, I've seen how good you are with the women, guy. Jersey especially seems taken with your manly charms."

"Hey, that's not fair. Jersey doesn't count. Hell, she's more manly than I am."

From behind Clements, a voice spoke up. "I heard that, you baboon!"

"Oh, shit," Coop mumbled, blushing scarlet. Jersey had heard him.

NINE

Helmut Schmidt, lead officer on the oil tanker *Grosse Hund*, was a different sort of man than Captain Jason Briggs. With a disposition like a German shepherd dog, he took no crap from anyone and suspected everyone of being against him.

When his second officer told him of the freighter adrift in their shipping lane with smoke pouring out of its forward hold, he was immediately suspicious.

"Hans," he told his second in command, "issue weapons to the men and stand by the radio. This does not look kosher to me."

"But Captain," Hans argued, "they are obviously in need of assistance."

Schmidt glared at him, daring him to question his orders a second time. "Perhaps a bit too obvious. If they are what they seem to be, we will certainly provide help," he growled. "But since they sent no radio message asking for help or declaring a Mayday, I intend to approach them with all due caution."

"Aye, Captain," Hans said, trying to hide his anger. He didn't know what the old man was worried about. They'd off-loaded all of their oil in Houston two weeks previously. What did he think he had for anyone to steal?

"While I prepare a boarding party," the captain said

just before leaving the bridge, "radio the port authorities at Bushehr and tell them about the freighter. They will need to warn other ships in this lane to be careful."

Schmidt put six men, all armed with side arms, in the captain's gig and told them to check out the freighter. "But be careful when you board her," he advised, touching his nose. "Something doesn't smell right about a disabled ship that sent no radio message asking for help."

Half an hour later, while watching through binoculars from his bridge, Captain Schmidt saw his gig appear out of the haze of smoke, which hung around the freighter. Several men could be seen lying in the boat with bloody bandages around their heads, covering their faces.

"Hans, come here and look. Tell me what you see," he said.

Since he hadn't sent any shortwave radios with his men, the captain had had no contact with his crew since they boarded the ship.

Hans took another pair of binoculars from a hook on the wall and peered through them. "It appears the men have found some casualties, sir, and are bringing them back to the ship for medical care."

"Look closely at the man at the helm, Hans. Look at his face."

Hans took another look. "I can't see much, Captain. His hat is pulled too low."

"No, you idiot, look at his chin."

Hans gasped. "Why, he seems to have a beard, Captain."

Schmidt nodded. He allowed none of his crew to have facial hair. "That means he is not one of our men, Hans, and yet he is wearing the uniform of one of our officers."

Hans looked up at Schmidt, alarm in his eyes. "Do you think they are pirates, sir?"

Schmidt snorted. "Whatever they are, they have no business on my ship. Alert the hands to stand by with weapons ready but out of sight. We will give these gentlemen a surprise when they try to come aboard!"

"Aye, sir!"

As the gig pulled alongside and the men in it started to climb up the ladder that had been lowered, all of the crewmen on the tanker suddenly raised their weapons and took aim.

Kemal Dervis, assigned by Al Hazmi to take over this last ship, peeked out from under the brim of the officer's hat he'd taken off the tanker crewman he'd shot dead.

When he saw the tanker's crew all armed and ready, he spoke briefly into a radio he held in his hand. "Al Hazmi, it is a trap! They are . . ." His transmission was interrupted by the captain yelling through a loudspeaker.

"Drop your weapons and hold up your hands or we will fire!"

Dervis whipped out the Uzi submachine gun he had hidden under his coat, and fired off a burst at the crewmen above.

One of the crewmen yelled and grabbed at his face, which exploded in a spray of blood.

The others began to fire down into the boat without hesitation. Dervis went down in the first hail of bullets, as did two of his men.

The three men lying in the boat with blood-soaked bandages over their heads sat up and began to fire assault rifles they had under the sheets.

Just as the last of the men in the gig were gunned

down, the Magna Marine patrol boat Hazmi kept next to the freighter came roaring out of the smoke and haze. The twenty-seven-foot-long boat was loaded with men, all of whom were firing automatic weapons at the tanker.

Two men at the rear of the boat aimed grenade launchers as the boat sped past the tanker, and fired. The fragmentation grenades exploded in a hail of shrapnel, killing over half of the men defending the ship.

As the boat circled, a man stood up holding a Stinger missile launcher to his shoulder, while another held a loudspeaker to his mouth.

"Captain, surrender your ship or I will blow it out of the water!"

Schmidt, from his position on the bridge, could clearly see the missile launcher aimed at his ship.

"Captain, you must surrender," Hans pleaded. "Most of our men are already dead, and that missile will sink the ship!"

"Damn your eyes, Hans, I will *not* give up my ship!" Schmidt roared back, his eyes still glued to the binoculars.

Hans, sweat pouring off his brow, took a deep breath. He had to save the rest of the men, no matter the cost.

He pulled his pistol out of its holster and stuck it in the captain's back. "I'm sorry, sir, but I can't let you get the rest of the men killed just to save your command."

Schmidt turned, his eyes blazing. "You damned traitor! I'll see you hanged for this!"

Al Hazmi stood on the bridge, his eyes dark with anger as he faced Captain Schmidt. "Are you the one who gave orders to shoot my men?" he asked, his voice harsh.

Schmidt glared at Hans, standing next to him, for a

moment, and then he answered, his voice firm. "Yes, and I would have killed the whole lot of you bastards were it not for this turncoat!"

Hazmi pulled a pistol from his holster and shot the captain in the face without another word. Schmidt's head snapped back, blood and brains spraying all over Hans's uniform.

As Hans gasped in terror and disbelief, Hazmi said to him in a conversational voice, "You are now in command of your men. Have them dump this piece of camel dung overboard and then get to work repairing the damage to your vessel. If they do a good job, I may let them live."

Just then, the radio crackled to life. "Vessel *Grosse Hund*, come in *Grosse Hund*."

Hazmi rested his hand on the handle of his pistol. "Captain, I suggest you answer that call, and be careful what you say or you will join the previous captain in hell."

Hans keyed the microphone. "*Grosse Hund* here."

"This is the port officer at Bushehr in Iran. What is the status of the disabled freighter you called about two hours ago?"

"Tell them it was a minor engine failure that has been repaired. There is no further cause for alarm," Hazmi dictated to the terrified Hans.

Hans did as he was told, and after the port officer signed off, Hazmi shoved him roughly toward the door to the bridge. "Now, get your men to work, or the fish will have more food before the day is out," Hazmi growled.

TEN

It took almost a day and a half for all of the Scouts and Buddy's team to be checked out on the heavy equipment they were learning to operate. After that was done, they took to the roads in a mile-long convoy headed south by southwest.

Buddy's team was loaded in the back of a deuce and a half truck, while the Scouts were divided up in other trucks and tanks and assault vehicles.

As they bounced along Highway 27 South, Coop asked Buddy where they were headed. He had to speak very loudly to be heard over the whine of the truck's big engine.

"Our final destination is what used to be the Big Bend National Park in the days before the big bang. But on the way, we're gonna stop off and do some training in the Glass Mountains near Alpine."

"Hey, a national park, huh?" Coop said, grinning. "That don't sound too bad."

Buddy laughed. "It may not sound too bad, but the Big Bend National Park is the last place God made. It's right in the middle of the Chisos Mountains and is the roughest, driest, nastiest country this side of Mexico."

"I've heard the rattlesnakes are so thick there, you have to shout to be heard over the rattling," Jersey said with a malevolent glare at Coop. She still hadn't forgotten his comment about her lack of femininity earlier.

Coop's face blanched. "Is that true?" he asked Buddy.

Buddy shook his head, his face serious. "Naw, not at all. I'm told the snakes there are nothing to worry about . . . now the bears, wolves, and cougars are something else again."

"Oh, shit," Coop moaned.

"That's not the worst of it," Jersey added. "I hear they're gonna train us to live off the land like the Scouts do—learn to eat lizards and snakes and bugs and stuff."

"You've got to be kidding me," Coop said.

"Those MREs you're always complaining about starting to sound better to you now?" Buddy asked, knowing of Coop's reputation as a chowhound.

"I've never complained about Meals, Ready to Eat," Coop protested.

"Yeah, but we could tell you didn't like 'em 'cause you never ate more than two or three at a time," Hammer observed wryly.

Coop turned his head. "Now don't you go getting on my case too," he said. "Guys are supposed to hang together."

Hammer leaned back and held up his hands. "Hey, just stating a fact, Coop, just tellin' it like it is."

The convoy stopped near the city of Alpine, and when Buddy and the Scout commander, Major Jackson Bean, found that the Glass Mountains were covered with pine trees and other evergreen varieties, they agreed the area wasn't suitable for the type of training their men needed.

"If we end up doing an intrusion into the Middle East, especially the mountainous regions of Afghanistan or the like, we're gonna need something a little more forbidding to train on," Bean said, staring at the peaks covered with a thick layer of pines.

"Then it sounds like we need to go further south, to the Chisos Mountains," Buddy said.

The convoy was loaded up again, and they moved toward the Big Bend area just north of the Texas-Mexican border.

"Buddy," Beth said, peering at a topographical map of the region, "It says here the highest peak in the Chisos is Emory Peak at 7825 feet."

He nodded. "That's right, and from what I've been told, that's roughly comparable to the ones we may be facing in the Middle East."

"I thought that area was relatively flat," Corrie said.

"Much of it is, especially the oil field regions," Buddy said. "But since we don't know where we'll be needed, or even *if* we'll have to go, headquarters figures we oughta cover all the bases."

After about an hour on the road, Coop leaned down, took off one of his combat boots, and held it up in front of his face.

"What the hell are you doing, Coop?" Jersey asked.

"I'm so hungry, I'm trying to decide if I can eat this boot without cooking it."

Buddy laughed. "Okay, hint taken. I'll radio Major Bean and see if we can pull over long enough to cook some chow."

Coop leaned over and looked at the map Beth was holding. "I see we're coming up on the town of Marathon," he said with a hopeful gleam in his eye. "Maybe they'll have a restaurant there."

"Yeah," Jersey said scornfully. "Maybe you can get a buffalo burger or something."

"Buffalo? Can you really eat buffalo?"

"My ancestors thought it quite a delicacy," Harley Reno said, licking his lips.

"Compared to what?" Coop asked. "Dog?"

Harley grinned. "Don't knock eating dog, Coop, unless you've tried it."

Coop grimaced. "I think I've just lost my appetite."

"That'll be the day!" Jersey said, causing the entire team to laugh.

That night, after they'd set up camp at the base of Emory Peak, Buddy and Major Bean issued night-vision goggles to all the troops and had them fit their weapons with the new Raptor night-vision weapon sights.

"If we do make an incursion, most of our fighting will probably be at night, so we want you to get used to coordinating your team movements in the dark. We've sent out some of the Scouts to set up targets so as you move up the mountain, you'll have something to shoot at besides each other."

"Uh, Buddy," Coop asked, raising his hand, "do snakes come out at night?"

"Only the poisonous ones," Jersey volunteered.

"Coop," Buddy said, "if you see a snake, you have my permission to shoot it."

"Hey, if you get bitten, we can practice cutting the wound open and sucking out the poison," Harley said.

"Unless you get bitten on the butt," Jersey said. "In that case, you're gonna die!"

After three days and nights doing intensive night and day training exercises, Major Bean met with Buddy to evaluate the troopers' progress.

They were in his command tent when Corrie stepped to the door. "Buddy, Major Bean, I've got Ben on the SOHFRAD calling for you."

"Come on in and put it on speaker-mode," Major Bean said.

Moments later, Ben's voice was heard. "How's the training going?" he asked.

"Fine, General," Bean answered. "I think the men are about ready for anything now."

"That's good, because we've got some worrisome intel from across the pond."

"Is it that Smeyth fellow again?" Buddy asked.

"Yes. He says there's been some trouble in the Persian Gulf he wants to brief us on personally. He's on his way now, but from the tone, I think you'd better round the guys up and head on back. When you get here, I'll give you a sitrep and we'll decide what we need to do."

"Roger that, Ben," Buddy said.

ELEVEN

While the C-130 transport plane was on the way to pick them up, Buddy and Major Bean had the troops use the heavy equipment they'd been training on to enlarge and flatten the civilian landing strip just outside the small town of Castolon in the Big Bend area.

"It doesn't have to be perfect," Buddy told the Scouts assigned to drive the big tractors and graders. "Those big C-130 birds can land on just about anything, if it's long enough."

"Shouldn't be a problem, sir," Sergeant Rutledge answered, staring out at the long expanse of caliche and sand, which comprised most of the ground in the area. "Main thing we have to do is plow down some of those mesquite trees and cactus patches."

"Good," Buddy said, glancing at his wristwatch, " 'cause the bird'll be here in three hours."

As Rutledge promised, the field was ready by the allotted time, and the C-130 transport landed without any problem. The troops and equipment were loaded aboard and less than an hour and a half after landing, the plane took off again, headed back to Ben's headquarters in Louisiana.

***

Abdullah El Farrar scheduled all of the tankers his men had taken over to dock at four o'clock in the morning, local time. He knew that was the time the guards and troops protecting the ports would be at their least alert—just over halfway through their watches. Various excuses had been radioed to the port authorities to explain the changes in the tankers' schedules. Most tankers had merely claimed engine trouble of different kinds, occurrences not uncommon in the aging tanker fleets.

The port at Dhahran in Saudi Arabia was darkened and appeared almost deserted. Normal port activities weren't scheduled to begin for another couple of hours.

Al Hazmi himself was in command of the tanker as it made its way slowly into the shallow waters of the port. The men manning the tugboats that helped pull the big ship gently into the docks were barely awake, having been rousted from their beds to work just hours after they'd gotten to sleep.

The tanker docks were some little ways offshore, almost a quarter mile, since the tankers that used the facilities were much too large to berth at the regular docks.

As soon as the tanker was tied down, the radio crackled to life. It was the harbormaster calling.

"Captain," he said, "would you come to the harbormaster's office, please. We need to go over some paperwork before we load your oil."

"Certainly," Al Hazmi answered, putting on a thick German accent. "My men have been at sea for some time, and I will bring them in to shore so they can have a few hours' liberty."

The harbormaster grunted. "They won't see much at this hour. Most of the shops and markets are still closed."

"That's all right," Hazmi said agreeably. "Most of them just want to feel firm ground under their feet for a change."

"We do have plenty of that," the master said with a short laugh.

"Will there be any problem with security?" Hazmi asked. "I wouldn't want my men detained for lack of appropriate documentation."

"Don't worry about that," the master replied. "Most of the U.N. soldiers are asleep, and I'll alert the two men on duty that you'll be coming ashore. They won't bother you."

Hazmi smiled. "That's good to know."

As soon as he got off the radio, Hazmi inspected his men, who were lined up ready to take the port by storm. They'd all been issued night-vision goggles and carried Uzis with silencers attached. Hazmi wanted the assault to be as quiet as possible, because they still had quite a ways to go before they got to the oil fields themselves and he didn't want to alert the U.N. forces that anything was amiss.

His men filed into the tanker's large tender and made their way toward the dock area at a sedate pace so as not to arouse suspicion. As they pulled into the dock and made the tender fast, Hazmi, wearing a captain's uniform with a pistol concealed under his coat, walked nonchalantly toward the guard post at the end of the pier with two of his men following.

When he got to the small booth, two guards emerged. One was yawning widely and the other had a cup of coffee in his hand. Neither had his weapon at the ready.

"Try not to get too much blood on the uniforms," Hazmi whispered over his shoulder.

He moved toward the guards, holding out his hand with a sheet of paper in it as if to give them a shore pass.

When the guard reached for it, Hazmi's men moved quickly. Knives were drawn and held under the guards' chins.

"Step back into the booth," Hazmi said, "and you won't be harmed."

Once the men were inside and out of sight, they were made to strip down to their underwear. "Lie facedown on the floor with your hands behind your backs so we can tie you up," Hazmi commanded.

When they complied, Hazmi nodded at his men, who calmly reached down and grabbed the men by the hair, pulled their heads back, and cut their throats. While the men were still writhing in their death throes, Hazmi's men donned their uniforms, noting the names of the guards that were stenciled on the shirts.

"You have approximately three and a half hours until the shift changes," Hazmi told them, glancing at his watch. "If anyone calls on the telephone, cough and speak with a raspy voice as if you have a cold." He'd picked these two men to man the guard post because of their command of English, the main language of the U.N. troops assigned to protect the ports.

"Thirty minutes before eight o'clock in the morning, leave the post, commandeer a vehicle, and follow the maps you have to the oil fields to join us."

Both men nodded, though they were sweating with the knowledge that the odds of them getting away were slim.

With the guard post taken care of, Hazmi went outside and gave a signal. The rest of his men came running. He sent them into the city to find suitable transportation for his troops and equipment to the oil fields.

In less than fifteen minutes, they were back with sev-

ENEMY IN THE ASHES 77

eral large trucks. "Make sure they are filled with gasoline," Hazmi warned as the men loaded the trucks with munitions, grenades, assault rifles, missile launchers, and most importantly, the containers of plutonium Hazmi had brought to put around the oil wells and storage facilities at the fields.

The entire process of landing and taking control of the port had taken less than thirty minutes—fifteen less than Hazmi had figured on.

The *Grosse Hund*, under command of Abdul Muttmain, had a similarly easy time when they sailed into the port at Bushehr in Iran. Hans, thoroughly cowed by the cold-blooded murder of his captain, talked to the harbormaster on the radio and cleared the way for the ship to be berthed at the tanker docking facilities.

Muttmain followed the same plan as Hazmi had, and his men had no trouble subduing and then killing the few U.N. soldiers standing guard at the port. In less than an hour after docking, Muttmain and his crew, with their weapons and plutonium, were on their way to the oil fields that dotted the countryside of Iran.

The *Exxon Marquis*, under the command of Dinise Jabagh, wasn't to be so lucky. Jabagh made the mistake of leaving Captain Jason Briggs in the bridge so he could communicate with the port authorities if necessary.

Briggs was an extremely intelligent man, and years of sailing in the Persian Gulf had allowed him to become conversant in most of the languages of the region. Jabagh and his men, when discussing their plans for the takeover of the port at Kuwait City among themselves, spoke in their native tongue, never guessing the infidel standing next to them would be able to understand what they were saying.

Once Briggs became aware of their plan, he knew it was imperative that he stop them, even at the cost of every life on the ship if necessary.

To make his plan work, Briggs knew he must make Jabagh feel that he would be incapable of going against the Arab's wishes. As they moved closer to Kuwait City, Briggs began to sob and moan, shaking and trembling as if in great fear.

Jabagh glanced at him with evident distaste. "What is wrong, Captain?" he asked, his voice dripping with scorn.

"I'm afraid you are going to kill me once we reach the port," Briggs moaned in a weak, rasping voice.

Jabagh spoke in a low tone to his second in command, Mustafa Harim. "This infidel dog is going to soil himself unless we let him believe he will survive all this."

He then turned to Captain Briggs. "Don't worry, Captain," he said, unaware Briggs had understood every word of his aside to Harim. "I have told you that if you cooperate fully, nothing will happen to you and your men."

"Promise?" Briggs groveled.

Jabagh had to fight to keep his disgust with the weakling captain out of his voice. "Yes, Captain, I promise."

As they neared the port, Jabagh tapped Mustafa Harim on the shoulder. "Keep your eyes on this sniveling dog for a moment. I must use the rest room before our arrival in Kuwait." He grinned. "I am afraid we will be much too busy killing infidels after that to take the time."

Harim grinned back. He patted the automatic pistol on his belt. "Do not worry, Dinise. This coward will give me no trouble."

After Jabagh left, Briggs wasted no time. He got to his feet, still crying as if in terror.

"What are you doing?" Harim asked harshly, his hand moving to the butt of his pistol.

"I need to get a handkerchief out of the drawer to wipe my eyes," Briggs moaned.

Harim spat on the floor. "Go ahead," he said, turning his eyes back to the course of the ship.

Briggs opened a drawer in front of the padded captain's chair he usually occupied, and wrapped his fingers around a silver ballpoint pen that had been a gift from his wife.

He looked up, his eyes wide with feigned terror, and pointed out the side window. "Look!" he yelled in alarm.

Harim turned his head to see what had scared the captain, and then he gasped as Briggs drove the point of the pen into his carotid artery.

Harim tried to scream, but his vocal cords were ruined and his blood was spurting in a steady stream all over the cabin. He jumped out of the captain's chair and took two steps, his hands outreached in claws toward Briggs, before he collapsed to the floor dead.

Briggs bent and pulled the pistol from Harim's holster, locked the bridge doors, and turned on the radio.

When the harbormaster at Kuwait City answered, Briggs quickly told him his ship had been taken over by terrorists and was out of his control.

"We will alert the U.N. forces in the city," the harbormaster said. "What are you going to do?"

Briggs grinned as he sleeved Harim's blood off his face. "I'm going to send the bastards to meet Allah," he growled, and then he smashed the radio beyond repair.

He turned the wheel of the ship all the way to the left, locked it in place, and then bent and reached under the counter in front of the wheel. He pulled all of the wires loose so the wheel couldn't be repositioned, just in case he failed in his mission. In that event, the tanker would move in a continuous circle and go nowhere.

Once that was accomplished, Briggs slipped out of the bridge and moved down side corridors toward the rear hold, where Jabagh had stored the munitions until they could be off-loaded at Kuwait City.

Luckily, there was no moon tonight, and the passageways were clothed in darkness. At the entrance to the hold, there were two men standing guard, but their attention was not on the task at hand. They were drinking what smelled like very strong coffee to Briggs, and chatting about how beautiful the women of Kuwait were supposed to be.

Briggs eased the safety off on the pistol, took careful aim, and fired twice in quick succession. The pistol, equipped with a silencer, as were all of the terrorists' handguns, coughed and the two men went down without a sound.

Briggs jumped over their bodies and hurried down the ladder into the hold. His eyes widened at the amount of munitions in the place. He'd never seen so many guns and rifles and missiles and grenades in one place since his days in the British Army as a teenager.

He put the pistol in his belt, picked up an Uzi and as many magazines as he could stuff into his pockets, and two fragmentation grenades, which he clipped to his belt.

As he climbed back up the ladder, he heard the ship's horn blaring. Evidently Jabagh had found Harim in the bridge.

Briggs took a deep breath. It was now or never. He took the hand grenades off his belt, pulled the pins, and then tossed them down into the hold.

Spinning around, he ran as fast as his legs could carry him toward the forward hold. He was going to rescue his men if at all possible, or die trying.

He never heard the shot that killed him. One of Jabagh's men, seeing him running along the corridor, let go with a burst from his Uzi. The first bullet fired hit Briggs in the back of his neck, killing him instantly.

Jabagh, hearing the shots, leaned over the rail that ran around the bridge, and saw Briggs fall.

"Good shot!" he yelled to the soldier, who was holding up his Uzi with a wide grin on his face.

When the grenades exploded in the rear hold, they set off over two tons of high explosives. The resulting fireball blew the back half of the ship off and sent a shock wave that knocked Jabagh over the rail he was leaning on. He screamed all the way down to the deck thirty feet below.

The *Exxon Marquis* took less than three minutes to disappear beneath the rolling swells of the Persian Gulf.

Thus, there was no one to hear when the harbormaster at Kuwait City radioed ten minutes later. "Captain Briggs . . . Captain Briggs on the *Exxon Marquis*. Can you read me?"

When his only answer was silence, the harbormaster turned to his assistant. "Get me the head of the U.N. security forces on the telephone. Now! This is an emergency!"

TWELVE

When Buddy's team assembled in Ben's office, they found Ben and Mike Post already meeting with the SAS soldier, Bartholomew Wiley-Smeyth. Since they'd come directly from the landing field after their flight home on the C-130, Ben arranged for his secretary to have the cooks at the mess hall bring them some food.

While they feasted on sandwiches, tea, and coffee, Ben filled them in on the reason for Bart's visit.

"Bart has come over to share with us some recent intel his security forces have come up with," Ben said, inclining his head toward Bart. "Why don't you tell them what you told Mike and me a little while ago?"

Bart cleared his throat. "You remember that two of my men were killed while trying to stop a man named Muhammad Atwa from delivering a shipment of plutonium to some unknown destination in the Middle East?"

When Buddy nodded, Bart continued. "Well, after I got back home from my visit here, I put all of our Middle Eastern resources on high alert to see if we could find out what was going on."

"Did you get any results?" Buddy asked around a mouthful of tuna on rye.

Bart nodded. "Yes. My agents reported a high degree of activity near Kandahar in Afghanistan. Rebels and old revolutionary troops were pouring across the border with Pakistan and out of the mountains, and they were all headed for Kandahar."

Harley Reno stopped eating to listen. "Any idea who they were going there to meet?"

"The name Abdullah El Farrar came up several times, along with a man named Farid Zamet, who at this point is unknown to our Intel resources."

Harley glanced at Mike Post. "I thought El Farrar was disgraced and out of favor after his failed coup attempt last year in the U.S."

"That is the information we had," Mike said, shrugging. "But as you all know, things can change rather rapidly in the Middle East. Alliances and loyalties can change almost by the hour over there, depending on who promises the most to the various tribal chieftains and their followers. Our information was that El Farrar as well as his family were on the verge of bankruptcy after the U.N. managed to freeze all of their banking assets."

"Evidently not all of the El Farrar family's resources were found and frozen," Bart said. "Some of the Arab banks don't exactly cooperate with the Western nations in matters that affect the Muslim world."

Buddy spoke up. "So what if that megalomaniac wants to come after us again? With our Intel and satellites, we should be able to keep track of what he's up to day by day. If he starts to send troops out of Afghanistan, it should be relatively easy to counter his moves almost before he makes them."

Bart nodded. "That's what we figured and why we weren't particularly concerned, until we got some worrisome information two days ago."

"What did you hear?" Buddy asked just before stuffing the last of his sandwich into his mouth.

"We got wind of a several freighters setting sail from the port of Karachi in Pakistan last week. When we sent men in to question the dockworkers, they said the ships were loaded with men and munitions."

Buddy shrugged. "So what? Farrar couldn't put enough men or matériel on a few old freighters to do much of anything."

"You're right, up to a point, Buddy," Bart conceded. "But the thing that worried us most was the dockworkers also mentioned noticing some rather strange metal containers that were guarded closely. They said the troops themselves loaded these metal containers, and wouldn't let any of the stevedores near them."

Buddy's eyes widened. "So, you think these ships were also carrying the plutonium Atwa delivered?"

"That's our best guess."

"Were you able to track the ships, either by airplane or satellite?" Harley asked.

"That's one of the things that has us worried. We thought for sure the ships would head out into the Arabian Sea toward one of the Western nations, but they didn't. Instead, they just proceeded to cruise around the Persian Gulf, making big circles, as if they were waiting for someone or something."

Harley's eyes became vacant as he stared at the ceiling. "Sounds to me, Bart, like they may be planning to move against one of the countries bordering the Gulf."

Bart sighed. "Our Intel agrees with you, Harley. I even went so far as to call Jean-François Chapelle at U.N. headquarters and ask him to put the troops guarding the ports along the Gulf on high alert."

Ben snorted through his nose. "Hah, I can probably tell you what he said."

Bart glanced at Ben.

"He probably said he couldn't do that because it would be a provocation to the poor law-abiding countries of the Middle East to accuse them of plotting terrorist attacks without any proof," Ben concluded sarcastically.

Bart laughed. "Damn if those weren't almost his exact words."

Ben shook his head. "The U.N. is nothing more than a bunch of lily-livered do-gooders who don't have balls enough to do what they're supposed to be in business to do. They sit around and talk and talk and talk until whatever is going to happen has already happened. They are the personification of that old cliché about locking the barn door after the horses have all gotten out."

"But Ben," Coop said, a puzzled look on his face, "I thought you like Jean-François."

Ben smiled a crooked smile. "Hell, I do like the man; mainly because he pretty much leaves us alone to do what has to be done without trying to interfere. 'Course, that don't mean the U.N. is worth a shit—not when you actually need them to do something."

Bart continued to chuckle. "Ben, it always amazes me when we talk, because you and I feel so much alike about so many things."

"So, what do you think is going to happen out there in the Gulf?" Buddy asked.

Bart had opened his mouth to answer when Ben's secretary stuck her head in the door. "I don't mean to interrupt, General," she said, "but Mr. Chapelle from the U.N. is on the phone."

Ben clapped his hands, laughing. "Speak of the devil," he said. "Put Monsieur Chapelle through, please."

When his phone buzzed a few seconds later, Ben picked it up. "Hello, Jean-François. I'm in a meeting with

Mike Post and Bartholomew Wiley-Smeyth, so I'm going to put you on the speaker if that's all right."

After a moment, Ben pressed a button on his phone and put it back on the hook.

"Good afternoon, gentlemen," Chapelle's voice said over the speaker.

Once greetings were exchanged, Chapelle got down to business. "It is good that you are there, Bartholomew, because you are part of the reason I called."

"Yes, what is it, Jean?" Bart answered.

There was a pause, and finally Chapelle cleared his throat. "I am sorry I failed to heed your warning of a few days ago, Bartholomew."

"So, the terrorists have finally made a move?" Bart asked.

"Yes, I'm afraid so. By means of faking distress at sea, the terrorists managed to board and take control of several tankers headed back to countries in the Middle East."

"But Jean, those tankers would have been empty," Ben said. "What did they gain by that?"

"Entry into the ports of Iran, Iraq, Saudi Arabia, and several other countries, Ben. In fact, Kuwait was only spared because one of the tanker captains was able to warn them and then blow his ship out of the water before they could get to the port."

"You mean they used the tankers as Trojan horses to get into the ports?"

"Exactly right. Once they'd overpowered or killed the U.N. troops stationed there as guards, they landed sizable forces and then headed for the major oil fields of each country."

"Can't you stop them?" Bart asked.

Another pause. "The U.N. is forbidden to send troops on a mission of war, at least not without a full vote of the General Assembly. I am working as hard as I can to do that even as we speak."

"And meanwhile, the troops you already have stationed guarding the oil fields are being slaughtered, right?" Ben asked, his voice dripping with scorn.

"I am well aware of your feelings about the rule of law that the U.N. has to follow, General Raines . . ."

"If you think I believe your organization to be a total waste of time, then you are correct!" Ben almost shouted.

Chapelle's voice remained calm. "Be that as it may, we will act to rid the countries of these invaders, although perhaps not as fast as you would wish, Ben."

"And you will be too little, too late, as always, Jean," Ben replied.

"What harm is there in a few days delay?" Jean asked. "After all, with the small number of troops in each country, they can't hope to hold the oil fields for long."

Bart snapped his fingers, his face blanching. "Damn! Of course, that's it!"

"I'm sorry, Bart," Jean said. "I didn't get that."

"It's plutonium, Jean," Bart said. "We have reports the terrorists recently acquired a substantial amount of weapons-grade plutonium."

"You can't seriously believe these men are capable of producing an atomic weapon?" Jean asked.

"They don't need to blow the plutonium up, Jean. Just use a conventional explosive to disburse the plutonium dust over the oil fields, and they will be radioactive for hundreds of years. They can make over half the world's oil supply unusable with what they have in their hands right now!"

"Oh . . . Jesus," Jean whispered.

Ben leaned forward on his desk. "Jean, I suggest you let me and Bart send in some troops posthaste. Do whatever you have to in order to get the countries involved to cooperate with us, or you're going to have a catastrophe on your hands."

"Yes—yes, I'll see what I can do," Chapelle said in a stricken voice. "I'll get back to you shortly."

"Better not waste any time, Jean," Ben said grimly. "Just tell the heads of those countries that they'll be poor as church mice without their oil, and I'm sure they'll see the light."

"Good-bye, Ben, Bart," Chapelle said, and hung up the phone.

"I've got an idea, Ben," Buddy said after Chapelle was off the line.

"Go on, Buddy," Ben said.

"Chapelle said Kuwait was spared and is still in control of its oil fields, right?"

Ben nodded.

"Instead of waiting for the U.N. to get permission for us to mount a counterattack from the countries involved, why don't we see if Kuwait will allow us to use their airfields? That way, we could be in the area and ready to go by the time Chapelle gets all of his bureaucratic bullshit out of the way."

Ben looked at Bart and smiled. "I think that's a great idea. What about you, Bart?"

"I agree," Bart said enthusiastically. "I'll get on the horn and have a squadron of my SAS chaps ready to go within six hours."

"Mike," Ben said, "get in touch with President Jeffreys and see if he can get permission from Kuwait for us to mount an operation out of their country."

"What if the Emir won't agree?" Mike asked.

Ben grinned. "Tell Cecil to remind the Emir that if the terrorists aren't stopped, his country will be next on the list of those to be attacked, and if his oil fields are destroyed, the entire royal family will have to go to work to earn a living like the rest of us."

Mike laughed. "That ought to do the trick. I'll get right on it."

"And tell Cecil if he needs to talk to me, I'll be right here getting ready to go kick some terrorist ass!"

"Correction, Ben," Buddy said. "You'll be here getting ready to send *us* to go kick some ass."

Ben's face fell. "Oh, yeah. I almost forgot I gave you command."

Buddy grinned and spread his hands. "You can always change your mind."

"No, I meant what I said. It's time for you to take over." He pursed his lips, "But of course, I'll still be around to give you some advice if you need it."

THIRTEEN

Luckily for Al Hazmi, the heaviest concentration of oil wells was in Eastern Saudi Arabia, near the port of Dhahran, so he and his men didn't have far to travel to reach their destination.

They arrived at the old Aramco offices, now redesignated Unoco, for U.N. Oil Company, well before dawn. As at the port, the U.N. soldiers guarding the facility were at minimum force at this time of the morning.

A small guard cubicle and a wooden board blocked the road into the office complex, which was on the eastern edge of a very large oil field. The board across the road could be raised and lowered by the guard.

There were two guards in the cubicle: one standing drinking hot tea, and the other slumped in a chair against the far wall, sound asleep with his chin on his chest.

Al Hazmi got out of the passenger seat of the lead truck and, holding his silenced pistol down by his leg, approached the guardhouse.

The guard stepped out of the door and held up his hand. "Yes, can I help you?" he asked in Arabic.

Hazmi talked as he walked closer to the man. "Why, yes," he said. "I have a shipment of oil field machinery to be delivered here today."

The guard consulted a clipboard in his hand. "I see no indication a shipment is due," he said.

When he looked up from the clipboard, he found he was staring down the barrel of a 9mm pistol. "Of course you don't," Hazmi said. "I lied."

With that, he pulled the trigger and shot the guard in the forehead, snapping his head back and dropping him to the ground. Hazmi stepped over the still-twitching body and leaned in the door of the guardhouse.

The sleeping guard stirred and opened his eyes. "Good morning," Hazmi said as he pulled the trigger, killing the man instantly where he sat.

Hazmi stationed four men at the guardhouse, along with a couple of LAWS antitank missile launchers and a fifty-caliber machine gun on a tripod.

"Don't let anyone pass," he told them.

"Yes, sir," one of the men answered.

Hazmi then directed the other trucks toward a building off to the side of the Unoco offices. It had several jeeps with U.N. insignias on the fenders, and he figured it was the barracks for the rest of the U.N. troops assigned to guard the oil fields.

He signaled for two men to follow him, and he walked in the front door, which was unlocked. When he stepped inside, he saw thirty bunks in the room, fifteen on each side, with a small office at the far end of the room.

He waved his hand, and a man took up stance on either side of the room while Hazmi walked down the aisle toward the office. He opened the door and saw a man sleeping, with a uniform hanging on a hook with lieutenant bars on it. Stepping to the side of the bed, he put his pistol inches from the man's face, and then he reconsidered. He didn't want to be covered with the poor man's blood and brains, so he picked up a nearby pillow and put it over the man's head. When he fired through the pillow, the man's legs jumped and bucked for a few seconds, and then he was still.

Hazmi holstered his pistol and walked back down the aisle. When he reached the end, he glanced over his shoulder and said, "Kill them all."

As he walked outside, he heard the chatter of the AK-47's his men were carrying as they assassinated all of the U.N. troops in the building. Other than a few scattered screams and moans, there was no sound other than the distinctive chatter of the Kalashnikovs.

Hazmi got in his truck and told the driver to drive toward the oil fields. "There is no need to check the offices," he said, "None of the workers will be here at this hour."

After setting up a defensive perimeter around the edge of the field, Hazmi instructed the explosives expert to set the plutonium bombs around the area, paying special attention to the huge storage tanks off to one side of the producing wells. The bombs, which had been prepared in advance, were camouflaged to look like ordinary pump motors, so they would be hard for a bomb squad to discover and disarm in the event it came to that.

By the time the sun was rising, Hazmi had everything prepared. He spread his men out and had them dig in around the perimeter of the oil field, preparing deep foxholes in case some foolhardy government tried to attack his forces. He carried a special radio-control device with him at all times. With it, he could detonate the plutonium bombs from anywhere within five miles of the fields.

Finally, he retired to his command tent in the middle of the field, and told his men to wake him when the officers of Unoco arrived. He had no illusions that his small force could defend their position against invaders, but he was counting on the threat of the plutonium bombs to keep them at bay until El Farrar's second phase of the plan could be initiated.

A similar attack was carried out by Abdul Muttmain on the plains of Iran, with the oil fields there also taken after all of the defending U.N. troops were killed. Unfortunately, by the time Muttmain and his troops got to the main oil fields, the Unoco officials were in their offices, and they were also killed without mercy by the bloodthirsty troops under Muttmain's command.

By noon of that day, oil fields in all of the major oil-producing countries of the Middle East were under the control of El Farrar's troops—all except Kuwait, where the intrusion had been prevented by the selfless sacrifice of Captain Jason Briggs.

In Kandahar, El Farrar, along with his associates Farid Zamet and Muhammad Atwa, was jubilant at the news of their almost total success.

"It is a shame that we weren't able to take control of the fields in Kuwait, but they make up only a small part of the total production under the control of Unoco," El Farrar said.

"However, after the second phase of your plan his been accomplished, we should be able to move on Kuwait without any sizable resistance," Atwa reminded him.

El Farrar nodded. "Yes, and it is now time to put the second phase into operation," he said. He picked up the phone on his desk and asked his radioman to get him in touch with Jean-François Chapelle as soon as possible.

* * *

"Monsieur Chapelle," El Farrar said twenty minutes later when the Secretary General of the U.N. was on the line. "I am sure by now you have heard of the events which have transpired over the past twelve hours."

"Mr. El Farrar, would you tell me what you hope to gain by this unwarranted attack against your neighboring countries? Surely you know that the meager forces you have in place cannot be allowed to stand?" Chapelle replied haughtily.

El Farrar permitted himself a small laugh. "Oh, but I think you will reconsider your attitude, Monsieur Le Secretary General, when I tell what will happen should your U.N. be so rash as to try and take the oil fields back."

"What do you mean?"

"My men have in each of the locations dozens of small packages of plutonium attached to high-explosive charges. These bombs, which are arranged so as to do maximal damage to the oil fields, will be set off if anyone tries to attack or otherwise interfere with my men."

"But . . . but that is insane!" Chapelle argued. "That would ruin most of the world's oil supply for generations."

"I am glad you understand, Chapelle," El Farrar said, all hint of civility gone from his voice.

"All right, it seems we are at an impasse. What are your demands?"

"Not now, Chapelle. First, I am going to airlift in some more troops to each location, just to be sure you don't try anything stupid. Would you be so kind as to instruct all of the nations involved not to attempt any interference with the planes delivering my troops?"

"You know I cannot tell sovereign nations what to do with their airspace," Chapelle reasoned.

"Then, just inform them that if they do interfere with

any of my transports, I will explode my bombs and render their oil fields useless to them."

"But that would mean killing your own men."

"My men are perfectly willing to martyr themselves in a good cause, Chapelle. But you'd better hope they don't have to, for it will mean everyone has lost in this game we are playing."

"All right, El Farrar. I will do what I can."

"I will contact you once again when my men are in place. And Chapelle . . ."

"Yes?"

"I would advise you to keep the general Assembly in close attendance. You will soon have some momentous decisions to make."

FOURTEEN

As Buddy and his team, along with Major Bean and his Scouts, boarded two large transport planes for the trip to Kuwait, he was surprised to see Ben Raines and Bartholomew Wiley-Smeyth approaching.

"Something else, Ben?" Buddy asked when they arrived at the ramp leading up into the transport.

"Yeah, Bart and I are going to hitch a ride."

"Oh," Buddy said, trying to hide the disappointment he felt. "So you are planning to resume command of the team?"

"Not at all, Buddy," Ben said. "I'm just coming along in case Mike Post and Cecil Jeffreys aren't able to convince the Emir of Kuwait to let us stage our operations from his country. And Bart here is going to ride with us to meet his troops when they arrive instead of flying all the way back to England first."

"But I assumed if we didn't have permission from the Emir by the time we got there, we'd just turn around and head back," Buddy said.

Ben shook his head. "That's not going to happen. This operation is much too important to let the stubbornness of one man decide the fate of the entire world."

"You mean, if he denies us permission to land, we'll do it anyway?" Buddy asked.

"Damn straight!" Ben said. "That's why I'm here. If we do have to land against the Emir's wishes, I'll take the heat for the decision, not you."

"You are aware that could lead to a war between Kuwait and the SUSA, aren't you?" Bart asked.

Ben shrugged. "I'm hoping it won't come to that. Cecil Jeffreys can be awfully persuasive when he needs to be. I'm sure we'll get the permission we need," Ben said. After a moment, he added, "And if we don't, to hell with all of them—we'll land anyway. It won't be the first time we've pulled Kuwait's fat out of the fire, will it?"

Three hours later, in the skies over the Atlantic Ocean, Ben was called to the pilot's compartment for a radio message.

"Who is it?" he asked the pilot as the man handed him a headset to wear.

"He says he's Jean François Chapelle from the U.N.," the pilot replied.

"Hello, Jean," Ben said into the mouth microphone. "Any news yet?"

"Plenty, I'm afraid," Chapelle replied. "I have just gotten off the phone with Abdullah El Farrar."

"What did the son of a bitch have to say?"

"He said he plans to airlift in some support troops to his positions in the oil fields of the various countries, and that if we try to interfere or shoot them down, he will explode the plutonium and contaminate the oil supply."

"He's bluffing," Ben said. "The plutonium is the bastard's only trump card. He won't dare play it so soon, at least not until he's told us what his demands are."

"We can't take that chance, Ben. I want you and your troops to stand down," Chapelle said.

"No," was Ben's short reply.

"What did you say?" Chapelle asked, as if he couldn't believe anyone would disobey his orders.

"I said no, Jean."

"You mean you are going to go against the orders of the United Nations?"

"Jean, the last time I looked, the SUSA was a sovereign country. We don't take orders from the U.N. or anyone else when our security is at stake."

"But Ben, you can't mean to risk the entire world's oil supply without the U.N.'s involvement."

"I'm not putting the oil supply at risk, Jean. You and your cowardly U.N. representatives are. Any time you give in to a despot's blackmail or threats, you weaken your organization. I would think you would have learned that from the debacles of three world wars, not to mention some minor conflicts like Vietnam, Bosnia, Haiti, the Gulf War, and Operation Enduring Freedom back at the turn of the century."

"Those were different circumstances, Ben," Chapelle argued, his voice short and clipped with anger.

"Bullshit, Jean. The U.N. was useless as teats on a boar hog in all of those wars, and this one will be no different if the world has to depend on you guys to solve it. You'll sit and talk and finally decide to give in to this terrorist, and then we'll all be under his thumb due to your inability to stand up to him."

"But we don't even know what his demands are yet," Chapelle said.

"It doesn't matter, Jean. The SUSA has never given in to blackmail and we never will. If that means we do without oil, then we'll find some other way, but at least we will be free, and that is what the SUSA is all about."

"Then you won't reconsider?"

"No. And you can tell this El Farrar that I'm coming for him. And this time, he'd better bend over and grab his ankles and kiss his ass good-bye. I won't let him run away and hide this time, 'cause I intend to give him the martyrdom he has ordered for so many of his followers in the past."

"I will tell him that, Ben, and I will also tell him you are acting as your own agent, outside of the authority of the United Nations."

"You do that, Jean. After all, it's way too late for you and the U.N. to grow some *cojones. Adios,*" Ben said, and clicked the radio off.

The pilot and copilot glanced at each other, and the pilot whistled under his breath. "Goddamn, that's tellin' him, Ben."

Ben grinned and handed the headset back, trying to stifle a yawn. "I'm gonna get some shut-eye. Wake me up when we're approaching Kuwait, gentlemen."

After Ben left the cockpit, the pilot shook his head. "Jesus, the man tells the head of the U.N. to kiss his ass and then goes calmly back to take a nap."

The copilot laughed. "That's Ben Raines, all right!"

Jean-François Chapelle clicked off the microphone, and turned to see his secretary staring at him open-mouthed. "Sir, what are you going to do about General Raines's blatant disregard of your authority?" the man asked.

Chapelle smiled and shook his head. "Oh, Henri, when will you ever learn the delicacies of diplomacy?" he asked.

"What do you mean, Monsieur Chapelle?" Henri asked, a puzzled expression on his face.

Chapelle took an unfiltered French cigarette from a box on his desk and lit it with a gold-plated lighter. As he let the pungent smoke trail from his nostrils, he smiled. "General Raines reacted to my news just as I knew he would—in fact, just as I hoped he would."

"You mean you intended for him to carry on with his plan to attack El Farrar?"

Chapelle spread his hands. "Of course, my dear boy, of course."

"But why?"

"So that now I can call this El Farrar and tell him that the entire world is doing as he asks, all, that is, except General Raines from the SUSA. I will explain that I tried my best to get him to agree to El Farrar's demands, but he went against my orders and is carrying on his own private war—against the express orders of the U.N.."

Henri cocked his head, clearly still not understanding Chapelle's point.

"Come on, Henri. Don't you see the beauty of what I've done? On the surface, the U.N. is acceding to El Farrar's demands, so he has no legitimate reason to detonate his plutonium bombs, while at the same time I've set loose a very determined dog to bite at his heels and take his mind off what we at the U.N. are really doing."

"So, you've set General Raines up as the bad guy?" Henri asked.

"Yes. And the beauty of it is that El Farrar cannot do anything about it. He can't blame us at the U.N. for what this rogue general is doing against our wishes."

"But Monsieur," Henri protested, "aren't you setting General Raines and his troops up?"

Chapelle grinned. "You obviously don't know General Raines, Henri. It is my belief that Raines will succeed where the might of the rest of the world would fail, and that is why I set him up, as you call it."

"But what if he fails?" Henri asked.

"Then I am afraid the world is doomed, Henri, doomed."

Henri sighed. "Perhaps the question will be moot. Perhaps Kuwait will not allow Raines and his troops to land."

Chapelle smiled enigmatically. "Oh, but that has already been taken care of, Henri. I called the Emir and told him in no uncertain terms that he is to cooperate with the general and to give him anything he needs, or the U.N. would withdraw all of its troops that are guarding his oil fields."

"So you really are playing both ends against the middle," Henri said admiringly.

"Of course," Chapelle said, leaning back in his chair and blowing a plume of smoke at the ceiling. "After all, I am a diplomat."

FIFTEEN

"Henri," Jean Chapelle said, "please get Mr. El Farrar on the phone. I might as well give him the 'bad' news about Ben Raines and his refusal to abide by my request to stand his forces down."

"Yes, sir," Henri said as he consulted his Rolodex and dialed an international phone number. After a few moments, he handed the phone to Chapelle, who immediately punched the button on his speaker so Henri could hear both sides of the conversation.

"Mr. El Farrar, this is Jean-François Chapelle from the United Nations calling."

"Hello, Mr. Chapelle," El Farrar said. "I hope you have good news for me."

"Well, the news is mixed, I'm afraid."

"Mixed?" El Farrar asked, his voice losing some of its cordiality.

"Yes. The good news is that I have persuaded the General Assembly to do as you've asked. U.N. forces will not interdict or otherwise try to stop you from bringing in additional troops to the oil fields while we are in negotiation about your demands."

There was a pause, and then El Farrar asked, "And the bad news?"

"Every one of the nations involved has agreed to your

request except Ben Raines from the Southern United States of America."

"What do you mean by that?"

"General Raines has informed me that as a sovereign nation, the SUSA will proceed on its own course without regard for any agreement between the U.N. and your forces."

El Farrar's voice became strident. "How can that be?" he almost shouted. "Is he aware of my threat to contaminate the world's oil supply should he disobey my orders?"

Chapelle grinned at Henri, but he kept his voice calm and professional. "Yes, he is, and he doesn't seem to be too concerned about it, Mr. El Farrar. In fact, he told me to give you a message."

"What message?"

"He said, and I quote, 'Tell El Farrar to grab his ankles and kiss his ass good-bye, because I am coming after him.'"

"What?" El Farrar yelled.

"I am only the messenger, sir," Chapelle replied calmly. "I do, however, want you to know that General Raines is acting outside of the power of the United Nations to stop him."

"Chapelle, you listen to me," El Farrar said gruffly. "If Raines or anyone else attacks any of my troops, I will blow up the oil fields!"

Now Chapelle paused for a moment, and then his voice became firm. "I am sorry to hear you say that, Mr. El Farrar. For if that is your response, I have no alternative but to join the U.N. forces with General Raines in an attack on your positions immediately."

"But . . . but you said you would agree to my terms," El Farrar said, his voice less strident now.

"That is true, Mr. El Farrar, but only if you promise

to refrain from any destruction of the oil fields. Since you now say that destruction is inevitable, there is no incentive for the U.N. not to press its attack."

For a full minute there were only faint sounds of static on the overseas line as El Farrar considered this ultimatum. Finally, in a more reasonable voice, he continued. "I guess it would not be fair to punish the entire world for the actions of one rogue general," he said. "All right, Chapelle, if the U.N. stays out of the fight, I will not destroy the oil fields on the basis of what General Raines does."

"That is very reasonable of you, sir," Chapelle said in an even voice, though his eyes glittered with amusement at El Farrar's capitulation to his threats. "As long as you keep your word and leave the oil fields intact, we can continue our negotiations with you. What happens between General Raines and your forces will be no concern of ours. Agreed?"

Both Henri and Chapelle could hear El Farrar's heavy sigh over the phone. "Yes."

"Then I suggest you make a formal list of your demands and cable them to me at U.N. headquarters as soon as possible so that they can be presented to the General Assembly."

"You will have them within forty-eight hours," El Farrar said.

"Good. Then I bid you adieu until we talk again," Chapelle said, giving Henri a silent thumbs-up sign.

"Good-bye Mr. Chapelle," El Farrar said, a loud snap as he slammed his phone down evident over the speaker.

Henri looked at Chapelle with approving eyes. "A masterful piece of diplomacy, monsieur," he said.

Chapelle put his hands behind his head and leaned back in his desk chair, smiling at the ceiling. "Yes, it was, wasn't it." Now, we have bought us some time and given Raines a chance to do our dirty work for us with little risk to the oil fields."

"Do you think he can possibly succeed?" Henri asked.

Chapelle shrugged. "If anyone on this earth can root out this fanatic El Farrar, Ben Raines can. And if he fails, then we will be no worse off than we are now. It is what the Americans call a win-win situation."

The pilot of the C-130 carrying the SUSA troops pulled the lever to disconnect the refueling line from the tanker after the air refueling was finished. "Better wake up General Raines," he told the copilot. "We're about an hour out of Kuwait airspace."

Minutes later, Ben Raines appeared in the cockpit. "Could you connect me with Mike Post back at our base?" he asked the pilot.

"Sure." The pilot fiddled with radio frequency knobs for a moment, spoke into his headset, and then handed it to Ben. "Mike Post is on the line," he said.

"Yo, Mike," Ben said. "Any word from the Emir of Kuwait yet on our request to stage our attacks from his country?"

"Yeah, Ben. It was the strangest thing. When I first called and asked for permission, he was emphatic in his denial. In fact, he said if you tried to land troops or matériel in his country, he would have the planes shot out of the air."

"Oh?" Ben said, his lips tight.

"Yeah. The son of a bitch was downright rude."

"So, then what happened?"

"Hell if I know. All I know is that he called me back four hours later and sugar wouldn't melt in his mouth. He said he'd reconsidered and we were welcome to use the airstrip outside of Kuwait City for whatever we needed."

Ben gave a short laugh. I smell the fine fingers of Jean-François Chapelle in here somewhere."

"But I thought Chapelle was furious about your decision to get involved in this fracas," Mike said.

"So he said," Ben replied. "But you've got to remember Chapelle is a master diplomat."

"In other words, he speaks out of both sides of his mouth," Mike said.

"Exactly. Now Chapelle can deny any U.N. responsibility for our actions, while at the same time hoping we'll somehow manage to pull his fat out of the fire." Ben chuckled again. "It was a masterful performance."

"Well, as I've said, you're cleared to land at Kuwait City," Mike said.

"How about the ships?" Ben asked, referring to the large tankers they had dispatched toward Kuwait loaded with Apache attack helicopters and other heavy equipment too large to be carried on the C-130s.

"They're on their way. They should arrive a few days after you do and once they're unloaded, the choppers and other heavy tanks and stuff will be forwarded to your positions."

"Great job, Mike. Thanks," Ben said.

"Okay, boss. I'll keep my ears to the ground over here. I've got all my Intel sources on high alert to find out anything they can about El Farrar's positions and troop strengths."

"Good. I'll talk to you later then," Ben said. "You can reach me on the SOHFRAD at any time."

"Signing off," Mike said.

* * *

ENEMY IN THE ASHES

The landing at Kuwait City Airport was anticlimactic after all of the intrigue involved in getting the Emir's permission to use the airfield. The two transports carrying the SUSA troops and their equipment landed without incident.

When Ben stepped off the first C-130, he was met by a delegation of men in traditional Arab garb. The leader stepped forward and inclined his head in a small bow. "General Raines, I am Abdullah Yassine," he said. "I am here to welcome you and your troops to Kuwait."

"Thank you, Mr. Yassine," Ben said, returning the bow.

Yassine pointed to a cluster of small buildings on the fringe of the airport. "The Emir has arranged for you to use those buildings as a command post, as well as the buildings nearby as barracks for your troops. I hope they are satisfactory."

Ben nodded. "I am sure they will be more than adequate, Mr. Yassine. As for the troops, they will only be here for a short while. Once we determine where El Farrar's men are, we will be sending the troops on their way."

Yassine glanced at Bartholomew Wiley-Smeyth standing behind Ben. "I assume you are Mr. Wiley-Smeyth from England?" he asked.

Bart inclined his head. "At your service, sir."

"I understand there are several airplanes due to arrive here from your country as well?" Yassine asked.

"That is correct," Bart said, glancing at his watch. "They should be here within the hour."

"There should be adequate room for your troops in the barracks, if that is all right?"

"Sure," Bart said with a smile directed at Ben. "We don't mind sharing our quarters with the Yanks."

"Good," Yassine said, "then if you will follow me, I will show you to your facilities."

Ben looked at Buddy and Major Bean. "Get the troops assembled along with their equipment and meet us at the barracks."

As Ben and Bart walked off with Yassine, Coop approached Buddy. "Sir," he said.

"Yes?" Buddy answered.

"Is there any chance of getting some chow any time soon?" Coop asked, rubbing his abdomen. "I'm so hungry my stomach thinks my throat's been cut."

Buddy winked at Major Bean so Coop couldn't see. "Sure, Coop. I'll bet the Kuwaitis have some figs and goat cheese all laid out for us in the barracks."

"Figs and goat cheese?" Coop asked, his face screwed up in a frown.

"Yeah, and if we're really lucky, they'll have some camel burgers on the grill," Bean added, trying to suppress a smile.

"Uh," Coop said, "any possibility of just having some good old MREs?"

Buddy and Bean both laughed. "That's the first time I've ever heard anyone request MREs over real food," Bean said.

"Well, you and your scouts are known to eat things that'll make a billy goat puke," Coop said. "But us regular troops require food that is at least partially digestible."

"I'll see what I can do, Coop," Buddy said. "Now, get your gear together and head for the barracks."

"Yes, sir," Coop said, throwing up a halfhearted salute.

As he moved back to the rest of the group, Jersey murmured, "Complain, complain, complain, Coop. That's all you ever do."

"Hey," he replied, "I'm a growing boy. I need my nourishment."

She patted his stomach. "You're growing, all right, but not in the right places."

He gave her a lascivious grin. "And just how would you know about that?" he challenged.

"Why, didn't you know, Coop?" she asked. "You're famous. There are detailed descriptions of your . . . shortcomings on the wall of the women's rest rooms back at the base."

"What?" Coop asked, his face flaming red.

"Yeah," Jersey answered. "There's a drawing of a couple of fingers like this," she said, holding up her thumb and index finger about an inch apart. "It says for a disappointing time, call Cooper, and it lists your phone number on the wall."

"Bullshit!" Coop exclaimed as he moved off to pick up his duffle bag. "The walls of the women's rest rooms ain't near wide enough to show my measurements."

Jersey and the other women in the group all laughed, and began to pick up their bags too.

SIXTEEN

El Farrar slammed the phone down and muttered a strong curse in his native tongue. Muhammad Atwa, who was sitting nearby sipping orange juice, looked up at him. He'd heard only El Farrar's part of the conversation.

"What is wrong, Abdullah?" he asked, wondering what had so angered his leader.

"That son of a whore Ben Raines says he is going to come after me in spite of the threat to the oil fields."

"Cannot the U.N. do something to stop him?"

El Farrar shook his head. "Apparently not. Raines has put himself above the U.N. and wishes to push the world to the brink of disaster."

The orange juice turned to acid in Atwa's stomach at the news Ben Raines planned to attack their forces. He knew full well just how effective the SUSA fighters could be. "Perhaps if we destroy one of the smaller oil fields as a warning, he would back off," Atwa suggested.

"I cannot," El Farrar answered. "Chapelle says that if any of the oil fields are hurt, he will have the U.N. forces join Raines and attack us."

"He wouldn't dare!" Atwa said.

El Farrar shrugged. "Probably not, but we cannot take that chance. Even with the troops promised us by our Al Nahda and Hezbollah brothers, we cannot possibly stand against the U.N. and Ben Raines. Our only chance is to bluff the infidels into giving us power over the oil without a direct confrontation."

Atwa belched softly, his stomach on fire. He doubted that even with the additional troops that were already on their way to the oil fields, they would be able to stand against the SUSA and Ben Raines. In his mind's eye, he could see their plan unraveling. Of course, he mentioned none of this to El Farrar, knowing it would only enrage him if he expressed any doubts.

"Do we know where Raines plans to attack first?" Atwa asked.

"No, but I would doubt that any of the countries we hold would let him use their airfields to stage an attack. That means he will have to use aircraft carriers to deploy his men and equipment, which should give us some time to fortify our positions."

Atwa nodded slowly. "That also means he will be limited in the amount of heavy equipment he'll be able to use." He stroked his chin. "And our men are well equipped to deal with helicopters and attack aircraft."

"Yes, the Stingers we bought on the black market will do nicely against them," El Farrar agreed.

Atwa sighed and got to his feet. This latest setback had caused him to desperately desire a drink of something stronger than orange juice.

"I am going to my quarters for a nap," he said, rubbing his stomach to take some of the sting out.

El Farrar glanced at him with hooded eyes. "Do not drink too much of the devil's spirits today, my friend," he advised in a soft voice, letting Atwa know he was aware of his habit of drinking whiskey. "We are going to be very busy overseeing the transfer of troops to the oil fields."

Atwa paled. He'd had no idea El Farrar knew he drank. "Yes, my leader," he said with a small bow. He left El Farrar's headquarters building resolving to be more careful in his imbibing in the future.

Over the next few days, there was a steady stream of aircraft arriving at the Kuwait City Airport, both from the SUSA and England. Ben arranged for Jackie Malone and her 512 Battalion to be brought over, along with the equipment they'd need.

When Buddy found out Jackie was on the way, he went to Ben's office. "Ben, I thought this operation was going to be a quick in-and-out guerrilla-type assault," he said as soon as he'd entered the room.

"I see you've heard that I had Mike send Jackie and the 512 over," Ben replied.

Buddy nodded.

"They're here strictly for mopping-up operations," Ben said. "You're correct that the initial attacks will be by small forces, but if Chapelle is right and El Farrar is sending large numbers of regular troops over, then we're gonna need a lot of men to keep the oil fields safe once we've taken control."

"Oh, so they're here as our backup once we've infiltrated and taken out El Farrar's men," Buddy said.

Ben nodded. "Yeah. You and your team are still going to be the first ones in."

Buddy smiled, relieved that he was still in command and would be leading his team on the initial assaults. Though he was an experienced field man, Buddy still lived somewhat in the shadow of his famous father, and was aching to show both Ben and everyone else how good he was.

Ben knew this, and was aware of just how difficult it was to have a famous father. When he'd decided to step down, he'd floated the names of several of his most senior men and women to his staff officers as possible replacements for him. He was both gratified and at the same time concerned that the staff had all agreed that Buddy should take his place as commander of the SUSA Army. He only hoped that he wasn't giving Buddy more responsibility than he could handle.

"Have the troops from England all arrived?" he asked Buddy.

"Yes, sir, and Jackie and the 512 should be landing any time now. Are you going to want to meet them at the airfield?" Buddy asked.

Ben smiled. "No, that's your place, now that you're commander in chief."

Buddy nodded. "All right. After they're set up in their quarters, I'll bring Jackie in to meet with you," he said, unable to hide his pleasure at Ben's giving him the job of greeting the new arrivals.

"I'll arrange for lunch to be served here and we can discuss your plans over a meal."

"Yes, sir," Buddy said.

Buddy stopped by his quarters and told the team about the imminent arrival of Jackie Malone and her battalion, and said he thought it'd be a good idea if the entire team was on hand to welcome them aboard.

Coop grinned when he heard Jackie Malone was going to be in the country. It was a poorly kept secret that he and Jackie had once had a short-lived fling. They'd run into each other in a bar several years back while both were on leave. For the next five days, they had stayed in his room and discovered they both liked sex equally well.

Realizing it was a one-time thing, once their leaves were over, they'd parted ways, but had remained good friends ever since.

Coop thought Jackie the most attractive and dangerous female he'd ever met, outside of Jersey.

Unfortunately, Jersey had found out about the affair, and had teased Coop unmercifully about it every time Jackie was in the vicinity. She wasn't exactly jealous, or so she told herself. Hell, it wasn't the first time Coop conquered a woman, and most assuredly wouldn't be the last. She just felt Coop could do much better.

When Buddy told the team that Jackie was on her way to join them, Jersey immediately glanced at Coop. Seeing his grin and obvious joy at the news, she felt her blood boil.

Coop got to his feet and moved toward the team's rest rooms. "Going to take a shower and put on some froufrou for your girlfriend?" Jersey taunted.

Coop blushed a bright red as the rest of the team laughed. "No," he replied testily. "I just thought I'd put on some fresh BDUs. I've been wearing these for a week."

"Want me to iron them for you?" Jersey asked maliciously.

Coop turned and grinned at her. "Why, Jersey, that would be nice. It's good to know you've finally realized just what a woman's duties are."

Jersey was halfway to her feet with her hand on her K-Bar when Coop decided discretion was the better part of valor and ducked into the men's room.

When Jackie deplaned, Buddy and the team were there to meet them. Jackie stepped up and gave Buddy a smart salute, which he returned with a slight blush.

"Good to hear of your promotion, Buddy," Jackie said where only he could hear. "You deserve it."

"Thanks, Jackie," Buddy said. "I'll have Harley Reno show your troops where the quarters are and you can join Ben and me for lunch in his office."

While he was talking, Jackie's eyes searched the team standing nearby and came to rest on Coop's. She gave him a quick wink, which Jersey noticed. When Coop winked back, Jersey gave him a dig in the ribs with her elbow.

"Down, boy," she hissed out of the side of her mouth. "Don't get too excited, you might bust your britches."

Coop grinned and hitched up his pants. "Yeah, it's a real shame you don't get this kind of response from men, Jersey. Perhaps if you were a *little* more feminine . . ."

"I'll remember you said that, Coop. The next time we're in a firefight and I have to save your scrawny ass, I'll just bat my eyes and be feminine. How's that?"

"Uh, forget it, Jerse," Coop replied as his eyes followed Jackie and Buddy as they walked away. "I guess you'll do just as you are."

Jersey shook her head in disgust. "Men," she growled. "Always thinking with your little heads."

Coop put his arm on her shoulder and smiled at her. "Come on, Jerse. You know that's what you love about us."

She laughed. "Well, it does make it easier to deal with you Neanderthals at that."

"What do you mean?" he asked.

"Oh, all us women have to do to get what we want is unbutton our blouses, show a little cleavage, and your IQs drop fifty points."

As she spoke, she stuck out her chest and let her breasts strain against her BDUs. When Coop's eyes involuntarily dropped to stare, she laughed and slapped him on the back. "See what I mean, big boy? Women's ultimate secret—the power of the big head over the little one."

SEVENTEEN

Al Hazmi, leader of El Farrar's troops in Saudi Arabia, sat at his desk in his headquarters on the outskirts of Riyadh going over reports from his field commanders. He wanted to make absolutely sure that all of the plutonium bombs had been set as per his orders.

His commanders, as experienced as they were with fighting guerrilla warfare, were not used to planting bombs designed to do maximal damage to existing structures. They were more used to fixing bombs to bodies of suicide bombers—a much less technical task.

His second in command, Taha al-Alwani, stood at attention in front of his desk while Hazmi went over the written reports al-Alwani had given him.

"You are sure the bombs are all in place and the radio transmitters affixed properly so the bombs can be exploded remotely?" Hazmi asked, glaring at his subordinate with hooded snake eyes.

"Yes, my leader," al-Alwani answered, nodding his head vigorously. "I checked each installation personally to make sure they were connected in the correct manner."

"Good. Now I want you to make sure your men are positioned around the perimeter of the oil field, and are dug in properly so as to repel any possible attacks on our positions."

"But sir," al-Alwani asked, "do you think the infidels will dare to oppose us now that the bombs are in place?"

Hazmi sighed, hating to explain himself to men under his command. "No. In fact I think it highly unlikely, al-Awani, but our commander, Abdullah El Farrar, has just sent me a radio message to be on the highest alert until our reinforcement troops arrive." He glared at al-Awani. "Do you wish me to radio El Farrar back and tell him my chief officer, Taha al-Alwani, does not think it necessary to follow his orders?"

Al-Awani's face looked horrified. "No, no, my leader. I did not mean any disrespect by my question. I will immediately do as you ordered."

"That is good, al-Awani, for if anyone manages to get into the oil field, I will personally cut off both your hands and make you eat them."

"Yes, sir!" al-Awani said, saluting smartly before turning on his heels and almost running from Hazmi's office.

Hazmi glanced skyward. "Allah, why must you plague me with idiots for officers?" he asked, and then blushed at his effrontery to question the Almighty God.

Ben Raines called a meeting of all of his staff officers in his office at the Kuwait City Airport. It was time to coordinate the attacks on some of the oil fields.

Buddy Raines, Major Jackson Bean, Jackie Malone, and the Englishman, Bartholomew Wiley-Smeyth, were all in attendance.

"Our Intel has detected radio traffic indicating several ships are on their way to the region carrying reinforcements for the relatively small forces that now occupy the oil fields," Ben said.

"Is there an estimate of when they will arrive?" Bean asked.

"Sometime between forty-eight and seventy-two hours," Ben replied.

"That doesn't give us much time to plan and mount an assault," Buddy said.

"No, it doesn't," Ben replied, a small smile playing across his lips. "That is why I'm only going to send in the very best troops in the world. There will be no plan, as such. You are going to have to take your troops in and proceed playing it by ear. We don't have any reliable intel on how many troops you'll be up against, where their positions are, or what kind of armament they have to use against you."

"Do we at least know where they are in a general sense?" Wiley-Smeyth asked.

Ben pointed to a map of the Middle East, with tiny oil derricks painted on it in various areas. "About all we know is where the major oil-rig concentrations are in each of the countries that have been invaded. It stands to reason the invaders will be positioned in some manner nearby to protect the booby traps they've planted."

"Do they have any idea we're coming?" Bean asked.

Ben shrugged. "That I don't know. It is my guess Jean-François Chapelle told El Farrar that I had not agreed to stand down, but whether he believes we will hit this soon is anyone's guess."

"How about transportation to the sites?" Wiley-Smeyth asked. "Since time is of the essence, I suppose we'll be going in by air transport."

"Yes. My Scouts and Buddy's team will all go in by HALO. That's High Altitude Low Opening parachute drops."

Wiley-Smeyth's eyes widened. "You're going to attempt HALO drops at night?" he asked as if he couldn't believe his ears.

Ben nodded. "Yes. Do you think your SAS men are up to that?"

Wiley-Smeyth shook his head doubtfully. "They would agree to it, of course, but they're certainly not trained for it. All of our parachute drops have been done in daylight or at the worst under a full moon in the past."

Ben frowned. "Then we probably shouldn't do it. You'd lose too many men in the drop and it would compromise your effectiveness. We'd better plan on inserting you via helicopters."

He hesitated. "The problem with that is it will be noisy, so we're gonna have to drop you a few miles away from the oil fields and your men will have to move across the desert a good ways."

Wiley-Smeyth smiled confidently. "That's no problem. My SAS chaps are in perfect physical condition. They're used to forced marches of up to twenty miles a day with full equipment packs on their backs."

"Good. Then here's the plan," Ben said, standing and walking to a large map of the entire region, which was on the wall. "The major oil fields in Saudi Arabia are in the southeast, near the city of Riyadh," he said, pointing to the city on the map. "My bet is that is where the enemy forces in Saudi are concentrated."

He moved his hand further north on the map. "Here in Iran, most of the fields are in the area surrounding the city of Tehran, so we'll concentrate our landing in that area."

"What about some of the smaller oil-producing states?" Bean asked.

"We don't have the forces to tackle all of them at this time," Ben answered, "so we'll just hit the two largest and hope for the best. If we can protect Iran and Saudi Arabia, that will be over half the world's oil supply the terrorists won't be able to destroy."

"Which will considerably lessen their bargaining power with the U.N.," Buddy added.

"Correct," Ben said. "Now, since a range of mountains which are a bit high for helicopter overflights is between Kuwait and Tehran, I'll send my troops that way. The course to Riyadh in Saudi is flatter and the choppers won't have to go around any large cities, so it will be perfect for your SAS troops, Bart."

Wiley-Smeyth nodded.

Ben moved back to his desk and picked up a stack of maps. "Here are some detailed topographic maps of each of the regions. I'll let you study them while you get your troops ready for their incursion," Ben said.

"Ben," Jackie Malone said, "you haven't told me what my job is going to be."

"Your troops are to be on standby for immediate reinforcement of the Scouts and SAS troops once they've secured their targets. By day after tomorrow, there're gonna be thousands of terrorist troops swarming all over these areas, and it's gonna be your job to make sure they don't retake the oil fields."

Jackie nodded, but it was clear she regretted not being able to go in first. She was not the kind of person who liked to let someone else do the dirty work.

"Okay. Then I'll divide my battalion up into two parts and have each ready to go on a moment's notice," she said.

"Excellent," Ben answered. He glanced at the watch on his wrist. "Now, get to work, gentlemen and ladies. It's three hours to dusk and I want you on your way by then."

* * *

Buddy Raines and his team, along with Major Jackson Bean and his contingent of Scouts, were loaded in a C-130 transport plane in readiness for their HALO drop in Tehran. Bartholomew Wiley-Smeyth and his SAS troops were loaded into a pair of Boeing CH-47 Chinook helicopters, each of which could carry forty-four men with their equipment at 138 knots.

As the sun set over Kuwait City, Ben shook hands with Wiley-Smeyth and wished him and his men good luck. After the Chinooks took off, their huge twin turbines whining with the effort, Ben walked over to the C-130, where Buddy and Major Jackson Bean were seeing to the loading of their troops.

Bean was talking with Willie Running Bear, Samuel Clements, and Sue Waters, his squad leaders, about the upcoming HALO drop when Ben arrived. Bean stopped and turned to Ben, holding out his hand. "Well, we're loaded and ready, General," he said.

Ben took his hand. "Major, I know we're asking a lot of you, but the world is depending on you to kick some terrorist ass."

Bean grinned. "That's what Scouts live for, General," he said.

"Since our Intel hasn't been able to find out the disposition of the enemy troops, I'm going to have your Scouts drop on the outskirts of the city of Tehran itself. Buddy and his team will be dropped a little to the north in the middle of the oil fields. You can keep in touch on the SOHFRAD, which I'll be monitoring from here at headquarters," Ben said.

Bean nodded.

"As soon as you've found the enemy base and secured the city, give me a shout and I'll have Jackie Malone's troops airlifted in to help you maintain control," Ben said.

"Tell her to be ready by dawn," Bean said. "If we haven't done it by then, it will mean we're in big trouble."

"Roger," Ben said, and he moved over to speak to Buddy, who was just finishing getting his team situated in the rear of the C-130.

Jackie Malone was standing next to Buddy talking to Coop. As Ben approached, he saw Coop give a sheepish grin and nod his head before he stepped into the plane.

When she saw Ben, Jackie blushed and moved off away from the men. Ben smiled to himself. It was the first time he'd ever seen Jackie embarrassed.

"Your team all ready to go?" he asked Buddy.

"Yes, sir," Buddy answered.

"Remember, keep in touch with the SOHFRAD, both with me and with Major Bean," Ben reminded him. "If you get in over your head, I can have some of Jackie's troops there within an hour or two."

Buddy gave a lopsided grin. "We'll be okay, mother hen," he said with a low laugh.

Ben returned the smile. "It's a lot harder than I thought it would be to send my old team off without me there to lead them."

Buddy put his hand on Ben's shoulder. "I know, Dad."

It was the first time he'd called Ben Dad in many months, and it touched Ben's heart.

"Be safe, son," Ben replied, and turned and walked away before he could make a sentimental fool of himself.

From the side of the field, he watched as the big C-130 lumbered down the runway and took off. He felt a strange foreboding, and the hair on the back of his neck stood up. He shook his head, trying to will away his misgivings about the upcoming mission, and returned to his headquarters to monitor the SOHFRAD frequencies.

EIGHTEEN

The ship appeared in space accompanied by a brilliant, though silent, display of light and energy as it exited from the subspace vortex that allowed it to travel at multiples of the speed of light.

The ship was silver-metallic in color, and slightly longer than a football field and almost as wide. The titanium-based metal of its surface was pitted and scored with thousands of tiny craters from collisions with space dust at speeds approaching that of light.

Inside the vessel, the change in velocity to sublight speeds triggered automatic sensors, which began to replenish the nitrogen/oxygen atmosphere and to heat up the interior from 175 degrees below zero to 110 degrees above zero.

Coffinlike containers arrayed along the walls of the many interior corridors began to vent a heliox gas mixture into containers, and the occupants inside the containers began to awaken after more than fifty years of a comalike deep hibernation.

The first to emerge was the commander of the ship. He was a little over five feet in height and resembled what humans had come to call "Grays" in the days of the UFO craze before World War III. He had two arms, ending in hands with three fingers and an opposable thumb, two legs, and large black eyes that were faceted like those of a fly. Two tiny holes in the middle of his face served as a nose, and he had no external ears. He was completely hairless, and his gray skin was the texture of old leather.

He stretched and flexed to ease muscles cramped by fifty years of immobility, and then he proceeded to the control cabin of the space ship. Easing into the captain's chair, he stuck his right hand into a depression on the console in front of him, and the liquid crystal display on the forward wall lit up, along with hundreds of other dials and indicators.

His eyes quickly roamed over the dials, noting they were all in a dark purple shade indicating everything was functioning properly.

He was about to get to his feet and process some food and water to fill his empty stomach, when a strident rapid buzzing sound erupted from a speaker and several of the lights changed from dark purple to brilliant orange and began blinking.

The captain ran back to his chair and began to twist knobs and punch buttons and move his feet over pedals under his chair as fast as he could.

A giant blue planet filled almost the entire surface of the view screen, while a smaller gray moon approached rapidly from the right.

The captain's second in command was running toward his chair next to the captain's when the ship suddenly veered sharply left and down, throwing the second officer to his knees and flinging him against a stanchion on the sidewall.

A nasty gash was opened in his forehead, and purplish liquid oozed from it to run down across his eyes.

Sleeving the blood off his face with his right arm, the

ENEMY IN THE ASHES

second officer got to his feet and moved with an unsteady gait toward his chair. Once there, he buckled himself in and began to assist the captain with his evasive maneuver to avoid Neptune's moon, Triton.

As they worked feverishly to change the course of the ship enough to miss the moon, they spoke to each other in a series of shrill whistles and clicks and low-pitched moans.

"By all the gods, how did this happen?" the captain asked, the tone of his whistles showing extreme anger. "The mass-proximity-avoidance device was supposed to bring us out of the vortex away from any large objects."

The junior officer glanced quickly at his captain, wondering if it was safe to explain to him how the much larger mass of the nearby gas-giant planet caused the MPA device to ignore the much smaller mass of the moon that even now was bearing down on them.

He finally decided not to attempt it. He had no desire to be thrown into the neutron disintegrator to be used as food for the rest of the crew members—something the captain had done to insolent underlings more than once on their long journey from their home planet.

The buzzing from the mass-proximity-warning speaker lowered in intensity as the moon flashed by less than five hundred meters from the ship and passed from view in the forward screen.

Seconds later, small flashes of light winked and flared as the ship passed through the twin rings of Neptune and the forward shields disintegrated the small bits of rock and ice that comprised the rings before they could penetrate the ship's hull.

When the buzzer abruptly ceased its warning, the captain leaned back in his chair and took a deep breath.

The slit in his face that served as a mouth curled in what

for him was a rare smile. "That was too close," he said, his whistles showing his mood was softening somewhat.

The junior officer nodded his agreement, his twin hearts slowing their beating as the danger passed.

All of the dials and lights on the console changed color from orange to purple, except one, which slowly pulsed green.

The captain pointed one of his fingers at the light. "I see the electromagnetic resonator has detected signals in this system," he said. "Run the sequencer analyzer on it to see if it indicates intelligent life or if it is merely the product of a magnetic emanation from a radio star."

The junior officer complied, twisting dials and keeping both his eyes on a small screen set in the console in front of his chair. After a few moments, he too smiled. "The sequencer analyzer reports the electromagnetic signals are organized, Commander. There must be intelligent life in this system!"

"Good," the captain said. He knew that the presence of intelligent life far enough along in the evolutionary chain to produce radio signals always meant there was a planet in the system that could support them. In all the thousands of years his people had been exploring space, they'd never come across higher life forms that didn't originate on a planet with oxygen and nitrogen as the main components of their atmospheres.

Though the physical forms of the various intelligent civilizations varied greatly, the one constant was an M-type star and a planet based on carbon with nitrogen and oxygen in the atmosphere.

"What are the radiation levels?" the captain asked.

"Well within the normals for a civilization that is pre-nuclear," the junior officer answered. "There is no sign of nuclear radiation in the system."

"Even better," the captain responded. He had found too many civilizations on his many journeys where intelligent life had progressed to the nuclear phase and poisoned their planets with radiation from internecine warfare, rendering them unsuitable for conquest.

"Begin the process of locating the planet where the radio waves originated. Once you've done that, send a pulse rocket message back to Zastar telling the supreme high commander we have found another planet suitable for colonization."

"Uh, shouldn't we wait until we are certain the climate and atmosphere are suitable for us, Captain?" the junior officer asked.

"You're right," the captain said. "I remember the time Captain Zistaake made the mistake of reporting a find, and later had to retract his claim when the temperature of the planet was too low to sustain us. The supreme high commander fed his atoms to the council members as punishment."

The junior officer breathed a sigh of relief. He too remembered the incident, and he also recalled that the entire crew of the unfortunate captain had been used as a foodstuff for their captain's mistake.

The supreme high commander was only slightly more unforgiving than their own captain.

The captain got up from his seat and turned to leave. "I am going to my quarters to feed and drink. Once you've located the planet with life on it, call me and I'll return and let you feed."

The junior officer's stomach growled at the mention of food, but he kept his mouth shut and his head down. Better to wait to eat than to anger the captain and become food.

Perhaps he'd get lucky and one of the females would

wander into the control room, and he could send her to get him some food. If he was really lucky, perhaps she'd even wait around and they could mate after he'd eaten. Fifty years in a sleep-cubicle tended to make one horny as well as hungry.

Just as the captain left the control room, a light began flashing on the console, and the junior officer bent to take a closer look at his computer screen. A tiny map of the system was displayed with nine planets revolving around a sun, which was indeed classified as an M-type star.

The third planet in the array of this solar system was blinking off and on, indicating it was the source of the radio waves the ship had detected.

The junior officer hurriedly set a course to intersect the orbit of the third planet. Once he was done, he swiveled in his chair and stared at the door, wondering if he dared to look out in the corridor and try to find a compliant female to fetch his food.

His dilemma was solved when a small gray head appeared peering in the doorway. He motioned her in and she entered. The females were identical to the males except for two small breasts on their chest used for feeding the young until they were old enough to eat solid food. The species wore no clothing due to the high temperature of their native planet.

The junior officer recognized the female as one he'd never mated with, which made her appearance all the more welcome. He couldn't remember her name, so he just whistled the equivalent of "Miss" and gave her his most engaging smile.

"Miss, would you be so good as to get me some food from the dispensary?" he asked. "I have been so busy guiding the ship through the perils of this solar system I haven't had time to eat since the awakening."

The female moved closer, her nostril openings dilating as she sniffed his body odor to see if he would be a suitable mate. After a moment, she nodded. "Of course, Navigator," she said, calling him by his official title.

"And after I eat," the junior officer added, his eyes moving over her body, "perhaps you could stay here a while and I could show you the planets as we pass them."

Her oral slit curved in a most fetching way, and she lowered her head an inch or two. "Is that all you want of me, Navigator?" she asked coyly.

Before he could answer, her eyes widened as his genitals changed color and began to respond to her flirting. She gave a low whistle of amusement. "Never mind, Navigator. I can see that is *not* all you want. I shall hasten on my way to get your food, and I eagerly await what will come next."

After she left, the junior officer swiveled in his chair and focused his attention on the screen in front of him. He hoped that the evidence of what he was thinking would disappear from his genitals before the captain returned. He would not want the captain to think he wasn't paying attention to his job. But like many species across the vast reaches of space, what his mind thought and what his sex organs decreed were two different things.

NINETEEN

The moon was a tiny crescent in a cloudless sky as the two Chinooks flew through the blackness. They were painted coal black and were flying without any running lights. In the cargo bays, men dressed all in black with black greasepaint covering their faces sat checking assault rifles, cartridge magazines, grenades, and just about everything else hung, strapped, or fastened to their BDUs. The loud whine of the turbines and the rhythmic *whup-whup-whup* of the rotor blades prevented talk of any kind.

Bartholomew Wiley-Smeyth checked his watch for the hundredth time, a knot of nervous acid in his stomach. He knew that no matter how cunning and brave his men were in the upcoming assault, he was going to lose some of them. Most were men he'd trained with for years, and he knew most of their families as well as his own. The loses were going to hurt terribly.

Bart had worked out a plan whereby the helicopters would split up ten miles short of Riyadh, with the lead chopper heading to the outskirts of the city and the second going on to the oil fields. Even though the oil fields and their plutonium bombs were the prime objective, Bart thought the bombs' detonators would probably not be trusted to field operatives, but would remain in the hands of the terrorists' leaders in the city itself. He couldn't risk a hurried radio transmission from the men guarding the oil fields getting through and the bombs being detonated while his men were among the derricks.

Bart was going to lead the contingent in the assault on the oil fields while his second officer, Major Hugh Holmsby, would take his men into the city of Riyadh.

Holmsby was one of the most dangerous men Bart had ever met. Trained in search-and-destroy tactics, Hugh, it was said, could sneak up and take a quarter off a rattlesnake's head and leave change without the snake ever knowing it had been visited.

Bart was no slouch at such maneuvers himself. In one of his early training days, he'd been sent into a completely darkened building containing ten men hiding in various rooms. His assignment had been to take each of them out without the others hearing him do it. He'd not only managed to take out all the men, but when his instructors entered the building thirty minutes later, there was no sign of Bart. He'd managed to sneak out of the building under their very noses, and was standing quietly at the back of their group as they searched for him.

He knew this was going to be even more difficult. He was going to have to lead a group of men over ten miles of desert in almost total darkness, and infiltrate and kill an unknown number of adversaries whose positions and displacements were also unknown to him. Hugh had grinned when told of the mission and said, "It's a cakewalk, Bart old chap."

Bart knew better.

The sound of the Chinook's engines changed as the pilot slowed for landing. Flying at only a little over a hundred feet to avoid radar, he wouldn't have to drop too much to let the men out.

A light on the wall just behind the pilot's compartment changed from red to yellow, and Bart signaled his men with a thumbs-up to tell them to get ready.

The chopper slowed and dropped, its wheels just inches above the gravel and sand of the desert, and the light went to full green.

Bart pumped his fist in the air, and twenty-five highly trained SAS soldiers rose as one and bailed out the door, immediately forming a perimeter around the Chinook in case of enemy presence.

Bart turned and gave the pilot a quick salute just before he exited the plane last.

After the Chinook eased around and headed back the way they'd come, the men gathered around Bart. He quickly checked his Global Positioning Satellite receiver, and noted they had to travel nine miles directly south to get to the outer ring of oil rigs.

The men spread out in an arrowhead formation, with Bart just behind the point man, and moved off toward their target.

The men in the other Chinook, led by Hugh Holmsby, were a little ahead of Bart's crew. Hugh's men were already at the outskirts of Riyadh. It was a fairly modern city, but there weren't a lot of streetlights burning and most of the windows in the city were darkened. Muslims didn't go in much for nightlife, and most were in their homes by dusk.

Hugh's first objective was to find out just which building contained the headquarters for the terrorists. Guessing it would be on the outskirts of the city on the side nearest the oil fields, he began his search there.

He spread his men out along a perimeter and told them to scan each and every building through their nightscopes. He figured the headquarters would be guarded, both on the ground and on the roof. He also thought the windows would be lighted, with men on radios keeping in touch with their leaders.

Sergeant Major Thomas Gifford gave a low whistle from off to Hugh's left. Hugh ran over and squatted down next to the man.

"We got lucky, Major," Gifford said, speaking in a whisper even though no one was nearby. He pointed at a five-story building just ahead of his position. "Check out the roof."

Hugh fastened his nightscope on the roof, and saw a man leaning against a parapet smoking a cigarette, the glow bright in Hugh's scope. The man had what appeared to be a Kalashnikov assault rifle slung over his back.

"Bingo," Hugh whispered. "Round up the men, Tommy, we're going in."

Once the men were reassembled, they all cocked their weapons and made sure extra magazines were readily handy. "From here on in, hand signals only," Hugh whispered.

When the men spread out and moved toward the building, not a sound could be heard. They moved through the night like ghosts on cats' feet.

They approached the rear of the building away from the entrances in groups of five men. When they got to within a hundred yards, Hugh waved his hand up and down and they went down on their bellies, crawling the rest of the way.

Twenty yards from the back wall, Hugh held up his

fist in a signal to stop. Two guards were strolling around the building, talking to each other in low voices as they made their hourly patrol.

Hugh pulled his assault knife from its scabbard and motioned to Tommy Gifford, who did the same. While the rest of the men held their positions, Hugh and Tommy crawled toward the two guards as silently as snakes on cotton.

When they were within six feet of the two men, Hugh and Tommy got to their feet and moved in unison. The left arm went around each man's neck to prevent him from calling out, while the right hand drove the blade of the knife up under the rib cage, severing the aorta and spinal cord and causing instant death. The two guards didn't even moan as they went limp in Hugh and Tommy's arms.

Hugh gently laid his man on the sand and stood up, signaling his men to join him up against the wall of the building.

He outlined his plan of attack. Two men would scale the side of the building, carrying only a knife and a silenced pistol, to take out the roof guards, while the rest of the men would go in through the front door in a storming action, also using silenced weapons.

While Jerry Albright and Keith Kilgore moved up the rear wall, Hugh peeked around the corner. A bored guard was standing in the doorway, leaning against the wall, snoring softly. He was asleep on his feet.

Hugh bared his teeth in a savage grin and moved quickly, his back against the wall to stay out of sight in case the man woke up.

Just as he got to him, the guard opened his eyes, frightened at the apparition standing in front of him. "Hello," Hugh said as he drove his stiletto into the man's throat.

Before the dead man's body hit the ground, the rest of Hugh's force was moving rapidly through the doorway, silenced Uzis at the ready.

A man carrying a sheaf of papers in his arms stopped on the staircase, and was cut down in a hail of bullets that made no sound louder than a cough.

The SAS men rushed up the stairs two at a time, the barrels of their weapons moving from side to side in front of them, ready to fire.

Peeling off by twos into the various rooms of the building, they began to fire at men awakened more by the smell of cordite than the sound of machine guns firing.

Al Hazmi glanced over his shoulder when he heard a thud from the stairwell. He was standing next to a radio, about to send a report to El Farrar that he'd had no contact with hostiles.

Frowning, he moved toward the door, and was startled when a black-faced man wearing dark BDUs stepped through the opening. He pointed an Uzi at Hazmi's gut and asked in a conversational tone, "Do you speak English?"

Hazmi considering lying and saying no, but the man raised the barrel of his gun to point at his face, and he changed his mind. "Yes."

"Then, step away from the radio and take a seat. My CO will be here in a minute to talk to you."

Hazmi's eyes moved to the remote control detonator lying on his desk next to the radio handset. He might just have time to press the button before the man could fire.

The soldier, seeing his eyes shift, grinned and said, "Don't even think about it, Abdul or whatever your name is. I'd cut you in half before you took two steps!"

Hazmi sighed and sat down in a chair against the wall.

He didn't even bother to ask who the men were who were invading his headquarters. He knew they were from Ben Raines, the infidel devil.

A few minutes later, Hazmi's second in command, Taha al-Alwani, was pushed by Hugh through the door. He had a deep gash on his forehead and was bleeding profusely.

"Sit over there next to your friend," Hugh said, giving al-Awani a shove.

"Now, who's in charge here?" Hugh asked.

Al-Awani and Hazmi glanced at each other, neither saying anything.

Hugh shook his head, a sad expression on his face. "So, it's going to be that way, is it?" he asked.

Al-Awani sat up straight in his chair and stuck his chest out. "You will get no information from us, infidel dogs! We are not afraid to become martyrs for our cause."

Hugh grinned crookedly. "Oh, I'm not about to make martyrs of you, sir," he said in a soft but dangerous voice. "That would be against all rules of warfare."

Al-Awani allowed himself a small smile, thinking these infidels were so stupid.

Hugh looked over at Sergeant Major Gifford. "Tommy," he said calmly, "kindly put a bullet through that gentleman's right kneecap."

As Tommy smiled and aimed his pistol at al-Awani, the Arab held out his hands. "But you said . . ."

"I just said I wouldn't make a martyr out of you, sir. I said nothing about maiming you a little."

"But I must protest . . ." al-Awani began, sweat appearing on the part of his forehead that wasn't covered with blood.

Hugh shrugged. "Protest all you want, sir, it will do you no good. After I have the sergeant major shoot out both of your knees, making you a cripple for the rest of your life, I will have him pluck out your eyes and perforate your eardrums. Then we will leave you to crawl around this city on your belly, blind and deaf, with only the ability to scream out your pain for all to hear. I think that will be a suitable lesson for all those who wish to join the terrorist forces, don't you?"

"But . . . but you can't do that!" al-Awani protested.

"Shut up, you cowardly dog!" Hazmi ordered. "He is only trying to trick you. He would never dare to do such a thing."

Hugh looked at Tommy and nodded his head toward Al Hazmi.

Tommy took dead aim and shot Hazmi in the right knee, blowing half the joint out the back of his leg to splatter against the wall.

Hazmi screamed, grabbed his ruined leg, and toppled out of his chair onto the floor, where he writhed in pain, moaning and crying.

When Tommy turned his pistol toward al-Awani, the man held out both hands. "Wait . . . wait! What do you want to know?" he asked as fear-sweat made dark stains on his clothes.

"That's better," Hugh said. He looked over his shoulder at the soldiers standing behind Tommy. "Get this piece of camel shit out of here," he ordered, indicating the still-crying Hazmi.

Once Hazmi had been dragged from the room, leaving a trail of scarlet blood on the floor, Hugh pulled up a chair and sat directly in front of al-Awani.

"Now, my friend, tell me all you know."

"What is it you wish to know?" al-Awani asked, sleeving sweat off his face with his arm.

"Who the commanding officers are at the oil fields, what frequency you use to contact them, and if they have the power to explode the plutonium bombs, to start with," Hugh said.

Al-Awani licked dry lips. "If I give you this information, I will be killed."

"It's your choice, friend," Hugh said. "Possible death, or sure maiming."

"All right," al-Awani said. "I'll tell you."

Hugh smiled. "I thought you might."

TWENTY

Bartholomew Wiley-Smeyth led his men through the darkness of the desert night, moving quickly but silently toward the outskirts of the oil fields around Riyadh. Directly behind him and to either side were his top two men. John Davidson and his brother, David, were two of the deadliest killers in his squad. Each had saved Bart's life on more than one occasion, and he relied on them to be his eyes and ears in the field when he was concentrating on tactics or leading the rest of the men under his command.

The Davidson brothers were fearless when it came to their own safety, and considered protecting their leader to be their most important job.

As they neared the area of the outermost oil wells, it was John who first noticed a brief scarlet glow in the distance. He quickly tapped Bart's left arm and held his hand out, palm down—the signal to hit the dirt.

When Bart flopped down prone on the ground, all of the men following immediately did the same.

Bart shifted his eyes to John, who pointed a bit off to their left and whispered, "Cigarette glow, 'bout two hundred meters."

Bart followed his directions, and after another moment

he saw it too, a sentry enjoying a cigarette in the early evening darkness.

"Damn fool," Bart mumbled to himself. Aware that noise traveled long distances on the desert, he patted John's shoulder in silent thanks for the warning, and crawled back to find his radio operator, Walter Johnson.

Walter had the radio on vibration setting so an incoming call wouldn't alert any nearby sentries.

Bart moved next to him and whispered, "Give Hugh a call and see what his status is in the city."

Walter nodded and keyed his mike in a prearranged code. That sent a signal that would sound a couple of low-pitched clicks on Holmsby's radio, another precaution against giving a warning to any nearby ears.

After a few seconds, Walter heard three answering clicks on his set and nodded at Bart, who took the mike and slipped on an ear-set. "He gave the response that says it's okay to transmit," Walter said.

"Lion Two, come in. This is Lion One," Bart whispered, his lips against the mike to maintain silence. He spoke so low that even the men lying on the sand a few feet away heard nothing.

"Lion One, this is Lion Two," Hugh Holmsby responded.

"What's your situation?" Bart asked.

"A-1," Hugh answered, indicating he'd achieved his purpose and captured the enemy headquarters in Riyadh.

"Excellent. Any intel?" Bart asked.

"Stand by, One," Hugh answered, and was silent for twenty seconds. When he came back on-line, he said, "Here are GPS readings for the locations of wells with bombs attached."

Bart held up his hand and made writing movements to

Walter, who quickly handed him a pad and pencil from his breast pocket.

"Go ahead," Bart said.

Hugh read off ten sets of numbers, giving the latitude and longitude readings on the Global Positioning Satellite receiver Bart would need to find the wells that had been mined.

Bart smiled quickly, his teeth gleaming white in the darkness. "How did you manage to get these?" he asked, admiration in his voice.

"I excel in the art of gentle persuasion," Hugh answered dryly.

"I'll bet it wasn't too gentle," Bart answered with a chuckle. "Anything else?"

"My source says the bombs in the wells can be triggered by the terrorist guards, but only by hand. They have no remote detonators with them. He says once they trip the switch, the bombs go off one minute later."

"Any description of the bomb mechanism itself?"

"Sorry. My source is not a technician, and the only man here who knew the precise layout of the bombs was killed in our attack. We're looking through all of the papers here to see if we can come up with a schematic, but so far no luck."

"That's okay, Lion Two. Post some guards on your prisoners and take the rest of your men out into the field. I figure we've got maybe twelve to twenty-four hours before the terrorist reinforcements show up. We've got to get these bombs unhooked and hidden before they arrive."

"Yes, sir," Hugh answered. "Looking at a map of the fields, my men are closest to the following wells with bombs." He read off four numbers, indicating the well positions he and his men would attempt to take, and Bart jotted them down.

"Lion One signing off," Bart said. "Be safe, Lion Two."

"Roger that, Lion One. You too. Over."

After he got off the SOHFRAD with Hugh, Bart gathered his men close around him so he could talk in a low voice. Each of his squad leaders carried a GPS receiver, and he told them to plug in the coordinates of the six wells they would have to capture and disarm.

"It's gonna be tough to get to all of them without the terrorists knowing we're attacking," Bart said. "We need to keep noise to a minimum, so make sure all your weapons have their silencers attached and use your assault knives whenever possible."

He divided his forty men up into six groups of six men each, with four groups having seven men, and assigned each of them a squad leader and a set of coordinates to move toward.

Glancing at his own GPS and then at his watch, he said, "I figure it'll take about half an hour for all of the squads to get into position, so we'll coordinate our attacks to begin in thirty minutes from . . . *now.*"

The men all set their watches and without another word, the squad leaders gathered their men and melted away into the darkness.

Bart kept the Davidson brothers with him. He knew they would have been very upset had he separated them from him, so he didn't try.

Bart led his group toward the well that was their target, and avoided sentries whenever they spotted them. Luckily, the sentries weren't expecting any trouble, and were not very well trained in the first place, so they talked and smoked among themselves and were pretty easy to spot and avoid.

Only once, when the men happened upon a sentry leaning back against a low bush sleeping were they surprised. As the sentry started to awake when John Davidson almost tripped over him, John stuck his left arm against the man's mouth, and quickly dispatched him by grabbing his throat with his right hand and ripping it out.

When Bart gave him a look, John shrugged. "I didn't have time to go for my knife," he said in a low voice.

David glanced at the man, who was gurgling and writhing as blood spurted from his torn carotid arteries. "I'll tell ya, bro," he observed dryly, "you're messy, but effective."

Bart and his men passed over twenty wells before they came to the one that was booby-trapped with the plutonium mine. They could tell without checking the GPS when they found it, for it was literally surrounded by sentries. These men were more alert than the others had been—perhaps because they knew they were guarding a bomb that would blow them to Allah if they relaxed their guard.

Bart checked his watch and whispered, "Five minutes." Using hand signals, he indicated he wanted the men to spread out and surround the well. "You guys take out the sentries and I'll make straight for the bomb," Bart said.

"That's the most dangerous place, boss," John Davidson said. "Why don't you let me do that?"

"Johnny," Bart answered, "now is not the time to question orders, okay?"

"Yes, sir," John answered sourly.

As the men moved off to flank the well, John whispered to David, "I'll take care of the sentries. You watch Bart's back."

"Roger that," David answered, a gleam in his eyes that would make a saint's blood run cold.

When the five minutes were up, Bart rose up off his knees and began sprinting for the well, holding his silenced Uzi in front of him.

A sentry standing next to the metal struts of the well straightened and stared at the apparition running toward him. He couldn't believe his eyes. He'd heard no warning from the others. He grabbed for his Kalashnikov, which was slung over his shoulder, and opened his mouth to yell.

Without breaking stride, Bart squeezed the trigger on his Uzi. A string of holes appeared in the man's chest, starting at his navel and running up to his throat.

The guard was thrown back against the strut and slid down it to the ground, blood pumping from his ruined lungs.

In the background, Bart heard a strangled yell cut short by the blade of an assault knife, and then he was at the well. He took a small flashlight from his belt and shined it around the base of the well, until he saw a box affixed to the pumping mechanism. It had a red switch protruding from the metal, with some Arabic scribbling underneath it that Bart could not read.

As he took out his knife and began to pry the top off the box, a man rose up from the other side of the pump and aimed his rifle at Bart's face.

Not having time to pick up his Uzi, Bart flipped the knife around in his hand and prepared to throw it at the guard.

A single cough from behind Bart, and the man's forehead exploded in a fine red mist of blood and brains.

Bart glanced over his shoulder and saw David Davidson grinning at him. "Go on with what you were doing, boss," he said. "I'll make sure no one else bothers you."

Bart returned the smile and went back to opening the black box with his knife.

Imad Yarkas stomped his feet to try and restore circulation in them. *This place is as cold at night as Afghanistan in winter,* he thought to himself. He decided to make the rounds of the sentries he'd posted to guard the well. He was very proud that the leaders had entrusted him with this very important job, and the bonus he'd been promised would keep his family back home in food for many years.

When he found a young boy of no more that seventeen leaning against a truck sleeping, he slapped him hard across the face, bringing him instantly awake. "Yassir," Yarkas growled, his face up next to the boy's, "if I find you sleeping while on guard duty again, I will cut off your left hand as a warning to others. Understand?"

"Yes, sir!" the boy replied, his eyes full of fear.

Yarkas grinned to himself as he strutted off. *That son of a camel won't fall asleep again any time soon,* he thought to himself.

Fifty yards farther along the sentry line, he saw another guard slumped on the ground, his Kalashnikov cradled in his arms. "Allah preserve me!" Yarkas snorted, angry to find yet another of his sentries asleep on the job.

He stepped over and kicked the man roughly in the stomach, and was surprised when the man didn't even groan in pain.

Yarkas bent down and grabbed the guard by the shoulder and rolled him over, gasping when he saw the gaping wound in his throat and the puddle of black-looking blood on the sand underneath him.

The hair on the back of his neck stood up when a soft voice behind him said, "Sorry, old chap. I don't think he's gonna wake up."

Yarkas whirled around, his finger searching for the trigger on his rifle.

A man dressed all in black with an equally black face was standing there, grinning at him.

As Yarkas brought the barrel of his AK-47 up, he saw the man's hand move and felt as if he'd been kicked in the stomach. When he doubled over, he saw the hilt of a large knife protruding from the man's hand against his abdomen.

The man grunted and jerked upward, slicing Yarkas's stomach open from groin to rib cage. Yarkas dropped his rifle and grabbed at his entrails as they flopped out of the gaping wound.

Yarkas dropped to his knees with his head bowed, and didn't see the gleam of the blade as the soldier buried it in the back of his neck, killing him instantly.

Things didn't go as smoothly for Major Hugh Holmsby at the first rig he attacked. One of the sentries managed to get a round off before Sergeant Major Tommy Gifford shot him through the heart.

The other sentries opened fire, pinning Holmsby and his men down long enough for the terrorist in charge to make it to the bomb affixed to the well.

He jerked the red switch down just as Gifford dove onto his back and plunged his assault knife into the man's throat. As Gifford and the dead guard fell to the ground, Holmsby hurriedly ripped the bomb casing off the well and bent over it with his knife, trying desperately to open the case before the minute he had was up.

Gifford rolled the dead guard off and got to his feet. He watched as Hugh finally managed to pop the top on the bomb casing. He looked over Hugh's shoulder into the box. Lying at the bottom, under a maze of wires and batteries, was a green-paper-wrapped brick of what looked like C-4 plastique.

Attached to the side of the box was a small lead container that had been spot-welded to the metal bomb container.

"That's got to be the plutonium," Hugh said in a whisper, as if the very sound of his voice might cause the bomb to explode prematurely.

He glanced at Gifford. "We have no time," he said.

"Hell with that, boss!" Gifford exclaimed. He grabbed the metal box from Hugh, stuck the point of his assault knife under the smaller lead box on the side, and pried at it until it popped off and fell to the ground.

He gave Hugh a quick wink, said, "See ya," and sprinted off away from the well, the box containing the C-4 under his arm like a football. He'd run about fifty yards when he stopped and hurled the box away from him high into the air. It exploded seconds later, the force of the blast and the metal fragments of the box blowing Tommy head over heels to lie still on the desert floor.

Hugh, his ears ringing and his face covered with black soot from the explosion, ran toward Tommy's body. Somehow, the shrapnel from the bomb had missed Hugh entirely.

He knelt in the sand and grabbed Tommy by the shoulder, rolling him over onto his back. Tommy's face was blistered and cracked from the heat of the explosion, and there were several small holes in his cheeks and forehead from the shrapnel. Hugh shook him back and forth. "Tommy . . . Goddamnit . . . wake up!"

After a few moments, Tommy opened bloodshot eyes and looked around, as if amazed he was still alive. "Hey, boss, did you see that throw? I should'a been a professional football player in the States."

Hugh smiled, tears of relief in his eyes. "Yeah, Tommy, but you held on to the ball a little long for my taste."

Tommy coughed, and then groaned from the pain it caused him. "Hugh, you got a cigarette?" he asked.

Hugh frowned in puzzlement. "But Tommy. You don't smoke."

Tommy grinned. "Oh, yeah, I forgot. Those things'll kill ya."

TWENTY-ONE

Once the SAS troops had all of the booby-trapped wells under control, Bart and Hugh made the rounds of the wells, separating the small lead containers containing the plutonium from the metal boxes holding the C-4 plastique bombs.

The bombs were carried off into the desert and detonated, minus the plutonium. After that was accomplished, all of the plutonium containers were placed in a trunk and buried out in the desert where there were no trees or rocks to mark the place. Bart checked his GPS receiver, and made a note of the exact location so it could be found later and the plutonium properly disposed of by experts Ben Raines would fly in.

Bart stationed his men around the wells, and asked Hugh to accompany him back to the terrorist headquarters in Riyadh.

"Sir," Hugh asked, "why are you stationing men around the wells now that the bombs have been removed?"

"Because the terrorist reinforcements are due here at any time. When they arrive, they won't know that we've disarmed the bombs and hidden the plutonium. The longer we can keep them from finding that out, the longer we'll have before they decide to try something else, or even bring in more plutonium bombs. With luck, they'll think the plutonium is still at the well sites, and will waste valuable time trying to retake control of the wells to bolster their bargaining position with the United Nations."

"That's all well and good, sir, but from what I hear, the terrorist reinforcements headed this way number in the tens of thousands. Do you really think we can hold them off with a handful of men?"

Bart's expression was grim when he answered, "That's what we're going to find out, Hugh. Remember, we're SAS and these terrorists are little better than camel jockeys." He sighed. "In any case, Ben Raines should be able to get us some help by first light in the morning."

Hugh glanced around at the small number of men guarding the wells and shivered in the frigid desert air. "Can't come soon enough for me, boss."

When they got back to Riyadh and entered the terrorist headquarters building, the first thing Hugh did was arrange for a medical corpsman to take a look at Tommy Gifford, who'd been carried in on a stretcher. After a brief examination, the corpsman reported to Hugh and Bart.

"The sergeant major should be all right after a couple of weeks of rest, sir," he said, speaking to Hugh. "He's got a couple of ruptured eardrums, some minor contusions and abrasions, and his left arm is broken in two places." He grinned. "Nothing that will keep a sergeant major off duty for more than a fortnight."

Hugh nodded, greatly relieved that his friend would suffer no permanent ill effects from his act of heroism. "Thank you, corpsman. Take good care of him," Hugh said.

As the corpsman was leaving, Bart's radio officer burst

into the room Bart was using as his staff office. "Sir, there's some important traffic on the terrorist radio I think you should hear."

Bart and Hugh followed the man down the hall into the communications room. A continuous chatter of Arabic was coming out of the speaker attached to the radio the terrorists had been using.

"You understand any of this, Riley?" Bart asked the radioman.

"A little sir. I took a second in Middle Eastern languages in college, but the accent is different from what I studied."

"What's going on?" Bart asked.

"What I can make out seems to indicate the terrorist reinforcements are arriving at the port of Dhahran right now. If I'm correct in my reading of this message, they're saying they should arrive at the city in about four hours, just before dawn. They keep asking for this Hazmi guy to answer their radio calls."

Bart slammed his hand down on the desk. "Damn!" He looked up at Riley. "Get me Ben Raines in Kuwait City on the SOHFRAD as soon as possible. We're going to need some help, fast!"

Ben, who'd had a cot installed in his command post, was lying in it but not sleeping when his communications officer knocked on the door. "Yes, come in."

"Sir," the man said, "Commander Wiley-Smeyth is on the SOHFRAD in the communications room."

Ben jumped to his feet and ran down the hall to the radio room. "Put it on the speaker," he ordered, and Riley complied.

"Bart, Ben here. What's your situation?"

"The good news is we've captured the terrorist headquarters in Riyadh and all of the booby-trapped wells with almost no casualties," Bart answered.

Ben grinned at the radioman. "That's great news, Bart!" he said. "And the bombs?"

"Separated from the plutonium and detonated. The plutonium is at the following GPS coordinates," Bart answered and read off the location where the plutonium had been buried.

Ben jotted the numbers down on a pad next to the radio receiver, and then asked, "And the bad news?"

"We have reliable information the terrorist reinforcement troops are landing right now and will be here in Riyadh before dawn."

"Shit!" Ben exclaimed.

"My thoughts exactly," Bart answered dryly.

"Listen, Bart," Ben said. "I haven't heard from my troops yet over in Iran, but the meteorologists tell me there's a big storm moving into the entire area from the desert. They say the sand will be so thick in the air, we won't be able to fly anyone in to relieve or reinforce your positions for at least twenty-four hours."

There was a short silence on the radio, and then Bart said, "That is disturbing news," with a voice so devoid of emotion it was as if someone had just told him the cook had burned his breakfast toast.

"Perhaps it would be best if you and your men beat a retreat back into the mountains," Ben said.

He heard a short chuckle over the radio. "Not the SAS way, I'm afraid. We'll hold our positions as long as possible and hope for a break in the weather, Ben."

"How are you fixed for weapons and ammunition?"

"We should be all right, with what we captured from the terrorists and what we brought with us."

"Hang in there, pal," Ben said. "We'll get some help for you as soon as we can."

"I know," Bart answered. "See you soon, Ben."

Just as Ben disconnected the radio, Jackie Malone strolled into the office, drinking a cup of what looked like black syrup in a chipped mug.

Ben arched an eyebrow. "What the hell are you drinking, Jackie?"

She stared down into the cup for a moment. "It's supposed to be coffee, but it tastes more like crankcase oil," she replied.

"Pour that crap out and have some of my coffee," Ben ordered, pointing at his coffeemaker in the corner of the office.

"Best offer I've had all day," Jackie replied. She walked to the window and pitched the dark liquid in her cup outside. "I'm afraid to dump this stuff down the drain, it'd probably stop it up," she explained as she filled her mug from Ben's machine.

"What's the latest news?" she asked, perching on the corner of his desk on one hip.

"I haven't heard from our troops in Iran yet, but Commander Wiley-Smeyth and his SAS chaps have taken control of the wells near Riyadh."

Jackie peered at him with discerning eyes. "You don't sound too happy about that, boss. What's going on?"

"Bart intercepted a radio message that the terrorist reinforcements are landing at Dhahran even as we speak."

Jackie's eyes widened. "Then we've got to get on our horses and get over there to back him up," she said, finishing the last of her coffee in one gulp.

Ben held up his hand. "Not so fast, Jackie. The weathermen tell me the entire area is going to be socked in by a winter storm for the next twelve hours or so."

"But Ben," she said, "they'll be overrun. They can't hold the area with only eighty or so men."

He nodded. "I know, Jackie. Believe me, I know, but there doesn't seem to be a damned thing I can do about it."

She set her mug on his desk and got to her feet. "Well, I can't just sit here doing nothing. I'm gonna get my men ready and have the pilot standing by. As soon as there's the least break in the storm, we're heading out."

Ben smiled. "Good. I'll alert the meteorologists to keep us informed and to let us know when and if the storm slackens."

TWENTY-TWO

The pilot of the C-130 air transport plane carrying the SUSA troops touched a switch on his console, and the drop light in the cargo bay turned from red to yellow, indicating they were approaching the drop zone.

Buddy Raines got to his feet and signaled his men to do the same thing. The large rear hatch in the tail of the C-130 began to open, providing a ramp down which the troops would run and dive off when it came time for them to jump.

The troops fixed their oxygen masks to their faces. Since they would be bailing out at almost twenty thousand feet, they would need oxygen supplementation until they fell to below ten thousand feet.

After what seemed an eternity, the yellow light changed to green and Buddy pumped his fist in the air. It was time for the Scouts to jump. They would hopefully be landing just on the outskirts of Tehran itself. Buddy and his men would jump a few minutes, later and would land among the oil fields where the bombs were located.

Major Jackson Bean nodded his head at Buddy in farewell as he sprinted down the ramp and dove into the blackness, followed by his Scouts.

Once the Scouts were gone, the light in the cargo bay

returned to yellow. The next time it changed to green, it would be time for Buddy and his team to jump.

The light changed, and Buddy led his team and their accompanying Scout troops down the ramp and out into the night air.

Once he was stabilized and falling at terminal velocity of miles an hour, Buddy took his D-ring to his chute in his right hand and held his altimeter in his left up close where he could read his altitude. When it showed a thousand feet, a hesitation of only a couple of seconds would cause him to fall too low for the chute to deploy and slow him down enough to survive the drop. On average, HALO drop casualties were upward of ten percent, but Buddy's men and women were not average. They'd trained unto exhaustion in this maneuver, and rarely had any injuries.

Abdul Muttmain, unlike his counterpart in Riyadh, Al Hazmi, was a hands-on leader. Instead of sitting in his headquarters building in Tehran, he preferred to remain in the field with his troops and to supervise personally the guarding of the booby-trapped wells. He left his second in command, Baltazar Garzon, in charge of the city command post to answer any radio messages from El Farrar, with instructions to send a messenger if any important transmissions were received.

Not trusting Garzon with the important task of deciding when or if the bombs should be exploded, he kept the remote control to the detonators in his possession at all times. Muttmain knew that in the unlikely event he had to trigger the bombs, it would mean his own death, but he was fully prepared to die to prevent the infidels from taking control of the wells from his men.

Muttmain had a tent set up in the center of the group

of wells that were equipped with bombs, thinking that in the event of an attack, he would have plenty of advance warning and would have time to detonate the bombs if necessary.

The tent contained a table with a shortwave radio on it along with a Kalashnikov assault rifle and a supply of ammunition. In the corner of the tent was an espresso machine to keep him well supplied with strong, bitter coffee to help ward off the chill of the desert air. A small Honda generator that he kept running continuously powered all the devices.

At eight P.M., Muttmain filled a small thermos with coffee and told his aide de camp, Khan Baz, he was going to make the rounds of the sentries to make sure they were all awake and alert.

"That is wise, sir," Baz said, "These shepherd boys who were assigned to us are not true jihadis as we are." *Jihadis* was a term meaning dedicated holy warriors, which Muttmain and his officers all considered themselves to be.

Muttmain gave the man a rare smile. "You are correct, Khan, and if I find one of them sleeping while on guard duty, I will bring you his head back as a souvenir."

Muttmain put the detonator on the table and picked up his Kalashnikov, unable to carry the thermos and rifle and detonator all at the same time. "I will return shortly," he said, dipping his head as he left through the flap in the tent wall.

As he made his way among the sentries, Muttmain was delighted, and somewhat surprised, to find all of the men awake and keeping watch as they had been told. *Perhaps these boys will become soldiers to be trusted after all,* he thought to himself.

When he finished his rounds, he began to walk back

toward his tent. A freshening breeze whipped his robes around his legs and he glanced skyward, looking for signs of an impending storm.

His mouth fell open and he gasped at the sight of several dark shapes drifting downward, blotting out stars behind them as they settled to the ground.

He dropped his thermos to the ground, his coffee forgotten as he jerked the Kalashnikov off his shoulder and pulled the loading lever back to put a shell in the firing chamber.

"Invaders!" he screamed in Arabic. "We are under attack!" he added, pulling the trigger and sending a dozen rounds into the air at one of the dark shapes drifting toward him.

Suddenly, the night was alive with flashes of orange and red as the invading troops returned his fire. Muttmain thought it strange he heard no gunfire save his own, not realizing the invaders' guns were fitted with silencers.

Coop, who'd been coming down almost directly over Muttmain, heard the bullets whiz by his head like a swarm of angry bees, and then his chute, ripped to shreds by the shells, collapsed around him. He plummeted twenty feet and hit the ground hard. He tried to roll, but he felt his ankle give way and he fell flat on his face, dropping his H&K MP-10 machine gun.

Muttmain crouched, replacing his magazine with a full one, and then he approached the black parachute billowing on the ground in front of him. He grabbed an edge and jerked it back, wanting to see just who was invading his oil field.

The stunned man in black fatigues rolled over onto his back, an expression of pain on his blackened face as he stretched out his hand for his machine gun, lying just out of his reach to the side.

Muttmain grinned and aimed his rifle at the man. "You are American?" he asked as his finger touched the trigger.

Coop stared up at the man standing over him with a gun. He grinned, shrugged through his pain, and said, "Fuckin' A, raghead!"

Muttmain's smile disappeared and he took aim at Coop's face.

Suddenly, a voice from behind him called, "Hey, Omar."

Muttmain whirled around to see a female, also dressed all in black and with black greasepaint on her face, standing ten feet away. She was cradling a terrible-looking shotgun in her arms, and her teeth were gleaming in the starlight as she grinned at him.

As Muttmain tried to bring his rifle around, she said, "Say good-bye, shithead!" and pulled the trigger.

The Franchi-FAS assault shotgun exploded, sending twelve-gauge flechettes across ten feet to shred Muttmain into hamburger meat. His body was flung backward to land spread-eagled on his back, gasping and gurgling as his blood spurted from hundreds of wounds.

Jersey glanced around to make sure there were no more terrorists nearby, and then she sauntered over to stand next to Coop. She squatted, the Franchi lying across her knees. "You okay, Coop?" she asked softly. "Are you hit?"

Coop shook his head. "Nope, but he shot hell out of my chute." He tried to get up and his face went white and pale, and he almost fainted from the pain in his ankle.

Jersey looked around again, making certain they were alone, and then she pushed him back down on his back and took his left leg in her hand. She quickly unlaced his combat boot and slipped it off. His ankle ballooned up around his sock to almost three times its normal size.

"Jesus, Coop," she said, grimacing. "It may be broken."

"Bullshit!" Coop said, sitting up. "It's just a sprain."

Jersey shook her head. "Nevertheless, you can't walk on that."

"Hand me that creep's rifle," Coop said, pulling his assault knife from its scabbard.

Jersey grabbed Muttmain's Kalashnikov and handed it to Coop, who used his K-Bar knife to cut the rifle's wooden butt and canvas sling off.

He handed them to Jersey. "Use the wood for a brace and tie it to my leg with the sling, then help me up."

Jersey shook her head. "You're crazy, Coop."

"Just do it, Jersey . . . please," Coop said. "I know I'll never hear the end of it from you if I spend this campaign flat on my back."

As Jersey worked to fasten the sling and brace to Coop's leg, they could hear sporadic shooting from the terrorists, along with screams and moans of wounded men as the battle raged all around them.

When she pulled Coop to his feet, he groaned and his face screwed up in obvious pain. He looked up, sweat pouring from his face even though the night air was frigid. "You're right, Jerse, I can't walk."

"Told you so, stubborn ass," she replied.

He pointed to a nearby well. "Help me over to that well. You can stand me up against one of the struts, and I'll guard the bomb and keep anyone from setting it off."

Jersey wrapped his left arm around her shoulders, put her right arm around his waist, and began to help him hobble over to the nearby well.

As they struggled through the sand toward the well, Coop's left hand happened to fall on her breast. Jersey glanced down at it just in time to see him cup it around her breast and give it a little squeeze.

She gave a short laugh. "Coop, you're such a fuckin' lecher," she said.

"What? Oh, excuse me, Jerse," he said, removing his hand. "Just an accident."

She looked up at him. "An accidental squeeze?" she asked skeptically.

"Must've been a spasm caused by the pain," he answered, a sly smile on his face.

"Just so you enjoyed it," Jersey said, continuing to walk him toward the well.

"Ummm, it was okay, I guess," Coop said.

"Okay?" she asked archly.

"All right, all right," he answered. "It was great!"

She took his arm from around her shoulder and leaned him back against the well strut. "For that, you get to keep your hand . . . so long as it doesn't happen again."

"But . . ." Coop started to say.

"Next time, try your moves on Jackie Malone," Jersey said, her eyes flashing. "Maybe she'll even let you succeed."

Coop grinned. "Now you're sounding like a jealous woman," he said.

"Hah!" Jersey replied. "Not jealous, and not easy either," she said, moving off toward the sounds of fighting.

"You can say that again," Coop muttered, jerking the slide back on his MP-10 to cock it.

When he heard the sounds of gunfire in the distance, Khan Baz hurriedly got on the radio and tried to raise the headquarters building, hoping to warn them of the attack. He got no answer to his repeated calls. Finally, he put the microphone down and sat staring at the detonator. He ran a tongue over dry lips and tried to decide if he should set the bombs off.

"Allah, give me strength," he whispered as he reached for the remote control.

The flap in the tent wall snapped open and Buddy Raines ducked inside, his Beretta M93R in his hand.

Baz grabbed the control and held it up, his lips moving in a final prayer to Allah as his finger searched for the button.

Buddy shot from the hip, firing three rounds into Baz's face, blowing him backward over his chair and spraying the walls of the tent with brains and blood.

The remote detonator slipped from the dead man's hand and fell to the sand floor of the tent.

TWENTY-THREE

Buddy bent and picked up the detonator, handling it very carefully so as not to inadvertently set off the bombs. He slipped the plastic back off the device and took the two AA batteries out, rendering it useless.

He didn't smash it because he wanted their experts to be able to examine it and perhaps determine if there was some way to block the signal, just in case similar detonators were in use by the terrorists in other oil fields.

Corrie entered the tent behind Buddy, turning slightly sideways so the SOHFRAD radio she was wearing like a backpack would fit through the doorway.

Buddy indicated the table containing the terrorists' radio. "Put the SOHFRAD there, Corrie. It's time to check in with the troops."

Harley Reno and Hammer Hammerick were pinned down, lying on their faces in the gravelly sand of the Iranian desert behind some old pump machinery as almost a dozen terrorist troops fired at them. The Kalashnikov slugs ricocheted and whined as they peppered the wrought iron of the pump housing they were behind.

Harley turned his head to look at Hammer. "I'm getting a little tired of this bullshit!" he growled.

"Yeah, but we don't dare spray the area with our machine guns," Hammer replied. "We might set the bomb on the well off."

"Time for a little precision shooting then," Harley replied. He put his H&K MP-10 down and pulled his .50-caliber Desert Eagle from its holster.

Peering around the edge of the pump, he saw one of the terrorists hiding behind a fifty-five-gallon drum, with only the top of a ragged turban showing in the starlight.

He took careful aim and fired one of his steel-jacketed rounds at the center of the oil drum, the explosion of the big pistol much louder than that of the Kalashnikovs the terrorists were using.

The large-caliber slug penetrated both sides of the drum and hit the terrorist square in the center of his chest. The man screamed and stood up, both hands clasping a hole in his chest you could put a fist in.

As he fell backward, one of his cohorts peeked out from behind the well strut he was hiding behind, and Harley fired again, his slug hitting the man just at the bridge of his nose and blowing the back of his head off. He dropped back out of sight like a sack of potatoes.

While Harley was picking the two men off, Hammer pulled a flash-bang concussion grenade from the webbing on his chest and lobbed it in the direction of the well. The concussion grenade, which contained white phosphorus and no shrapnel to speak of, was safe to use in the vicinity of the bomb affixed to the well.

Hammer and Harley both ducked and closed their eyes against the brilliant white flash and loud noise of the flash-bang.

When it went off, it lit up the surrounding desert like a miniature sun and sounded like a large mortar round going off.

Several of the terrorists, blinded and deafened by the concussion, dropped their weapons and staggered from cover, their hands over their eyes and ears.

Harley stood up and, holding his Desert Eagle in the classic two-handed grip, proceeded to shoot them as fast as he could pull the trigger.

Hammer also got to his feet and with the MP-10 on single fire, began to fire repeatedly as he walked calmly toward the rest of the terrorists.

Those brave or stupid enough to try to return his fire were soon lying on their backs in the sand bleeding profusely.

Three of the terrorists, deciding enough was enough, threw their weapons down and stepped out from cover with their hands held over their heads.

Hammer didn't hesitate. He thumbed the MP-10's lever to full auto and gave the men a quick burst, killing them where they stood. "Sorry boys," he said in a harsh voice. "You invade a country and try to take over the world, you got to pay the price."

When they were sure the area was secure, Harley and Hammer dismantled the bomb mechanism attached to the well and separated the plutonium container from the package of C-4 inside the bomb itself. Hammer disconnected the wiring from the C-4, making it safe from explosion, and then put the plastique in his pocket along with the fuse he'd taken out of it. He grinned at Harley. "Never know when some of this will come in handy," he said.

"Roger that!" Harley agreed.

Once the well was safe from explosion, they dragged the bodies of the terrorists into a pile and removed all of their weapons and ammunition, placing it in a separate area.

Sporadic and intermittent gunfire could be heard all around the area as the remainder of the Scouts assigned to Buddy's team did much the same thing to the wells nearby. In less than three hours, the entire oil field was deemed to be secure. Over twenty bombs had been removed from the wells and deactivated by the troops.

Many of the terrorists, when they saw they were defeated, ran off into the desert rather than die at their posts. The Scouts didn't chase them, as their primary responsibility was to make the wells safe.

Major Jackson Bean and his Scouts were having a little trouble locating the terrorist headquarters in Tehran. The largest city in the country, with over five million inhabitants, Tehran stretched over many square miles.

Bean, figuring the terrorists would want to be in close proximity to the airport, centered his search for their headquarters there.

He spread his men out, dividing them into squads with Willie Running Bear, Samuel Clements, and Sue Waters as squad leaders. Each was told to search a different quadrant around the airport area and to check back by radio if they hit pay dirt.

It took almost two hours before Sue Waters and her squad came upon a three-story building near the northern section of the airport. Unlike surrounding buildings in the area, whose windows were dark, this building was lit up like a Christmas tree. Additionally, Sue could see several large jeeplike vehicles parked next to the structure that were painted with desert camouflage. "That's got to be the place," she whispered to her radioman, Mike

Nugent. "Give Major Bean a buzz and tell him we think we've found the nest."

While she was waiting for Bean and the other squads to arrive, Sue watched the building through her night-vision scope. Sure enough, she began to see armed sentries moving around on the roof, as well as men patrolling the adjacent areas on foot.

When Bean arrived, she filled him in on what she'd seen, and he agreed with her that this was most likely the place they'd been looking for.

"You want to go in soft or hard?" Sue asked, her tone making it clear she preferred hard.

"Let me check with Buddy before we do anything," Bean said. "I don't want to go barreling in there until Buddy has secured the wells. They might set them off at the first sign of an attack."

Nugent began to fiddle with some dials and after a few moments, he grinned up at Major Bean. "General Raines is on the line, sir."

"Buddy," Bean said, "this is Jackson. We've found the main building housing the terrorists and we need to know is it safe to take it out."

"Roger, Jackson," Buddy Raines answered. "My men report all of the wells have been cleared of bombs. You are free to proceed with all due dispatch."

"Thank you, General. That's just what we wanted to hear."

"And Jackson," Buddy added.

"Sir?"

"If at all possible, try to take any officers alive if you can. Mike Post and his boys at Intel would dearly love to have a couple of live ones to interrogate."

"Roger that, sir," Bean said.

He turned to Sue Waters. "Spread the word among

your troops. The general wants some of the officers taken alive if at all possible. Intel wants to talk to them."

Moments later, Sue and her squad, along with the other squads, were moving silently through the night toward the terrorist headquarters.

Sue's orders were to go in through the front door, while Sam Clements's squad took the rear door and Willie Running Bear's squad concentrated on taking out the sentries as silently as they could. This was the sort of assignment Willie lived for. He liked nothing better than to stalk and kill the enemy with his knife. He said it was much more satisfying to look into a man's eyes when you slit his throat than it was to kill him at long distance with a rifle or bomb.

Sue held her squad back for a moment to let Willie Running Bear and his men do their work on the guards. His squad was so expert at this, Sue didn't even see them moving toward the building. After about five minutes, she saw Willie Running Bear stand up near the front door and motion her forward with his arm.

When she and her squad got to the front door, she saw Willie Running Bear wiping his knife on the shirt of a dead guard. She also noticed that a significant portion of the man's scalp was missing, but she decided not to remark on that. Willie Running Bear had strange ideas about taking souvenirs from his victims. Sue had always wondered what he did with the scalps he collected, but had never had the nerve to ask him.

"Remember," she cautioned her squad, "shoot low if the target looks like an officer."

One of her men, named Barney, gave a low chuckle. "All them ragheads look alike to me."

"The officers will be the ones hiding behind their desks sending the grunts out to get killed," Waters remarked. "The Arab headmen have always been high on letting others be the martyrs."

Sue jerked the loading lever back on her Uzi and put her left hand around the silencer on the barrel as she crouched and moved toward the doorway, her men spread out behind her.

Just inside the door was an alcove with a desk in the center. A young Arab-looking boy was dozing behind the desk, his head resting on his hand with his elbow on the desk.

Sue moved silently toward him, noting that his rifle was leaning against a nearby wall out of his immediate reach. She handed her Uzi to Barney, and pulled her assault knife from its scabbard.

She slipped behind the sleeping boy, grabbed his hair, and yanked his chin up and back. Pressing the razor-sharp blade against his throat, she whispered in his ear.

"Do you speak English?"

The boy gulped once and nodded his head, his eyes wide with fear as sweat began to run down his face.

"Where are your leaders?" Sue asked, moving the knife slightly so a thin trickle of blood oozed from his neck.

"If I tell you that, they will kill me?" the boy pleaded, his voice almost a sob.

Sue moved quickly, putting her left arm around his neck and pulling his chair back from the desk. She put the point of the knife in his lap against his genitals. "And if you don't tell me, I will cut your balls off and make you eat them!" she growled. "Do you understand?"

"They're all on the third floor," the boy whimpered, his face as pale as the stucco walls of the room.

"Thank you," Sue said. She flipped the knife around and used the steel hilt to knock the boy unconscious with one sharp blow to the back of his head.

She holstered the knife and held out her hands. Barney pitched her Uzi to her and she bounded up the stairs.

On the second-floor landing, three men walked from a room, their Kalashnikovs in their arms. Sue didn't hesitate for a second. She loosed a quick burst at the men, spraying them across the chest with a stream of 9mm parabellum slugs.

Barney and two other men didn't have to be told. They vaulted over the bodies and ran into the room the men had just come out of. Sue heard the soft coughs of their Uzis as they killed the rest of the men in the room.

Jerking her head for the remainder of the squad to follow her, she ran lightly up the last flight of stairs. A closed door was at the head of the stairs, and was the only door on the floor.

Sue raised her right leg and kicked the door, which splintered and disintegrated into small pieces.

Baltazar Garzon was sitting at a table, talking rapidly into a radio to Abdullah El Farrar. When the door exploded and Sue Waters walked through the doorway, he screamed something into the radio and grabbed for an old Colt .45 on the desk next to the radio.

Sue shot from the hip, emptying her clip into the radio, and then moving her aim slightly to center on Garzon's hand, which was picking up the .45.

Three bullets hit the back of his hand, nearly taking it off at the wrist and sending the Colt spinning across the room.

Garzon screamed again as he grabbed his shredded hand, and rolled out of his chair onto the floor just as two more men came from an adjoining room brandishing assault rifles.

Barney dropped to one knee and triggered off a quick burst, aiming low. The two men's legs shattered and folded and they fell to the floor, screaming and moaning in pain.

Sue quietly ejected the spent magazine from her Uzi and replaced it with a full one. "Some of you get tourniquets on those men," she ordered. "We wouldn't want them to bleed to death, now would we?"

TWENTY-FOUR

Corrie twiddled with the dials on the SOHFRAD radio, and finally managed to contact Harley Reno. She looked up and nodded at Buddy, who picked up the microphone attached to the radio.

"Harley, this is Buddy Raines. How goes it?"

"So far so good, Boss," Harley replied into his headset. "The squad leaders of the rest of the Scouts tell me they've managed to gain control of all of the wells they've found that have bombs attached, and have disconnected the C-4 packages from the plutonium cases. Unless we've missed a couple of wells with bombs, we should be in good shape."

"Are you facing much resistance?"

"Not so far. According to the Scouts, most of the terrorists that are still alive have taken off into the desert. They may be trying to regroup there, but I think most of their leaders have been killed, so I doubt it's a credible threat."

"Good job, Harley. I'm here in a tent where the leader of the oil field group was holed up. I've disabled his remote detonator, so we shouldn't have to worry if you've missed any bombs. Tell the men to hold their positions until I check in with Major Bean and find out the status of the terrorist headquarters in Tehran. I'll get back to you soonest."

"Will do, Boss Man," Harley answered, and clicked off the radio.

Buddy spoke to Corrie. "See if you can raise Major Bean on this thing, would you?"

After another few moments fiddling with the dials, Corrie grinned up at him. "Go ahead. Major Bean's on the line."

"Jackson, Buddy here."

"Yes, sir," Bean answered.

"What's your status?"

"We've taken control of the terrorist headquarters building," Bean answered. "And even managed to capture a couple of the officers—relatively undamaged."

"That's great news, Jackson. I'm here in the fields and we've got them secured. There's a jeep nearby and I'm gonna head your way right now. I'm sure Ben will want us to find out everything the officers can tell us."

Bean chuckled. "I'll keep them on ice for you, Buddy. The headquarters building is right next to the airport. It's the only three-story building in the area. I'll alert the sentries you're on the way so they won't take any potshots at you. See ya soon."

Buddy broke the connection. "Corrie, get that radio packed and get in the jeep outside. We're going for a little ride."

It took Buddy less than half an hour to make the journey from the oil fields to the outskirts of Tehran. He found the airport with no problem, and pulled up right next to the building Bean had indicated.

The guards posted waved him in and Corrie followed.

A guard in the main foyer stood up and saluted. "Major Bean is on the third floor, sir. He's waiting for you."

"Thank you, soldier," Buddy said, flipping him a quick salute as he jogged up the stairs.

Major Bean was sitting behind a desk on the third floor, and got to his feet when Buddy and Corrie entered.

Buddy glanced around the room at the bullet holes and blood that covered the walls and floor.

"Looks like you had a little excitement here, Jackson."

Bean shrugged. "Oh, not too much."

"Let me check in with Ben and then we'll talk to the prisoners," Buddy said, nodding at Corrie to set up her radio.

After a few minutes, she had Ben on the line.

"Ben, Buddy here."

"Good to hear your voice," Ben said, relief evident in his tone. "What's your sitrep?"

"We have control of all threatened wells, and the bombs have been rendered useless. Also, Major Bean has captured a couple of terrorist commanders and we're ready to interrogate them. Anything in particular you want to know?"

"We have information that terrorist reinforcements are on their way to both Iran and Saudi Arabia. See if you can verify expected time of arrival, troop strength, and which ports they'll be arriving at."

Buddy glanced out the window of the room he was in, and saw increasing darkness as the sandstorm outside continued to build in force. He could hear the wind howling even through the thick walls of the building.

"Ben, the weather here is getting pretty bad. I don't think there's any way you're gonna be able to send Jackie Malone and her troops here any time soon."

"Roger that, Buddy," Ben replied. "It looks like you

guys are going to have to hold the fort on your own for a while."

"I figured that. Any suggestions?"

Ben laughed, but the sound had little humor in it. "Are you asking the old man for advice, young'un?"

"It never hurts to get a second opinion."

"What do you plan to do?" Ben asked.

"I thought I'd spread my forces out, placing them as high up in various buildings as I can to give them a good field of fire on the advancing terrorist troops. I'll make it into a guerrilla-type fight so the enemy's superior troop strength will be nullified."

"Good idea. I can't improve on that," Ben said.

"I plan to have Harley and the Scouts do the same thing. Break up into small, very mobile groups and have them spread out in the oil fields where they'll have plenty of cover. That way they'll be able to hit and run and never stay in one place long enough for the heavy weapons the terrorists will probably bring to do them much good."

"Excellent plan, Buddy. Good luck to you, and let me know if you find out anything useful from your prisoners."

"Hope to see you soon, Dad," Buddy said, and clicked off the connection.

"Ring up Harley on the radio and tell him what I told Ben about breaking up into small squads, Corrie," Buddy said. "I'm gonna go see what our prisoners have to say."

Buddy handed her the microphone, and followed Major Bean to the room where Willie Running Bear was standing guard over the prisoners.

Running Bear was leaning back against a wall, his Uzi pointed in the general direction of three men who were stretched out on blankets. One had a blood-soaked bandage on his right hand, while the other two had field dressings applied to their lower legs. All were moaning in pain and were covered with sweat and blood.

Running Bear stood up at attention when Buddy and the major entered the room.

"Have the prisoners said anything?" Buddy asked.

"No, sir. They've been too busy crying and moaning to talk much."

"Do they speak English?" Buddy asked Bean.

Bean pointed to the man with the bandage on his hand. "That one does, but I don't know about the other two."

Buddy moved over to squat next to the man. "What is your name?" he asked gently.

The man turned hate-filled, pain-ridden eyes on Buddy, clamping his lips tight.

Buddy sighed. "Okay, I tried the easy way. Now for the hard way. Mister, whatever your name is, you are in a foreign country in a uniform of an enemy state. That makes you a prisoner of war. You are required to state your name and rank when questioned."

The man turned his head and spat at Buddy's boots. "I don't speak to infidel dogs," he growled through gritted teeth.

Buddy looked down at the spittle on his boot. He stood up and casually wiped his dirtied boot on the rags covering the injured man's hand, causing him to scream in pain and grab at Buddy's boot with his good hand.

Buddy ground the boot down harder. "Now, I'll ask you once again. What is your name?"

"Baltazar Garzon," the man gasped through pale lips.

"Rank?"

"Field commander of our headquarters," Garzon answered, panting in pain.

"He was on the radio to his boss when we captured him," Bean said in a low voice.

"What did El Farrar tell you?" Buddy asked.

"You can kill me, but I will say no more," Garzon gasped as sweat poured from his forehead and cheeks.

Buddy looked over at Willie Running Bear. "Would you call the medic in, please?"

A few minutes later, a soldier with a red cross on his shoulder patch entered the room carrying a medical bag.

"Hello, Tommy," Buddy said.

"Hello, sir," Corpsman Tommy Garza replied.

Buddy winked at him. "I think our guest is in some pain, Tommy. Would you fix him up a cocktail that will make him feel better?"

"Aye, sir," Tommy said, hiding his grin by ducking his head. He got out several small bottles, and added a mixture of each to a large syringe.

"What are you using?" Buddy asked quietly, so the prisoner couldn't hear him.

"Phenobarbital, scopolamine, and just a touch of morphine," Tommy replied. "It'll put him in a twilight sleep, but he'll be able to respond to your questions, and the beauty of it is he won't even remember doing it."

"Carry on, son," Buddy said, stepping aside so the corpsman could give the injection.

Garzon, when he saw Tommy approach with the syringe began to scream insults and curses in Arabic and to thrash around on his blanket.

"Willie," Bean said.

Willie Running Bear put his Uzi down and straddled Garzon, holding the man's arms still so Tommy could insert the needle.

Seconds later, Garzon's eyes rolled back in his head and he began to snore softly, his body completely relaxed.

"He's ready for you, sir," Tommy said.

"Baltazar," Buddy said in a low, soothing voice. "Tell me what El Farrar and you talked about."

Garzon's eyes opened to tiny slits and he grinned drunkenly. "The leader told me reinforcements were on the way. Soon we will drive the infidels from the oil fields."

"How many troops is El Farrar sending to do this?" Buddy asked.

"Ten thousand here to Iran, and ten thousand to Saudi Arabia," Garzon answered proudly in a slurred, dreamy voice.

"When are they due, and where are they going to land?" Buddy asked.

"They will be here by dawn," Garzon said. "They will land at the port in Khorramshahr."

"Khorramshahr is about three hundred and fifty to four hundred miles southwest of Tehran," Major Bean said quietly.

Buddy stroked his chin thoughtfully. "That means it'll take them at least twelve to fifteen hours to get here after they unload."

"Yeah, considering the lousy roads and the weather, that's about right," Bean agreed. "Even if they bring some choppers with them, they won't be able to fly in this storm."

"Good. That gives us some time to prepare some surprises for the troops," Buddy said.

Buddy addressed Garzon again. "What about Saudi Arabia? Where will the troops land there?" he asked.

Garzon gave a half shrug. "I do not know. Probably Dhahran, but I do not know for sure."

Garzon's eyes closed and he began to snore again.

"That's about all you're gonna get out of him for now, sir," Tommy said.

"That's enough," Buddy said. "Good job, son."

Back in the office Bean had appropriated, Buddy began to give orders. "Jackson, get your men spread out in as many of the surrounding buildings as you can. Try to get them high up so they'll have a clear field of fire when the terrorists arrive."

"Sir, we found a storage room full of explosives in the basement of this building. How about if I place some of them around the area as mines? It might give the ragheads something to think about and slow them down a bit."

"Good idea, Jackson. You should have plenty of time before they get here to make sure they get a hotfoot when they attack."

"What are you going to do, sir?" Bean asked.

"I'm heading out to the oil fields to be with my team. I'll keep in touch via the SOHFRAD."

Bean stuck out his hand. "Good luck, sir."

"And to you," Buddy replied, taking his hand. "As soon as Corrie can tell Ben what we've found out, I'll be on my way."

TWENTY-FIVE

Abdullah El Farrar slammed the microphone down on his desk and muttered a curse under his breath in Arabic.

Muhammad Atwa and Farid Zamet, who were sitting nearby, glanced at each other. It was unlike their leader to lose his composure so openly. Usually, his volatile temper was hidden under a sarcastic demeanor.

"What is troubling you, Abdullah?" Zamet asked in a deferential tone. When El Farrar was in such a mood, it was best to be very circumspect lest his murderous attention fall on the wrong person.

"That son of a Babylon whore Ben Raines is attacking our positions in Saudi Arabia and Iran," El Farrar answered hotly.

"Perhaps if we explode a bomb or two, it will dissuade him from continuing to provoke us," Atwa offered.

"I am afraid it is already too late for that. I fear he has taken control of the oil fields in those countries away from us."

"Oh?" Zamet asked, a worried frown on his face. Saudi Arabia and Iran represented the largest oil fields in the region, outside of Kuwait, which had never been under their control. Loss of those countries as bargaining chips would indeed put a crimp in their plans of world domination.

"Yes. I was cut off while talking with Baltazar Garzon in Tehran, and I have been unable to reach Abdul Muttmain for the past two hours. I fear the worst."

"What about Al Hazmi and Taha al-Alwani in Riyadh?" Atwa asked, struggling to keep the sound of fear and defeat out of his voice.

El Farrar shook his head. "They too have been unreachable." He slammed his hand down on his desk and glared across the room at his two confederates. "The good news is that from what Garzon said before he was cut off, the invading forces are but small contingents, and my sources in Kuwait tell me the larger reinforcement brigades are stuck in Kuwait City due to deteriorating weather in the region."

"What about our forces that were sent days ago?" Farid Zamet asked.

For the first time in hours, El Farrar gave a small smile. "They are even now landing at the ports of Dhahran in Saudi and Khorramshahr in Iran."

Atwa pursed his lips, visualizing the region in his mind. "Then our forces should be in Riyadh in three or four hours and in Tehran in ten or twelve," he said.

"Exactly," El Farrar exclaimed. "Long before the weather clears enough to permit Ben Raines to reinforce his troops in either area."

Zamet stroked his beard. "Perhaps our men would benefit from your leadership in the area," he said.

El Farrar nodded. "I believe you are correct, Farid."

He picked up the telephone on his desk and dialed a number. "Have my personal jet readied for takeoff," he said when it was answered. "We are flying to Dhahran as soon as you can get it ready."

Atwa tried to keep the fear out of his face when he asked, "We, Your Excellency?"

El Farrar's expression turned to stone. "Do you have any objections to going into a battle zone, Muhammad?" he asked, his voice as cold as his face.

"Uh, why, of course not, Abdullah," Atwa answered, though it was clear from the worried look on his face that he was in fact not at all happy about the turn of events.

"Good, because I will need the wise counsel of both you and Farid during the upcoming engagement."

"You have but to ask, my leader," Zamet said, his eyes alight with the fervor of a true fanatic.

Atwa, on the other hand, was fervently wishing he were back in his room with his fingers curled around a straight scotch whiskey.

Ben had his radioman contact Bartholomew Wiley-Smeyth in Riyadh.

"Hey, Bart, this is Ben."

"Hello, General," Bart said.

"I have some news, but none of it is good," Ben said, trying to keep the worry out of his voice.

"That seems to be the case lately, doesn't it, General?" Bart answered with a chuckle, betraying not the slightest amount of fear.

"Buddy managed to interrogate one of the officers he captured in Tehran. It seems the troop strength of the terrorist reinforcements numbers about ten thousand each in Saudi and Iran."

"A little over a hundred to one," Bart mused. "Not too bad odds at that."

"Bart," Ben said, "you cannot stand against ten thousand troops with eighty men. It'll be suicide."

"Not to worry, old chap," Bart replied, still sounding

as if in good humor. "The SAS are brave lads, but we're not stupid or suicidal," he added. "I don't intend to make a stand, as you call it."

"Oh?"

"No, sir. I'll divide my men up into groups of four or five each, and send them out into the desert between here and the port. The weather here is so bad that visibility is virtually nil, so the transport vehicles bringing the troops toward us will of necessity be moving very slow and will be confined to the major roads between here and the port."

Ben gave a low laugh. "Absolutely perfect for ambushes and hit-and-run tactics."

"My thoughts exactly," Bart replied. "We'll be like the mongoose going up against a king cobra. The cobra is much bigger and his poison is very deadly, but the mongoose is much quicker and never stays in one place long enough for the cobra to get at him."

"By the way, Bart," Ben said.

"Yes?"

"My people will be brought in by airdrop, so you don't need to spare the roads, if you get my meaning."

"Certainly," Bart replied. "We have plenty of high explosives left here by the recently departed terrorists, and if we get right on it, time to mine portions of the road to slow the convoy down quite a bit."

"Good hunting, Bart," Ben said seriously.

"Thank you, sir," Bart responded crisply, and broke the connection.

He turned from the radio and looked at Major Hugh Holmsby, who'd been listening. "You have your orders, Major," Bart said. "Let's get the men cracking. We only have a few hours to get set up."

"Yes, sir!" Holmsby said, snapping off a salute and stamping his heels on the floor as only British soldiers do.

* * *

At that very moment, Abdullah El Farrar's plane was landing at the airport next to the port city of Dhahran. His troops were lined up in a caravan almost four miles long and waiting for his arrival. Most of the men were being carried in two-and-a-half-ton trucks, called deuce-and-a-halfs by Americans. There were also numerous light tanks and armored personnel carriers, and other motorized assault vehicles of various names, depending on which country they'd been purchased from.

The leader of his Saudi contingent, Jamal Ahmed, stood at rigid attention as El Farrar and Farid Zamet and Muhammad Atwa deplaned.

"Excellency," Ahmed said, saluting, "it does us honor for you to be here to witness our great victory over the infidel dogs."

El Farrar nodded. "Thank you, Ahmed. I will set up headquarters here in Dhahran and monitor your progress as you take our oil fields back from the interlopers."

"I have already arranged quarters for you, Excellency. Radios have been set up on our frequency so you can stay in constant touch with the field commanders when we get to Riyadh and start the assault."

"Remember, Ahmed," El Farrar said, pointing his finger at his commander. "The city itself is a secondary target. Your primary mission is to gain control of the oil fields. Only after that has been accomplished are you to attack the city."

"Yes, sir. I understand," Ahmed said, bowing his head.

El Farrar covered his mouth as he yawned widely. "I haven't had any sleep for twenty-four hours, so I am going to go to bed. By the time I wake up, you should be in control of the oil fields . . . do you understand me, Ahmed?"

"Yes, sir."

"Good," El Farrar said harshly, "because your life and the life of your family in Afghanistan depends on your success today."

Ahmed swallowed and licked suddenly dry lips. "Of course, Excellency," he croaked.

He turned on his heel and waved his arm in a circle over his head, signaling the trucks to begin the four-or-five-hour journey to Riyadh.

TWENTY-SIX

The road from Dhahran to Riyadh was a little over 150 miles, and was a fairly good road as roads in Saudi Arabia go. Jamal Ahmed hoped to make the journey in three to four hours, but the weather was so bad, with visibility reduced to fifty meters or less, his trucks were only able to travel at twenty miles an hour or less.

He radioed El Farrar back at his headquarters building that due to the weather, his expected arrival in Riyadh would be sometime in the midafternoon.

El Farrar was furious, but even he couldn't change the weather. Muhammad Atwa reminded him that he shouldn't curse the weather, since it was the only thing keeping Ben Raines from sending reinforcements to his troops around Riyadh, which didn't help El Farrar's mood any at all.

Meanwhile, Bartholomew Wiley-Smeyth had divided his men up into fourteen groups of five men each, and stationed them at various points along the winding road from Dhahran to Riyadh. Though the terrain held few hills or mountains, unlike much of the Middle East, there were plenty of sand mounds and small hillocks to give his men cover, and the blowing sand and gravel kept visibility low enough that they could attack with little fear of being seen.

Major Hugh Holmsby, along with the ever-present Davidson brothers, took the point position, and was among the first to encounter the long convoy of troops and equipment headed by Ahmed.

Heading the column were a pair of ancient used Bradley Attack Vehicles. The Bradley, designed to haul small assault teams, carried five men: a crew of two to run the vehicle, and three men that could exit quickly and attack on foot. They were armed with a 120mm cannon and a .50-caliber machine gun, and were capable on good terrain of speeds in excess of fifty miles an hour.

Holmsby and his men were behind a small rise in the ground less than fifty yards from the road just around a bend. They'd armed themselves with two Stinger missiles and a CPAD Tech rocket grenade launcher with a case of twelve fragmentation grenades.

Holmsby held up his hand as the first Bradley came into view around the bend. "Hold off a minute and let him get a little ahead of us," Hugh ordered, peering at the road through sand-encrusted goggles. He and all of his men had wet bandannas over their noses and mouths, looking much like old-time stage robbers.

Following the two Bradleys was an old Russian tank, of uncertain parentage. It was well used, and had been scraped together out of so many old used parts, it was impossible to tell what model it was.

Hugh pointed at the tank. "Take out the tank first with the Stinger," he said. "That'll block the road right at the bend, and then we'll use the rocket grenades to destroy the Bradleys."

John Davidson, with the Stinger launcher on his shoulder, nodded once and squeezed the firing trigger. A loud *whoosh* sound was followed by a whistling wail as the Stinger missile shot toward the tank.

It hit just under and to the rear of the turret, exploding in a giant fireball as the ammunition in the tank, along with its fuel supply, exploded. The tank jumped fifteen feet in the air, and then came apart like a cheap suit in the rain, sending molten shrapnel in all directions.

The man driving the lead Bradley made the mistake of stopping his vehicle and opening the door to take a look behind him to see what had happened.

David Davidson, with a perfectly still target, fired off the CPAD and launched a fragmentation grenade directly at the lead Bradley.

It was a perfect shot. The grenade hit the front of the vehicle, bounced once, and then exploded with a loud bang. The hood of the Bradley was blown completely off, and the men inside were shredded into mincemeat as the shrapnel entered the open door and killed them all.

The driver of the second Bradley gunned his engine and tried to drive around the disabled lead vehicle, running off the road in the direction of Holmsby and his men.

All of the SAS troops opened fire with their Uzis, and David Davidson jammed another rocket grenade onto the CPAD and fired again.

This one wasn't as accurate, and it exploded harmlessly behind the Bradley as it raced across the gravel next to the road and then disappeared from sight.

A deuce-and-a-half, directly behind the tank that had exploded, tried the same maneuver, but its tires dug into the soft gravel and it got stuck as it tried to go around the tank.

Holmsby and his men raked the truck with machine-gun fire, emptying clip after clip into the canvas cover

over the back of the truck. Four terrorists managed to jump clear of the truck, but in the blowing sand they couldn't see where the attack was coming from, and ended up firing wildly in all directions. The wounded men in the back of the truck filled the air with their screams of pain and horror as Holmsby and his men continued their firing, until all of the men from the truck were dead or wounded.

No other vehicles appeared around the bend. Evidently, they were afraid to go any farther until they could see what was happening up ahead.

"Come on," Hugh shouted. "Time to get the hell out of here before that Bradley figures out where we are and comes back."

"I've still got another Stinger left," John Davidson protested.

"Save it," Hugh ordered. "We'll have plenty of chances to use it again."

They backed down off the small rise, jumped into one of the terrorists' jeeps they'd used to get there, and drove off into the desert away from the road as fast as they could considering the limited visibility in the storm.

As luck would have it, they almost sideswiped the Bradley, which was coming back toward them. Bob Foster, who was driving the jeep, jerked the wheel to the right so hard the jeep almost tipped over, and the Bradley zoomed by with inches to spare.

"Jesus, that was close!" Foster yelled as he floored the accelerator to escape.

Hugh, riding in the front passenger seat, leaned over and hollered in his ear, "We can't outrun a Bradley! Our only hope is to lose it in the storm."

David Davidson, who was looking back over his shoulder, yelled, "He's turning and coming after us!"

Hugh grabbed a handful of grenades from a box at his feet and said to Bob Foster, "We'll bail out over the next ridge and try to get him with these grenades."

As the jeep jumped over a small rise in the desert, Bob slowed enough for Hugh and the Davidsons to dive out of the jeep, leaving one man and Bob to remain with the jeep as it sped away.

Hugh and John and David spread out, each clutching a grenade in each hand, and hunkered down, trying to become invisible in the blowing sand.

The Bradley crested the hill and let go with its 120mm cannon at the jeep fifty yards ahead. The shells must have hit the gas tank, for the jeep exploded in a huge ball of fire just as Hugh and the Davidsons threw their grenades under the wheels of the Bradley.

One went off in front, two underneath, and the others to the side, flipping the Bradley over onto its side and throwing it twenty feet away.

Two men, their faces blackened by soot and smoke, stuck their heads out of the crumpled door, and were cut down by Hugh and his comrades.

Once they'd made sure all of the men in the Bradley were either dead or out of commission, the three men ran to where the jeep lay in a smoking, shattered ruin. The flames were so intense they couldn't get close enough to see the bodies of Foster or the other SAS man, but it was clear they couldn't have survived the explosion.

Hugh's body slumped and he shook his head. "Damn!" he muttered, his face turning red from the heat of the fire.

John Davidson put his hand on Hugh's shoulder. "At least it was quick, Hugh," he said, his eyes smarting from the smoke and heavy odor of gasoline and charred flesh.

Hugh got out his GPS instrument and clicked in their

position and the position of Riyadh. He looked up and pointed. "We go that way," he said, and began to walk toward the town over a hundred miles away.

After a few steps, David said, "You think we can make it that far on foot in this storm?"

Hugh gave a grim smile. "I don't intend to try. With any luck, the boys will slow the column down enough for us to find another way home."

"Yeah?" John asked.

Hugh looked at him. "You ever do any goose hunting, Johnny?"

"Uh, not to speak of. Why?"

"When you're hunting geese and they fly over in a line, you shoot the last one so as not to spook the others," Hugh said.

David laughed. "I see what you've got in mind. We'll catch up to the terrorists and take out the last vehicle in the column."

Hugh nodded. "Sounds better than walking a hundred miles or so, doesn't it?"

"Damn straight!" David said.

"What if we can't catch up to them?" Johnny asked, wiping sand out of his eyes with the back of his hand.

"Then you'd better hope these boots the quartermaster gave us have thick soles," Hugh replied.

"Oh, my feet will hold out," Johnny observed. "It's my lungs filling up with sand I'm worried about."

"That's easy to fix," David said, punching his brother in the shoulder. "Just don't breathe so often."

Hugh laughed. "Reminds me of a saying I read about the Mississippi River in school. They used to say it was so muddy, it was too thick to drink and too thin to plow, kinda like this air. Too thick to breathe and too thin to walk on."

TWENTY-SEVEN

Jamal Ahmed instructed the driver of his large armored personnel carrier to move around the stalled convoy and go to the head of the line.

Ahmed, never one to take a personal risk needlessly, had been riding in the middle of the line of trucks and tanks and other equipment. He'd realized early in his career that taking point was the job for someone far less valuable than he.

As Ahmed's vehicle pulled up to the crushed and ruined Bradley Attack Vehicle and the scorched and still-smoking Russian tank, he slammed his hand down on the dashboard of his car. He looked out through the windshield to make sure all of the hostile forces had gone, and then he exited the vehicle and strutted up next to the wrecks.

"What in Allah's name happened here?" he demanded of a junior officer who was in the process of questioning those who'd been nearest to the action.

Sohail Shaeen responded with a quick salute and a deferential tone of voice. "It is still unclear, Commander," he said, glancing over his shoulder at the troops he'd been interrogating. "The men here were around the bend in the road when the incident occurred. They heard a series of loud explosions and when they came around the turn, they saw what you see here."

Ahmed slapped his thigh impatiently with his open palm. "What of the troops in the two vehicles? What do they have to say for themselves for allowing such an ambush to take place?" he asked.

Shaeen shook his head and shrugged. "All of the men in the lead vehicles are dead, sir." Shaeen hesitated, dreading giving this next piece of bad news to his leader. "And there is another vehicle missing and unaccounted for."

Ahmed's eyes turned dangerously dark. "Oh?" he asked in a low voice that made Shaeen cringe at the thought that he might be forced to take the blame for this too.

"Yes, sir. Another Bradley vehicle like that one"—Shaeen paused and pointed—"is missing. It took off the road after the hostiles and hasn't returned. The crew does not answer our calls to them on the radio."

"Why have you not sent another vehicle to go and see what has happened?" Ahmed asked, his voice growing harsher.

Shaeen spread his hands. "I was waiting for your orders, Commander. I did not want to risk another vehicle or any more men unless you ordered it."

Ahmed took Shaeen by the arm and pulled him off to the side where no one could hear their conversation. "And just what do you recommend we do?"

Shaeen's face paled. "I think we should continue on, sir. The infidels have obviously set a trap for the other vehicle and it has most probably been destroyed. I see no need to send another to the same fate, and I understand we have a deadline to meet in getting to Riyadh."

"You are correct, soldier," Ahmed said. "We gain nothing by risking another vehicle. Now, get this mess off the road and get that truck unstuck so we can be on our way."

"Yes, sir," Shaeen said, giving another salute.

Ahmed ignored the salute and returned to his personnel carrier, which was filled with his personal guards. "Take me back along the convoy," he said to his driver. "I want to review the troops."

"Yes, sir," the driver said, knowing full well that Ahmed wanted to get out of the line of fire as quickly as possible. He'd driven for the man for several years now, and knew Ahmed took few risks with his own neck, though he thought nothing of sending his troops and other officers into dangerous situations. This was just as well with the driver, who also valued his own neck above that of others.

Bartholomew Wiley-Smeyth, like Hugh Holmsby, was not one to send his men to places he was unwilling to go. Therefore, it was he and a group led by Staff Sergeant Alphonse Green who were the next in line to greet the terrorist convoy.

Alphonse Green, called Al by everyone who didn't desire their nose broken, was a thirty-year veteran of the SAS. He'd refused retirement the year before on the grounds that a man with his training and experience wouldn't be able to retire and grow roses. If the service forced him out, he told them, he'd probably just get into trouble. His commanding officers, relieved that he'd be staying, had granted his wish and waived the mandatory retirement rules to allow him to continue his career.

Bart had chosen as his engagement point an area of the road that had a small bridge over a washed-out gully that was five or six feet deep. He'd had Green and his men wire the bridge with some of the C-4 plastique explosives left behind by the terrorists.

Once the bridge was mined, Bart instructed Green to blow it when the first vehicle was on top of the bridge. He then split his group up into two portions, with three men on one side of the road and Green and Wiley-Smeyth on the other.

Bart told the men to spread out and pour as much firepower into the stalled convoy as they could for exactly five minutes, and then they were ordered to retreat back out into the desert out of sight. The men were given GPS coordinates where they would rendezvous after the convoy had gotten on its way again.

One of his men asked, "Sir, do you mind if I ask why we are to fire for only five minutes?"

"Because," Bart answered, "we're here to delay the convoy as much as possible with as little loss of life as possible. I figure we'll have about five minutes of total confusion when we attack, and after that, they'll begin to get their shit together and come after us." He paused. "Do you really want to face ten thousand men with only five of us?"

The soldier grinned and shook his head. "No, sir. I understand now."

"All right then," Bart said. "To your places and hunker down until the convoy arrives."

"Yes, sir," the men said, and disappeared across the road into the blowing sand.

Sohail Shaeen rode in a HumVee at the front of the line of trucks. He had a fifty-caliber machine gun mounted on a post just behind the front seat, and he was determined not to let the convoy be ambushed again. He rode in the passenger seat, and had two men in the backseat, and they were all using binoculars to scan the road ahead and the desert hills off to the sides of the road. The soldier manning the machine gun continually swiveled the barrel back and forth, his finger caressing the trigger while he hoped for an excuse to use the big gun.

As the HumVee began to cross the twenty-foot-long bridge over the gully, Shaeen glanced at the drop below and thought, *This would be an excellent place for an ambush.*

Just as he turned his head to tell the men in the back to be especially careful and observant, the bridge erupted in a giant explosion, blowing man-sized chunks of concrete and steel in all directions.

The front of Shaeen's HumVee was lifted off the ground and slammed back down so hard, all of the specially made tires burst and flattened. The soldier on the machine gun was thrown head over heels to land flat on his face in the gully below. He rolled over, groaning, just in time to see a ton and a half of cement smash him into hamburger.

The second explosion picked the HumVee up and tossed it like a toy into the gully, where it landed upside down. Only luck kept Shaeen in the seat and saved his life as the big car crashed over him. Shaeen awoke some five minutes later to the sound of machine-gun fire and exploding grenades all around him.

At first, he couldn't figure out where he was. Feeling with his hands, he soon discovered he was in the wheel well of the HumVee, stuck up against the floorboards that had saved him from being crushed to death.

Unable to open the crumpled door, he finally managed to dig down into the gravel and dirt enough to squeeze out from under the HumVee. When he stood up, unable to see more than a few yards in the whirling sand and dirt of the storm, he heard the gunfire suddenly cease.

Pulling out his side arm, an old Reuger Arms .38-caliber revolver, Shaeen scrambled up the sides of the gully and stood there, his mouth open, unable to believe his eyes.

Two of the deuce-and-a-halfs that were following his lead vehicle were tipped on their sides with their metal sides twisted and scorched. Bodies of his fellow soldiers lay sprawled all along the road, bloody bullet holes in their uniforms. More than a few were missing arms and legs. It was a scene he thought he'd never be able to forget.

He whirled and pointed his pistol as a car screeched to a stop behind him. He lowered it when he saw it was the personnel carrier used by Commander Ahmed.

Ahmed jumped out of the vehicle and walked rapidly toward Shaeen, his eyes angry and looking for someone to blame.

"Lieutenant Shaeen," Ahmed shouted before he got within twenty feet of Shaeen. "What is the meaning of this?"

Shaeen took a deep breath. It was all he could do not to shoot the arrogant bastard where he stood.

"The bridge was mined, Commander," he said, struggling not to add, "as any fool could see who would open his eyes."

Ahmed spun around, waving at the dead bodies and the two ruined trucks nearby. "And this?" he shouted, his eyes wild with anger and fright.

"Evidently, sir, the hostiles waited in ambush just over that rise over there. When my vehicle got onto the bridge, they exploded it. The trucks stopped to avoid falling in the gully, and the infidels must have opened fire on them with automatic weapons and hand grenades or rockets."

"Allah give me strength," Ahmed growled as he looked at the ruined bridge and trucks. "It will take us hours to clear the way and construct a new bridge," he almost wailed.

Shaeen took another deep breath. The man's arrogance was exceeded only by his stupidity, he thought. "Not really, sir. We have several repair trucks in the convoy. They will be able to construct metal rails to allow the trucks and other heavy equipment to pass within an hour."

Ahmed seemed to calm down at the news. Shaeen took the opportunity to step up close and speak in a low voice. "Sir, in the future, it might be best if we sent a couple of scout vehicles ahead. That way, if the convoy is hit again, we should have some warning of it in time to counterattack."

Ahmed pursed his lips, nodding slowly. "That is just what I was about to suggest, Lieutenant Shaeen. Good thinking."

While the convoy was halted, making the necessary repairs to the road to continue along the way, Hugh Holmsby and the Davidson brothers were crawling on their bellies alongside the road, inching their way closer to a jeep parked next to a deuce-and-a-half full of soldiers.

They'd been watching when the two men in the jeep parked it and got out to chat and smoke with the men in the truck. The sound of the storm and the talking and laughing of the men were enough to cover the sound of Hugh and the Davidsons moving up behind the jeep.

John slipped behind the wheel, checked to make sure the keys were still in the ignition, and then nodded at Hugh and David to climb aboard.

Hugh and David readied their Uzis, and when John

started the engine, they began to rake the deuce-and-a-half with fire, killing the two men from the jeep instantly and causing the men in the truck to dive for the floor.

By the time the soldiers had recovered from their surprise enough to begin to return fire, the jeep was disappearing in the swirling clouds of sand like a ghost.

TWENTY-EIGHT

After Jamal Ahmed began to send his point guards out ahead of the convoy, it was much harder for Bartholomew Wiley-Smeyth's troops to completely disrupt the movement of the long line of vehicles and equipment.

The small groups of men continued to hit the terrorists every few hundred yards, and while they didn't do quite as much major damage to the vehicles, they did manage to cause a significant drop in the terrorist troops' morale. Instead of a nice, quiet ride to inundate a vastly inferior enemy, the troops found themselves in a constant series of battles and confrontations with an enemy who wouldn't stand still and fight.

It became like the plight of the bull moose in the north woods, pursued and attacked by swarms of small black flies until it runs out of the woods to escape the constant irritation. So it was with the terrorist soldiers, who became quite paranoid, and jumped and even fired weapons at every noise or change in the wind. Soon, they were fighting among themselves over cigarettes, bits of food or drink, or where they would sit in the trucks that were hauling them; no one wanted to be by the back of the truck, since many men sitting by the open rear of the trucks had already been picked off by SAS snipers alongside the road.

Jamal Ahmed began to doubt El Farrar's claim that they would be facing only a handful of SAS troops. He didn't realize that as soon as one small group broke off from an attack, it would leapfrog ahead, traveling parallel to the road, and then would attack again. Ahmed began to feel that they were going to face thousands of hardened troops, and he wondered how his inexperienced troops would stand up against them.

Prior to taking his nap after arriving in Dhahran, Abdullah El Farrar instructed his pilot to take his second-in-command, Farid Zamet, on to Khorramshahr, where he could oversee the troops there.

Zamet frowned. "Do you think it wise, my leader, for me to try and fly in this weather?"

El Farrar glanced at his pilot, who'd broken into a sweat while trying to land in the high winds and reduced visibility at Dhahran. "What do you think, Muhamar?" he asked.

The pilot shrugged, though his face did pale a bit at the thought of flying again in such inclement weather. "It should be no problem, Excellency. I will curve out over the Persian Gulf, where the sand will not be so strong."

"There, you see, Farid?" El Farrar said. "The pilot says there is little risk."

Zamet nodded, but it was clear he would much rather stay on the ground.

The pilot was correct. The flight was fairly uneventful since the weather out over the Gulf was much less turbulent than that over land. In less than an hour and a half, Zamet was at the port city of Khorramshahr, where the leader of the troops there, Haji Kuchkool, had his men ready for the journey to Tehran.

"Will you be traveling with us, or do you wish to remain in Khorramshahr?" Kuchkool asked Zamet.

Figuring he was much safer with the troops in the event the weather cleared and Ben Raines's reinforcements arrived, Zamet said he would travel with the troops. "However, you will remain in command, Haji," he added. "I have no desire to usurp your leadership authority."

Kuchkool nodded, thinking how rare it was to find an administrative leader who knew his place.

"The journey should take us until late afternoon, providing we meet no resistance along the way to slow us down," Kuchkool told Zamet.

"Resistance?" Zamet asked. "How could we face resistance? We've been told the forces against us here number in the hundreds, not thousands."

Kuchkool laughed. "Mr. Zamet, you will soon learn not to believe everything you are told. Remember, these forces managed to defeat our troops after they were dug in and heavily prepared, so they cannot be too inferior."

Zamet grinned weakly. He hadn't considered that.

Zamet and Kuchkool became increasingly confident as their journey progressed without any signs of significant opposition forces. By late in the afternoon, they were almost at the city of Tehran, and the thousands of oil derricks could be seen off to the left, standing like skeletonized trees in the dead of winter.

"Perhaps, for once, our intel was correct," Kuchkool said, glancing at Zamet, riding behind him in the large HumVee that served as Kuchkool's command vehicle.

ENEMY IN THE ASHES

"Perhaps the foreign forces have retreated in the face of our superior numbers," Zamet suggested.

Kuchkool shrugged as he looked at the oil fields through his field binoculars. "Perhaps, but I seriously doubt it. I have heard about this Ben Raines, and nothing I have heard indicates his troops are overly concerned about the numbers of troops arrayed against them. From what I hear, Raines's men would fight the very devil himself if Raines told them to."

"Well, for whatever reason," Zamet said, "I am sure Abdullah El Farrar will be happy that we've seen no sign of the foreign devils."

Before Kuchkool could reply, a truck carrying twenty-five of his soldiers that was ahead of them in the convoy suddenly exploded, bouncing twenty feet in the air before turning into a raging fireball after being hit by a rocket grenade.

Kuchkool's driver immediately veered sharply to the right and ran off the road into the desert for a short distance.

Kuchkool grinned over the seat at a terrified Farid Zamet. "See, what did I tell you? Never count your blessings too soon. It angers Allah, and he will smite you for it."

Kuchkool turned back around, grabbed a radio microphone off the dashboard, and began speaking rapidly into it to his unit commanders.

"We've been attacked by hostile forces! Pull your vehicles off the road and unload the men! We must stage a counterattack immediately!"

Suddenly, from out of the swirling sand and dirt, a pair of old U.S. Army jeeps careened alongside the road. Each had a man standing in the rear of the jeep behind a post on which sat what looked to Kuchkool like an M60 machine gun.

As the jeeps roared past, the machine guns began to chatter, sending thousands of rounds of molten death into the trucks and other vehicles carrying troops.

Men began screaming in pain and fear as they poured out of their vehicles and ran as fast as they could away from the jeeps and their death and destruction.

"Bastards!" Kuchkool screamed between gritted teeth at the sight of his men running away in terror. He grabbed the microphone and shouted into it, "Commanders, kill any of your men who try to run away! Shoot them down like the dogs they are!"

The jeeps continued down the line of the convoy and out of Kuchkool's sight. Over 150 of his men were killed or wounded before a HumVee in the middle of the convoy that was fitted with its own fifty-caliber machine gun returned fire.

The lead jeep was hit, and veered off in a sudden circle and overturned when the fifty-caliber bullets penetrated its gas tank and it exploded in a huge ball of fire, incinerating the two men inside.

The second jeep, seeing it'd lost the element of surprise, turned away from the road, and disappeared in a swirl of sand and dust seconds later.

The sounds of the wounded screaming for help continued until unit commanders went up to them and told them to shut up or they would slit their throats. Soon, the sound of the wind covered the moaning and crying and praying of the wounded men lying alongside overturned trucks and vehicles riddled with bullet holes.

Kuchkool put out a call on his radio for his unit commanders to come to his HumVee for a strategy meeting as soon as possible.

* * *

In the middle of the oil fields, Buddy Raines keyed the mike on his SOHFRAD and spoke to all of his squad leaders. "The terrorists have arrived. Time to show 'em what we're made of. It looks like they're going to try and clear the oil fields before hitting the city, Major Bean, so you've got a while yet to continue to prepare."

"Roger that, Eagle One," Bean said. "Good luck, Buddy."

"Thanks, Jackson, same to you and your men."

Buddy handed the microphone back to Corrie, who switched off the set and packed it into its pack so she could carry it on her back. Wherever Buddy Raines went, she would follow with the SOHFRAD so he could keep in touch with the troops, and with Ben back in Kuwait City.

Buddy stepped outside the tent. Harley Reno was on one side and Hammer Hammerick was on the other side of the doorway, standing guard. The rest of Buddy's team was scattered out in a rough circle around the tent, making sure no one got within range while he was on the radio.

"Time to boogie, guys," Buddy said, taking the H&K MP-10 Harley handed him. As they moved off away from the tent, Harley bent and pulled tight a string that was hanging four inches off the sand and ran in a circle around the tent. Anyone who approached the tent from now on would get a nasty surprise. The string was attached to the pins in a fragmentation grenade that was duct-taped to four other grenades.

"Harley, take the point," Buddy said. He swiveled his head. "Coop, you take our six."

"Aye, Buddy," Coop said, trying to hide his disappointment at being told to bring up the rear. After all, he thought, his marksmanship wasn't all that bad, especially after he'd gotten used to the new weapons Harley had provided them with.

"Don't look so down-in-the-mouth, Coop," Jersey said, walking beside him as he moved toward the rear of the team. "He probably put you at the rear so it wouldn't put so much strain on your ankle trying to lead the group."

The field medic had injected Coop's ankle with a local anesthetic and steroids to reduce pain and swelling, and then he'd taped it tight to give it support so Coop would be able to walk on it. Coop, whose dislike of needles was well known, had gritted his teeth and closed his eyes during the injection. Now he could walk, although still with a pronounced limp and a moderate amount of pain.

Coop gave a half grin, doubting what she had said was the reason. "Bullshit, Jersey," he responded. "It's just because he thinks Harley and Hammer are the lead dogs around here."

Jersey smiled, knowing there was some truth in what Coop said. Harley and Hammer had shown everyone they were excellent guerrilla fighters many times over, and were in fact just about the toughest men she'd ever met.

"Bringing up the rear is a job for a doofus," Coop groused as he limped toward the rear of the group.

Jersey laughed, trying to gibe Coop out of his bad mood. "Just remember, Coop, unless you're the lead dog, the view never changes," she said.

Unable to resist her levity and stay solemn, Coop leaned his head to the side and craned his neck until he was staring at her buttocks, moving sensually under her BDUs. "Yeah, but the rear dog gets a view the lead dog can only dream about," he said with a leer.

Jersey laughed again, relieved to see Coop snapping

out of it. She really enjoyed her repartee with Coop. "Well, looks are free, rear dog, but a touch will cost you a couple of fingers."

"Who said I was going to use my hands?" Coop asked, sticking out his tongue and wiggling it obscenely.

Jersey made a face. "Oh, Coop! You really are disgusting," she groaned.

He made a smooching sound with his lips. "Don't knock it if you ain't tried it, little girl."

"That'll be the day!" Jersey said, and moved off to take her place in the line of troops led by Harley Reno.

Coop laughed to himself. "Coop, old son," he mumbled, "perhaps you were a bit too gross for Ms. Jersey."

After a moment of quiet reflection, he laughed again. "No, on second thought, you weren't at all, old chap," he told himself.

When the last of the team had passed, Coop checked the rear perimeter through his night glasses. Seeing no one in the near vicinity, he took his place in line and followed the team out into the oil fields among the hundreds of oil derricks that were outlined against the darkening sky.

TWENTY-NINE

Buddy led his team out into the oil derricks away from the booby-trapped tent toward the periphery of the oil fields. He'd instructed the other squad leaders to do the same with their men, spreading his forces out so there would be no concentration of troops for the enemy to attack.

As the skies darkened, dusk falling rapidly in the cold clear air of the desert, the temperature fell to just above freezing.

Limping along at the rear of the team, Coop pulled his field jacket tight and shivered. "Who'd think the desert got so cold at night?" he said to Jersey, who was walking just ahead of him. She'd elected to stay near her friend in case his ankle got to bothering him. She wanted to make sure he was able to keep up with the group. Of course, she'd never in a hundred years admit this to Coop, who would've been insulted at the thought he might need help.

Jersey glanced up at the swirling sand that was still in the air. "Just be glad we've got this storm still hanging around," she said over her shoulder. "Otherwise, the temperatures would be even lower."

"Yeah, it's a great choice," Coop replied. "Choke on sand or freeze your balls off."

Jersey chuckled. "Well, at least I don't have to worry about that."

Coop started to reply that she had bigger balls than most of the men he knew, but decided against it. He didn't want to piss her off. He enjoyed having her hang back and keep him company. Not that he'd ever let on to her he enjoyed it.

When they got to the edge of the oil fields and the derricks began to be spread farther apart, Buddy called a halt to the march.

"Let's hunker down here, guys," he said, looking around at a cluster of small storage sheds and outbuildings that housed extra pumps and other oil-field equipment. "These buildings will give us some cover when the terrorists arrive."

Harley set the huge M-60 machine gun he was carrying down on the sand and pointed off in the distance. "Looks like we won't have long to wait, Buddy," he said.

A string of lights could barely be seen through the swirling sand, snaking across the desert like a giant luminescent caterpillar as the terrorist convoy made its way along the road toward the oil fields.

"Jesus," Hammer, who was standing next to Harley, muttered. "There must be thousands of them."

"About ten thousand, if Intel is correct," Buddy said, shaking his head. *This is going to be one mother of a fight,* he thought.

He glanced at Corrie. "Better radio the other squad leaders and tell 'em to get ready. The dance is about to begin."

Anna, who'd fallen in love with Harley, moved to stand by his side. She preferred to be near him whenever there was action. Hammer moved over to take up a station near the corner of one of the buildings, next to where Beth was standing. Coop and Jersey walked off to another nearby building and got ready for the upcoming firefight by laying out extra magazines for their H&K MP-10 machine guns. The Franchi FAS shotguns were leaned against the building out of the way, to be used only if the fighting became close-range.

Buddy moved Corrie back to the rear of one of the structures, with orders to protect the SOHFRAD at all costs since it was their only contact with the rest of the squads.

Harley and Anna moved to the front of the group, and lay down behind an oil-well pump, where Harley could position his M-60 on a tripod. Its range was longer than the assault rifles the rest of the group was using, and he would be the first to open fire when the terrorists got close enough.

Buddy climbed up on top of one of the smaller buildings with the ECAI, the European Combined Arms Initiative experimental assault rifle. This was the first time the SUSA would use the gun in actual combat. He was counting on the integral grenade launcher that was able to control the grenade trajectory to give him enough extra range to be able to target the terrorists before they got within rifle range. The integral holographic aim-point sight with its infrared vision would allow him to sight in on and target the terrorists through the sandstorm long before they could see him . . . he hoped.

Once he was up on top of the building, Hammer handed him a large crate of fragmentation grenades and HE (high-explosive) grenades. The frags he'd use against troops, while he'd save the HE ones for heavy equipment and vehicles.

As he lay there on the roof, Buddy went back over in his mind the instructions he'd given to all of the squads.

Their defense of the oil fields was contingent upon them being able to halt the advance of the terrorist troops. If the troops were unable to be stopped due to superior numbers, the squads were all instructed to break off the engagement and scatter out into the desert. They would then rendezvous at a prearranged site at dawn, and then proceed into the city to help with the defenses there.

Buddy had no illusions that his meager force of less than two hundred men and women could defeat ten thousand enemy troops, no matter how inexperienced the terrorists were. His only hope was they could delay their advance long enough for the storm to dissipate and for reinforcements from Ben to arrive.

As the lights from the enemy convoy grew closer, Buddy peered through his holographic infrared sight. The sighting mechanism had small markings on it that indicated when the targets were in range. As soon as the dim outlines of the trucks and other enemy vehicles centered on the marks, Buddy began firing.

Haji Kuchkool, riding in his HumVee near the head of his convoy with Farid Zamet, was encouraged by the lack of resistance they'd met on their way from the port to Riyadh.

As they moved along the road toward the darkened oil fields, he turned to Zamet, sitting in the rear seat. "It shouldn't take us long to secure the oil fields, Farid," he said. "I see no lights of an enemy encampment, so we are evidently facing a much smaller force than El Farrar had feared."

Zamet nodded. "Perhaps the enemy forces have all retreated to the city of Tehran," he suggested. "Maybe they hope to be able to hold the city against us by concentrating their forces there."

"Perhaps," Kuchkool agreed. "But I fear they have miscalculated. With the number of troops and equipment at my disposal, we shall easily be able to surround the city and pound it into rubble with our mortars and heavy guns."

He gave a short laugh. "By Allah, we won't even have to invade the city to destroy the infidel dogs."

Just as he finished speaking, he heard a shrill whistling over the low groan of the wind.

"What the . . . ?" he began, just as one of the large trucks ahead of his HumVee exploded in a brilliant flash of light and sound.

Kuchkool's driver jerked the wheel, and managed to pull the HumVee off the road before it was engulfed in the raging fire from the destroyed truck.

The sounds of his troops screaming in pain as they were incinerated echoed in Kuchkool's ears as the HumVee jerked to a halt.

More explosions began to come as the fragmentation and high-explosive grenades rained down on his convoy. A Bradley Assault Vehicle two cars ahead of the burning truck was blown on its side as a grenade went off under its right front wheel, while seconds later, the HumVee was peppered by hundreds of tiny shards of shrapnel from a fragmentation grenade that just missed its target.

The troops, seeing the trucks being targeted, scrambled to exit their vehicles as fast as they could, running in all directions to escape the holocaust.

Kuchkool jumped out of the HumVee and began shouting orders to his field commanders. "Tell the men to return fire!" he hollered.

One of the commanders, who was crouching nearby,

shouted back. "At what, sir? We can't see where the rockets are coming from!"

"Then get the men out and have them attack on foot until they *can* see the targets!" Kuchkool ordered. "Tell them to advance toward the oil derricks. That must be where the enemy is."

"Yes, sir," the man said, and began to round up the scurrying troops and order them to attack.

A light tank moved off the road and moved toward the oil derricks in the distance, with a line of soldiers walking behind and beside it.

After the tank had traveled less than fifty yards, a fragmentation grenade hit the front of the tank and exploded. Though the grenade wasn't powerful enough to destroy the tank, it tore the man riding in the turret in half and killed several of the nearby troops.

"Haji," Zamet said as he stood next to the HumVee. "They're targeting our vehicles."

Kuchkool nodded, his teeth gritted in anger. "You're right, Farid." Kuchkool got on the radio and ordered the drivers of the vehicles to pull them back out of range. "We'll let the troops attack on foot, and save our equipment until the enemy mortar has been destroyed. That will give them fewer targets for their bombs," Kuchkool said, mistaking the grenades for some sort of mortar attack.

After two more trucks and another Bradley were destroyed, the terrorist convoy finally managed to pull back out of the range of Buddy's grenade launcher.

Buddy saw the enemy's strategy, and pushed the HE grenades to the side and concentrated on firing only fragmentation grenades, spreading them out among the advancing troops to do maximal damage.

Harley watched the soldiers through his night-vision goggles until he saw they were within range of his M-60. He elevated the barrel to forty-five degrees for maximum range, jerked the loading lever back to insert a shell into the chamber, and gently squeezed the trigger. The troops were too far away for him to concern himself with individual targets, so he merely swung the barrel back and forth, sending a devastating stream of bullets into the mass of soldiers walking toward them.

The troops, though inexperienced in combat of this magnitude, had been thoroughly indoctrinated that if they were killed in battle, Allah would welcome them into heaven and each would have seventy virgins for all eternity. No one bothered to explain where Allah would find so many virgins, but then the men so indoctrinated were not the brightest to begin with.

As the number of soldiers killed and wounded mounted, the terrorist troops finally realized they should spread out and not make such easy targets of themselves. The screaming and crying of the wounded and dying became loud enough to be heard even over the howling of the wind and the booming of the guns arrayed against them.

Soon, the troops were in range of the assault rifles of the Scouts defending the oil fields, and the hoarse chatter of the M-60 was replaced by the higher-pitched rattle of the H&K MP-10's and the Uzis of the rest of the Scouts. The silencers had been removed from Buddy's troops' weapons, and the din of the firing on all sides was deafening.

The terrorist troops, their numbers depleted by ten percent, finally got within range of their Kalashnikovs and

Army-surplus M-16's and M-14's. They began to return fire. Since they couldn't see in the dark and the sandstorm, they just aimed ahead of them and fired until their magazines were empty, and then they reloaded to fire again and again.

When Harley's M-60 finally jammed, its barrel glowing a dull red it was so hot, he put it down and picked up an Mp-10 and began firing it as fast as he could.

Soon, the enemy troops were too close for Buddy to use his grenade launcher, and he jumped down off the roof to join his comrades behind the buildings, firing his MP-10 with the rest of them.

Soon it became evident the terrorist troops could not be stopped. For every one they shot down, two more seemed to take their place.

Buddy emptied his magazine, and then squatted down next to Corrie. He put his lips close to her ear so he could be heard over the noise of the firefight. "Radio squad leaders and tell them it's time to retreat!" he said.

Corrie put her rifle down and began to speak into her microphone.

Buddy ran from one to the other of his team, and told them it was time to get the hell out of Dodge.

Buddy took what was left of his crate of grenades and placed a brick of C-4 plastique in it. He turned the dial on a timer to ten minutes, and then signaled the team to follow him.

The team began to trot backward, firing behind them until they had the buildings between them and the enemy troops, and then they sprinted into the desert as fast as they could.

Coop, bringing up the rear, slipped and fell when his foot snagged on an electrical line lying on the ground.

He dropped his rifle and sprawled facedown on the

gravel and sand. Jersey, running a few feet ahead of him, heard his grunt as he hit the ground.

She whirled around, and saw him struggling to get to his feet just as three enemy soldiers ran around the side of the building behind him.

"Coop, down!" she screamed as she leveled her MP-10 and fired from the hip.

Coop didn't hesitate when he heard Jersey's command. He hit the deck and covered his head with his arms.

He could hear the 9mm slugs whining inches from his head as they plowed into the enemy soldiers mere feet behind him.

Jersey was back next to Coop and grabbing him by the arm before the men she'd shot were dead. Once he was on his feet, she took Coop's right arm and draped it over her shoulders, leaving her right arm free to handle her rifle.

As they hobbled along, Coop bouncing on his good foot and trying to keep up, they began to fall further behind the team.

Coop jerked his arm off Jersey and pushed her ahead. "Go on, Jerse," he shouted.

"I'm not leaving you," she shouted back.

He shook his head. "Go! No need of both of us buyin' it!"

Suddenly, Harley Reno materialized out of the blowing sand. Without a word, he handed his MP-10 to Jersey and bent, grabbed Coop by the thighs, and lifted him over his shoulder in a fireman's carry.

"Cover me!" he shouted to Jersey, and began to trot off into the night after the team.

Jersey held the two MP-10's at waist level, one in each hand, and began firing into the enemy troops as she backed quickly after Harley and Coop.

A slug tore into her left shoulder, burning a crease in the muscle as it ripped through her field jacket and making her drop one of the machine guns.

The next thing she knew, Anna and Buddy were beside her, firing their weapons into the group of enemy soldiers that kept coming.

As the last of the soldiers went down under their fire, Buddy grunted loudly and doubled over. When Anna grabbed his arm, he straightened up and yelled, "Let's go. I'm all right!"

Thirty minutes later, the team was assembled a couple of miles out in the desert behind a small rising in the desert floor.

"Is everyone here?" Buddy asked, his voice harsh as he flopped down on the sand.

Harley nodded. "Yeah, Boss. We all made it out."

"Good," Buddy said, his head nodding and his eyes half-shut. "Harley, take over for me, will ya?"

Harley squatted next to where Buddy was half-lying. He noticed a bright red splotch of blood on Buddy's stomach.

"Beth," Harley said urgently. "Bring me your field pack! Buddy's been hit."

Beth, who acted as the team's medic when in the field, rushed over and jerked Buddy's shirt and jacket open.

A small, neat hole was slowly oozing blood from his left abdomen. She rolled him to the side, and saw a much larger hole in the rear flank.

Jerking her pack open, she pulled a pair of field-dressings from it. "He took a through-and-through hit," she explained as she slapped the two dressings on the wound and began to circle his body with tape.

"Pop one of those morphine ampoules open, would you, Anna?" she asked.

Minutes later, with Buddy's wound dressed and the morphine dulling his pain, Harley asked if he was going to be okay.

Beth shrugged. "If the slug missed his colon and his kidney, he should do all right. If he makes it through the next hour, it'll mean he's probably safe."

"Okay," Harley said. He reached down, took the GPS receiver from Buddy's jacket pocket, and took a reading on the location of the scheduled rendezvous with the other Scouts. He then addressed the rest of the team. "We've got a couple of hours to make the rendezvous point. Let's see if we can fashion a stretcher out of a couple of rifles and a field jacket. We'll take turns carrying Buddy."

THIRTY

While most of Bartholomew Wiley-Smeyth's troops were busy attacking the convoy from Dhahran to Riyadh to slow them down, a handful of men with explosives training were left behind to arrange a suitable surprise for the terrorists when they finally made it to the oil fields.

These SAS troops took all of the C-4 plastique and Semtex plastique they'd captured when they took the oil fields from the terrorists, and began to fashion makeshift mines from the small bricks of explosives. The same radio-control switches the terrorists had used to make the plutonium bombs were used in the mines.

The only problem with this arrangement was that the controls were all on the same frequency, so the mines wouldn't be able to be detonated individually, but would have to be set off all at the same time.

George Rearden, the sergeant in charge of the mining, decided to arrange the mines in a huge semicircle in front of the oil fields. Once the terrorists entered the circle, mines would surround them and the effects of the shrapnel would be devastating. The plastique bricks were buried a couple of feet deep in the sand and gravel of the desert and covered with nuts, bolts, screws, and nails his men had found in the supply sheds of the oil field.

Small flags were set in the ground at each end of the semicircle so the men responsible for detonating the mines would know when the terrorists were fully in the trap.

Private Bill Blakely met with Sergeant Rearden after the last mine was buried. "Sarge, I think we're about ready for the buggers now," Blakely said, dusting sand off his SAS fatigues.

Rearden took two of the controls, one to be used as a backup in case the first one didn't work, and placed them on a wooden table in one of the supply sheds, next to the SOHFRAD radio receiver they were using for communications with Wiley-Smeyth.

"Excellent, Bill," Rearden said. "Now, your job, your *only* job, is to guard this remote control with your very life."

"Sir!" Blakely said, snapping off a salute.

Rearden smiled at the very young man, who was still full of piss and vinegar. "No need to be so formal, soldier," he said. "There aren't any officers present."

Blakely blushed. "Yes, sir."

"And don't call me sir," Rearden said with mock anger in his voice. "I'm not an officer . . . I work for a living!"

Even Blakely laughed at this old enlisted man's joke. "All right, Sergeant," he said.

Rearden glanced at the radioman standing nearby next to the SOHFRAD. "Stephen, would you ring up Commander Wiley-Smeyth on that contraption and tell him we're ready for him to return?"

Stephen Bales nodded and began to twist dials, and after a moment gave the message to Bart.

Rearden could hear the sounds of gunfire and explosions in the background as Bart said, "Thanks, son. I'm a mite busy here at the moment, so would you mind calling the other squad leaders and telling them to call off the attack and return to base?"

"Certainly, sir," Bales said, and he began to call the other frequencies of the various squad leaders to tell them what Bart had said.

Rearden picked up his assault rifle and walked to the door of the shed. Before exiting, he looked back over his shoulder. "I'll be outside getting the men to their stations," he said. "Give me a shout if there's any news I need to hear."

"Certainly, Sarge," Bales said.

"And remember, Private," Rearden added, "we're counting on you to keep that remote safe until it's needed."

"Right-o, Sarge," Blakely answered, and barely stopped himself from saluting again.

Bart tapped his driver, Alphonse Green, on the shoulder and jerked his head to the side after he put the microphone down. "They're ready back at base," he shouted to be heard over the roar of automatic weapons from the two men in the rear of the jeep. "Let's head home."

The driver jerked the wheel to the side, and the jeep skidded sideways as it made a sharp turn and began to head back toward the oil fields.

Four slugs from the soldiers they'd been shooting at slammed into the side of the jeep, but did no real damage. Seconds later, the jeep was out of sight in the blowing sand and headed for the oil fields to take up the fight there.

As they raced down the road, Bart picked up the microphone again and punched in the frequency of Major Walter O'Reilly, the man he'd left in charge of the forces in Riyadh. He'd tried to order Hugh Holmsby to stay there in charge, but Hugh had threatened to disobey the order. He'd wanted to join Bart in the assault on the convoy. Knowing he'd need his most experienced men on the assault, Bart had given in and appointed O'Reilly instead.

"Sir?" O'Reilly said.

"Bart here. The surprise package at the oil field is ready to be delivered, and so I'm calling off the attack and sending everyone back there. I don't know if the enemy will elect to try and take back the oil field first, or head directly into town, so keep your guard up."

"Aye, sir," O'Reilly said. "The men are spread out all over the town. We intend to give the camel jockeys a warm welcome ourselves if it comes to that."

"I'll meet you for a pint when this is over, Walter," Bart said.

"I'll look forward to it, sir. Are you buying?"

"Of course," Bart replied, with a laugh at the cheek of the man.

By the time Bart and his men had assembled on the edge of the oil field, it was nearing dusk. The SAS assault teams had managed to delay the convoy and make a four-hour trip into almost eight hours.

When taking stock, Bart found they'd lost six men in the assault, almost a tenth of his total forces. Three others were wounded, though not so badly they couldn't still fight. The men got a kick out of Hugh and the Davidson brothers arriving in an enemy jeep, but Hugh refused to explain how it'd happened.

Sergeant Rearden pointed out the locations of the mines to Bart. "Good job, Sergeant," Bart said. "The way you've positioned the mines, the enemy forces will have to enter the trap if they come straight at us."

Rearden nodded. "Yes, sir. I only hope they're not smart enough to try a flanking maneuver first."

Bart shook his head. "I doubt they'll bother with that, George. They know they've got us seriously outnumbered, and their commander will be under some pressure not to lose the daylight, so I think he'll come straight in from the road over there," he said, pointing at the opening to the trap. "A lot of his heavy equipment won't do too well in the sand, so I figure he'll try to keep them on solid ground."

"I don't know how much damage the plastique will do to tanks and things, sir, but it'll damn sure make mincemeat of the ground forces," Rearden said.

Bart laughed. "Equipment's not worth spit without men to run it, Sergeant," he said, slapping Rearden on the back.

Once the men had eaten some field rations, Bart began to deploy them around the various oil derricks in the oil field, stationing them near derricks that had outbuildings or other large structures that would give them some cover in the upcoming battle.

He put Rearden on top of the supply shed with a pair of night-vision goggles, and told him to give the signal when the majority of the enemy forces were within his trap. Then Bart moved to take up his own position next to an oil derrick in the very front of the field. Hugh Holmsby and the Davidson brothers stationed themselves on either side of him, along with Staff Sergeant Alphonse Green. The terrorists were going to have to go through them to get at their commander.

* * *

Jamal Ahmed couldn't understand why the multiple attacks on his convoy had suddenly ceased, and things he couldn't understand made Ahmed nervous.

Lieutenant Sohail Shaeen pulled up next to Ahmed's HumVee in his smaller jeep. "I've gotten all of the men transferred from damaged vehicles into those that are still running, Commander," Shaeen said. "Do you want us to proceed toward the oil fields now?"

"Lieutenant," Ahmed asked, his eyes thoughtful and focused on the road leading toward Riyadh and the oil fields, "why do you suppose the enemy troops broke off their attack on the convoy?"

Shaeen shook his head. "I don't know, sir. Maybe they were losing too many men. Remember, our intelligence sources say they are very shorthanded here."

Ahmed glanced at the junior officer, hoping he was correct in his assessment of the situation. "How many confirmed kills do we have?"

Shaeen shrugged. "Only six confirmed, sir, but there may have been many more than that."

"Do you think they could be setting a trap for us farther up the road?" Ahmed asked.

"No, sir, I doubt it. I think they've pulled their forces back to make a last stand at the oil fields and in the city."

"Well, then, Lieutenant," Ahmed said, making up his mind. "Let us give them the chance to die for what they believe. Move the convoy out!"

"Yes, sir!" Shaeen said, and tapped his driver on the shoulder, pointing to the head of the convoy.

THIRTY-ONE

As his convoy neared the divide in the road, with one branch heading toward the oil fields and the other toward Riyadh, Jamal Ahmed called a halt to the column of trucks and equipment.

He pulled his HumVee up next to the jeep Lieutenant Sohail Shaeen was riding in, and leaned out of the window.

"Lieutenant," Ahmed said. "I want you to take the first ten trucks and several of the Bradley vehicles and lead an assault on the oil fields. I will take the rest of the convoy toward the city itself, where I suspect the majority of the hostile troops are located."

"Yes, sir," Shaeen replied. "After I secure the oil fields, what are your orders?"

"I want you to mine as many of the oil derricks as you can with the supplies you have. Our leader, Abdullah El Farrar, says this is our primary mission. We must regain control of the oil fields as soon as possible before the enemy can send in reinforcements."

"Yes, sir. Consider it done," Shaeen said.

"Radio me as soon as you've driven out all of the enemy troops. El Farrar is waiting anxiously for word of our success in this matter."

Shaeen nodded, and told his driver to proceed to the

front of the convoy so he could direct the troops in their assault on the oil derricks, which could be seen in the light of the moon looming like prehistoric skeletons against the night sky.

After the lead trucks and vehicles had turned toward the distant fields, Jamal Ahmed took the point position in the convoy and headed toward the lights of Riyadh in the distance.

Shaeen, who was an experienced field commander, pulled the trucks to a stop some five hundred yards from the first of the oil derricks, and had his men deploy in a wide line behind the Bradley Assault Vehicles, which he planned to have lead the attack.

Once the Bradleys drew the fire of the enemy, he would have his troops make a frontal assault on their positions. It was the classic maneuver for a commander attacking a numerically inferior force, and Shaeen thought it would be a routine assault.

He keyed the microphone on his radio and told the drivers of the Bradleys to proceed at a slow speed toward the oil derricks so his troops could keep up on foot.

In the cluster of oil derricks, hidden among the outbuildings and shacks, Bartholomew Wiley-Smeyth and his men watched the approach of the enemy forces.

"Let the lead vehicles get well within the minefields before we explode them," he told Rearden, who was lying on top of the building observing the approaching enemy troops through his night-vision goggles. "I want to wait until the foot soldiers are in the trap before we spring it."

"Aye, sir," Rearden answered, keeping his eyes on the

troops and ignoring the Bradleys as they drew closer to his position.

By the time the last of the troops had entered the jaws of the trap, the Bradleys were less than fifty yards from Bart's position.

"Now!" he yelled, and opened fire on the Bradleys with his Uzi.

As his men followed suit, their bullets sparking as they ricocheted and caromed off the metal armor of the Bradleys, Rearden pushed the button on the remote detonator.

The multiple packages of C-4 and Semtex exploded in a blinding flash of light, followed by a tremendous booming series of explosions that sounded as one.

Over five hundred terrorist troops were killed outright, their bodies blown into pieces as the shrapnel whistled through the air, while hundreds more were wounded by the flying shards of metal.

The Bradleys, who'd escaped the worst of the explosions, slowed as their drivers looked to see what had happened behind them.

Staff Sergeant Alphonse Green stood up from behind his cover and lobbed a grenade at the closest Bradley. It landed just under the right front tire and exploded, blowing the front tire completely off and tipping the vehicle on its side.

As its occupants scrambled to get out of the burning vehicle, they were cut down by murderous fire from Bart and his men.

The other two Bradleys opened fire on their position, driving them back behind cover and wounding David Davidson in the left shoulder.

More grenades were thrown, and they exploded harmlessly off the armor of the Bradleys, but did make the drivers reverse their courses and race away from the derricks back toward the hundreds of bodies of the troops behind them.

Sohail Shaeen's driver was decapitated by the blast from the mines and thrown bodily out of the jeep, which spun to the side and almost overturned before slowing to a stop.

Shaeen, his left leg punctured in three places by shrapnel, managed to scoot over into the driver's seat and get the jeep turned around, headed away from the oil field.

Once out of the smoke and airborne debris, he could see the extent of the damage done to his troops, and got on the radio and instructed his squad leaders to pull back and regroup behind the Bradleys, which were racing back toward his position.

During the confusion, Bart pulled his men back also and led them toward the city, a couple of kilometers away.

"Radio Walter O'Reilly and tell him we're coming in," Bart said to his radioman. "We'll pull back into the city and take up positions there. We've done all we can here."

It took Lieutenant Shaeen almost an hour to regroup his forces and get them headed back toward the oil fields. He left the dead and wounded where they lay, intending to come back for them once he'd taken control of the oil fields.

He moved the men slowly, expecting another trap, and was pleasantly surprised to find the oil fields unguarded on his second assault.

Once he'd made sure there were no enemy forces remaining in the field, he set his explosives experts to mining the oil derricks, while he set up defensive positions around the perimeter of the field.

Only after that was done did he send men out into the desert to try to rescue any wounded that were still alive.

Jamal Ahmed, hearing the explosions and seeing the huge fireball that lit up the night sky, slowed the convoy he was leading toward the city, fearing they'd underestimated the number of opposing forces they faced.

As the convoy neared the city, he came to the airport, which was off to the left of the city. He stopped, trying to decide what to do next. Then Shaeen radioed him that he had control of the oil fields and was in the process of mining the oil derricks.

"What happened?" Ahmed asked.

"The enemy had mined the desert in front of the oil field, sir. I lost over a thousand men, dead and wounded, but did finally manage to secure the fields."

Ahmed nodded. That was indeed good news. El Farrar would be pleased. "Any sign of opposing forces?" he asked.

"No, sir. It appears they've all retreated toward the city."

"Good. Then they're trapped there," Ahmed said. "I shall take control of the airport to prevent the enemy from using it for reinforcements, and then I shall take the city."

THIRTY-TWO

By early in the evening, the skies over the Middle East began to clear and the winds dropped down to almost normal levels. For the first time in almost a week, the moon and stars could be seen.

In Kuwait City, after being assured by his meteorological team that the storm was over, at least for the next twenty-four hours, Ben Raines scrambled the pilots that had been on standby for the past few days and told them to get their engines warmed up. His second call was to Jackie Malone, telling her to get her troops ready to roll.

Jackie put the phone down, called her second in command, Johnny Walker, and told him the good news. She had already divided her battalion up into two equal groups, with Walker scheduled to lead the second group while she retained command of the first group.

The men and women of her battalion were on active standby, which meant they'd be able to take off within one hour from the battle-stations call.

As soon as he had everyone moving toward the planes, Ben took the time to call his commanders in both Saudi Arabia and Iran to tell them help was on the way.

His first call was to Tehran to check in with Buddy's group. He was a little surprised when Harley Reno answered the call instead of Buddy.

"Harley, this is Ben. How come Buddy isn't available?" Ben asked, sweat beginning to break out on his forehead at the thought of what might be wrong.

"Hey, Ben," Harley answered, his voice more serious than usual. "Buddy's okay, but he's taken a hit in the gut."

"How serious?" Ben asked.

"The medic thinks he'll be fine. The bullet passed completely through and there doesn't seem to be any serious internal damage, but he's not in any shape to fight."

"You in charge?" Ben asked.

"For right now," Harley answered.

"Can I talk to Buddy?" Ben asked.

"Uh, I don't think so, sir," Harley replied. "The medic's just given him a shot of morphine and he's kinda out of it right now."

Just then, a soldier walked into Ben's office.

"Wait one, Harley," Ben said, and turned to the young man. "Yeah?"

"The ship with the helicopters on it just arrived, General," the man said. "They're unloading and fueling them now."

"Great!" Ben said. He keyed the mike again. "Harley, the choppers from our home base are here. Do you have control of the airport?"

"For the time being, sir, but it'll be dicey holding it. We've got a bunch of hostiles on our doorstep."

"Well, the weather's cleared and I'll be sending Jackie and half her battalion to see you. I'll have the choppers make a pass over the airport first. Pop a green canister if it's safe. If you can't hold it, then I'll have the choppers strafe it until it's safe for Jackie and her troops to land."

"Roger that, General."

"Oh, and Harley . . ."

"Sir?"

"Tell Buddy I'll be coming along with the troops."

"That's good news, sir," Harley replied, relief in his voice at the news.

Ben signed off, and immediately called Bartholomew Wiley-Smeyth's headquarters in Riyadh.

When Bart was on the line, Ben asked, "How're you holding up, Bart?"

"By the skin of our teeth, Ben," Bart replied. "The hostiles are thick as thieves here. So far we've managed to keep them out of the city, but I'm afraid we lost the oil fields."

"Hang in there, buddy," Ben said. "Help is on the way."

"We'll do our best," Bart replied. "We've retreated from the oil fields and are holed up in the city."

"How about the airport?" Ben asked.

"We had to abandon it, Ben. I'm pretty sure it'll be in the terrorists' hands by the time you can get reinforcements here."

Ben thought for a moment. "Okay, that's no problem. We have some helicopters that should be able to clear the way for our troops to land."

"We'll do what we can, Ben, but tell the pilots not to spare the gas."

"Roger that, Bart," Ben said, and broke the connection.

As soon as he was off the radio, Ben went into his quarters, changed from his uniform into battle fatigues, and ran toward the airport to join Jackie and her troops.

Ten C-141 StarLifter aircraft were lined up on the tarmac, waiting to take off. The StarLifters, longer and wider than the older C-130's, could handle more cargo and troops than the C-130 Hercules could. Whereas the C-

130s could transport, only ninety-two paratroopers or 128 battle-ready troops, the C-14s could transport 168 or 208 respectively, and at a slightly faster speed.

The first two StarLifters were loaded with paratroopers, while the other eight were loaded with regular troops.

Ben ran up to Jackie, who was preparing to board one of the planes with her paratroopers.

She turned and raised an eyebrow when she saw Ben in battle fatigues. "You comin' to this party, boss?" she asked.

Ben nodded as he slipped into a parachute and strapped on his weapons. "Buddy's been wounded, Jackie, and I'm gonna take over his command in Tehran."

Jackie grinned. "Then, I'll go with the plane that's headed to Riyadh."

"Let the choppers lead the way, Jackie," Ben said. "Commander Wiley-Smeyth says the hostiles control the airport there."

"That shouldn't be a problem," Jackie drawled in her thick Texas accent. "We'll let the whirlybirds soften 'em up while we jump on the outskirts. By the time we hit the dirt, they should be on the run."

Ben stepped in close and shook her hand. "Be careful, Jackie. Remember, we'll still be outnumbered ten to one."

She grinned. "Those odds oughta be about right then. We wouldn't want it to be too easy."

Ben turned and climbed into the cargo bay of the big StarLifter that was headed for Iran.

When the Scout paratroopers saw who was joining them, they all broke into wide smiles. "Welcome aboard, General," one of the gunnery sergeants said, snapping off a quick salute.

"It's been a while since I jumped, Gunny," Ben said. "You may have to kick me off the plane."

"Not to worry, sir," the sergeant said as he stepped up to Ben and gave his equipment a quick going-over. "It's just like riding a bicycle . . . you never forget how."

"From your lips to God's ears, son," Ben said, taking his seat alongside the rest of the Scouts.

"You get a sitrep from the target zone, sir?" the sergeant said, sitting next to Ben.

"Yeah. It's gonna be a hot zone," Ben replied.

The sergeant grinned. "Wouldn't have it any other way, sir."

As the StarLifter gunned its engines, readying for takeoff, six McDonnell Douglas AH-64 Apache helicopters were already in the air heading toward the targets, three to Iran and three to Saudi Arabia. Since both Riyadh and Tehran were around three hundred miles from Kuwait City, the choppers would be at the extremes of their three-hundred-mile range when they arrived. There would be no time for refueling on the way, so the helicopters would only be able to make one or two passes on the airports before they ran out of fuel.

Ben gave a silent prayer the six Hellfire antitank missiles and the M230 30mm chain guns each of the Apaches carried would be enough to clear the airports so the troops could land. If they weren't, the C-14s would have to try to land on the desert, which wasn't a happy thought.

THIRTY-THREE

As the C-141 StarLifter carrying Jackie Malone and her Scout paratroopers approached the airport just outside of Riyadh, Jackie made her way to the cockpit and asked the pilot if she could be put through to the lead pilot in the Apache helicopters that were leading the way in.

"Sure, ma'am," the pilot said. He twisted a dial on the instrument panel and spoke a few words into his headset microphone. He slipped the headset off and handed it back over his shoulder to Jackie.

"You're gonna be talking to Major Juan Gomez, ma'am," he said.

"Major Gomez," Jackie said after slipping the headset over her head.

"Yes, ma'am," the pilot responded, his voice soft with the slight Mexican accent Jackie remembered from her home state of Texas.

"How's your fuel, Major?"

She heard a low chuckle. "No problem. Probably got at least a teacup left," Gomez replied.

"You have enough left for a couple of strafing runs over the airport?"

"That depends on how well this baby flies on fumes," Gomez answered. "We'll make at least one and we can try for another. I'll try to position my birds so if we run out of fuel, we'll drop on the heaviest concentration of hostiles. How's that?" Gomez asked, only half kidding.

"Don't take any chances, Major," Jackie advised, grinning at the bravery of the man. "If you get too low, put the choppers down on the east side of the airport. That's where we're gonna be dropping, so we can give you and your men some cover."

"I'll try, ma'am, but my fuel warning light's been blinking for the past ten minutes, and these birds have all the gliding characteristics of rocks. When the engine quits, we're gonna go straight down."

Jackie shook her head. There was just no reasoning with pilots. "Roger that, Major. Good luck," Jackie said, and clicked off the mike and handed the headset back to the pilot of the StarLifter.

"As soon as the Apaches make their first run, drop us off to the east of the airport," she said. "I'd like us to be on the ground by the time they line up for their second attack."

The pilot didn't answer, but just nodded his head.

Jackie walked back into the cargo hold and pumped her fist in the air, signaling her men to get ready to jump.

Minutes later, the StarLifter turned to the east and the loading ramp at the rear of the plane began to open. When the light changed from red to yellow to green, Jackie and her troops simply ran out of the back of the plane and dove into thin air.

The pilot had them at the very lowest possible altitude for a regular jump so as to minimize their time in the air, when they would be helpless against ground fire.

After instructing his fellow pilots to try to avoid doing any damage to the runways, Major Gomez tilted the nose of his Apache down and increased his throttle, going in low and fast along the edges of the runway. Through the

Plexiglas windshield, he could see numerous vehicles and even some foxholes the enemy troops had dug in the desert along the runways. Taking the eastern side first to give some protection to the paratroopers, Gomez triggered his M230 30mm chain gun, and watched as thousands of slugs tore into the enemy troops and shredded the vehicles parked alongside the runway.

Major Billy Thornton, in the second Apache, concentrated his fire on the buildings and control tower on the west side of the airport. He could see many hostile troops on the roofs and as he began his run saw the glittering red dots of their guns as they fired at him.

Deciding against using his chain gun on the first run, Thornton instead fired his 2.75-inch rockets at the bases of the buildings. He pulled up over the buildings just as the rockets exploded, sending up huge billows of smoke and flame.

As he passed over the buildings, a line of holes stitched across his windshield, shattering it and sending razor-sharp shards rattling against his helmet visor.

"Bastards!" he yelled, and jerked the nose of the Apache around for a second run over the ruined buildings.

As his engine coughed once and then caught again, Thornton could see dozens of enemy troops scrambling to get away from the buildings and out of his line of fire.

He bared his teeth in a savage grin and opened fire with his chain gun, decimating the running troops and mowing them down like so much wheat.

Just as his engine faltered again, Thornton caught sight of a tank coming out from behind one of the buildings. He had time to fire one Hellfire missile before the rudder became heavy in his hand and he began to lose control of the Apache.

It took all of Thornton's strength to hold the rudder and collective as he auto-rotated down to a rather hard landing next to the runway.

He grabbed the Uzi off the floor next to his feet and bailed out of the cockpit, crouching next to the rocket tubes as several bullets pinged off the fuselage next to his head.

A group of eight or ten hostiles were running across the tarmac toward him, firing Kalashnikovs as they ran.

Thornton raised the Uzi and triggered off a burst that dropped three of the men, but the rest kept coming, driving him back behind cover with their fire.

Thornton reached up and wrapped his fingers around the cross that hung around his neck on a silver chain, figuring it was his time to die.

A roaring *whup-whup-whup* sounded overhead and Major Gomez's chopper zoomed by, not more than twenty feet off the ground, and cut the men down with his chain gun before they could get to Thornton.

Thornton stood up and watched helplessly as Gomez's Apache tilted crazily to one side and dropped onto the desert sand, crumpling like it was made of tin instead of reinforced titanium.

"Crazy son of a bitch," Thornton growled as he ran toward the wreckage. He knew Gomez had used the last of his fuel to save his life rather than landing safely.

Luckily, the lack of fuel in the Apache kept it from bursting into flames. By the time Thornton arrived at the crash site, Gomez had kicked his door open and was dragging himself out of the cockpit. Both his legs were at funny angles, but he was alive.

Thornton pulled him free of the helicopter and laid him back up against one of the wheels. Then he reached inside the cockpit and took out the medical kit strapped to the sidewall.

Popping it open, he took out a morphine syringe and stuck it in Gomez's thigh.

"Thanks, Juanito," he said as Gomez's eyes slowly closed in blissful sleep.

Thornton grabbed his Uzi and whirled around as a roaring, coughing sound came from behind him. He relaxed when he saw it was only Jack Ashford, the pilot of the third Apache, landing a dozen yards away. He'd timed it so close that his engine quit just as the wheels touched down.

Ashford jumped out of the helicopter and ran over to Thornton. He too had his Uzi in his hands. "Thought you boys might like some company," he said as he took up position next to Thornton and Gomez.

"Hell, yeah!" Thornton yelled back. "There are never enough rednecks around to suit me."

Ashford grinned and took a couple of long, fat cigars from his flight suit. It was a tradition among the chopper pilots to light one up after a successful mission.

He flicked his Zippo lighter and they both puffed clouds of evil-smelling smoke as they watched for hostiles.

As Jackie Malone and the other 167 paratroopers floated to the ground, they came under some small-arms fire from terrorist troops, but it was slight, and ceased as soon as the Apaches began to strafe the enemy positions along the runways.

Once on the ground, the Scouts jettisoned their chutes, formed into a wide line, and began to jog toward the enemy positions, firing as they advanced.

When they arrived at the foxholes of the enemy troops, they found hundreds of bodies torn asunder by the murderous fire of the Apaches' chain guns. The few enemy troops left alive threw down their guns and rifles and held up their hands in surrender.

Jackie assigned a couple of men to take charge of the prisoners, and led the rest in a frontal assault on the ruined, smoldering buildings on the other side of the runway.

The slight resistance they faced was soon overpowered by the ferocious fighting of the Scouts, and in less than half an hour, they had complete control of the airfield.

Jackie motioned her radioman to her side and called the other C-14's and told them it was safe to land. She spread her men out along the runways as a guard until the big birds had landed safely.

As the troops poured out of the StarLifters, Jackie began to get them organized for an assault on the enemy troops that were laying siege to the city in the distance.

Appropriating every vehicle that wasn't damaged too much to be operative, she loaded her troops into the jeeps and Bradleys and tanks, and had them lead the way toward the city.

Some of the troops were assigned to carry fuel to the two Apaches that were still functional so they could aid in the counterattack on the city.

In Riyadh, Bartholomew Wiley-Smeyth had his meager force of men spread out among the city buildings, on rooftops and top stories so they'd have a good line of fire at the enemy troops that were attempting to enter the city.

As the Apache helicopters, with full fuel tanks, flew

toward the city, Bart had his men pop green gas grenades to show the pilots where the friendly troops were.

Jamal Ahmed's troops, caught between the pincers of several thousand SUSA troops and Bart's men, were no match for the Apaches' withering fire and Hellfire missiles.

By mid-afternoon, it was all over. Jamal Ahmed had been killed when his HumVee was blown to splinters by a Hellfire missile. Lieutenant Sohail Shaeen, seeing there was no hope of victory, had surrendered the few enemy troops remaining alive to Jackie Malone's Scouts.

Of the ten thousand troops El Farrar had sent toward Riyadh, only three thousand remained alive, many injured severely. The prisoners of war were gathered in a large, open field and surrounded by guards.

Bart climbed down out of the building he'd been fighting from and walked up to Jackie. He saluted and then stuck out his hand. "Thanks for coming so soon, ma'am," he said, not able to ascertain Jackie's rank from her battle fatigues, which were without an officer's ranking on them.

"Glad to oblige, Commander," Jackie said, taking his hand and gripping it hard enough to make him wince. "And the name's Jackie."

"What's the status of the oil fields, Jackie?" Bart asked, his face blushing at the informality of the American.

Jackie shook her head. "We haven't cleared them yet," she said. "I figured they'd be booby-trapped, and we might want to let the ranking officer of the terrorist forces try to get the hostiles there to give up without destroying the oil wells."

Bart nodded. "Good idea. Any idea who that might be?" he asked.

Jackie motioned to a small group of men behind her, and they moved aside to reveal Lieutenant Sohail Shaeen standing there, his wrists restrained by a plastic restraint.

She waved her arm at him. "Be my guest, Commander. You are still the officer in charge of this city."

"Thanks," Bart said, moving to stand in front of Shaeen.

"Do you speak English?" he asked.

Shaeen nodded. "Of course, Commander," he answered with a heavy accent.

Bart waved his arm at the numerous forces around them. "As you can see, Lieutenant, we have more than enough troops to take the oil fields back from your forces."

Shaeen's eyes followed Bart's gesture. "Yes, Commander, I can see that."

"Have your men mined the oil wells?" Bart asked.

Shaeen gave a sad half smile. "I'm afraid I cannot answer that, Commander. You are aware of the Geneva Convention and its rules concerning treatment of prisoners of war, I take it?"

Bart smiled grimly back at Shaeen. "Lieutenant, let me give you some facts. You and your men are *not* prisoners of war. You belong to no recognized country's armed forces and you are not fighting in a declared war. You are terrorists and spies, nothing more."

When Shaeen started to speak, Bart held up his hand. "And as such, I am sure you are aware we would be perfectly within our rights to execute you and your men on the spot."

"But . . ." Shaeen began.

Bart glanced pointedly at his wristwatch. "You have

ten minutes to make up your mind, Lieutenant. After that we will begin to execute your men one by one until you are all dead. And then we will attack the oil fields and wipe our your troops there to the last man."

Shaeen glanced around at the stony faces of the troops around him. "But surely you do not want the oil wells destroyed."

Bart shrugged. "The most your men can do will be to blow up the derricks. The damage from such an act could be repaired in a matter of days." He glanced at his watch again. "You now have eight minutes, Lieutenant, or the lives of all of your men will be on your head."

Shaeen's eyes dropped and his shoulders slumped. "I will see what I can do, Commander."

Bart glanced at Jackie and winked so Shaeen couldn't see him. "Give the lieutenant a jeep, please, Jackie. We'll let him go and have a talk with his comrades."

THIRTY-FOUR

Haji Kuchkool, with Farid Zamet riding in the rear of his HumVee, stayed well to the rear of the advancing troops as they moved closer to the oil fields.

He winced in sympathy and anger as he saw hundreds of his men cut down by the withering fire from the defenders, as well as the rocket grenades that, with no vehicles to concentrate on, were now landing in the middle of his troops and cutting them down by the dozens.

By the time his men overran the oil derricks and found the defenders had retreated, the field in front of the oil field was covered with dead and dying men, and the screams and moans were pitiful to listen to.

Kuchkool turned to one of his lieutenants. "Go out into the field and shut those men up," he ordered. "Their cowardly crying is bad for morale."

The young soldier nodded, not having the slightest idea how he was going to accomplish this, short of killing the men himself. However, as young as he was, he knew it was certain death to defy or question Commander Kuchkool's orders, so he moved as rapidly as he could to get out of the sight of his temperamental leader.

As Kuchkool approached the area where the defenders had last been sighted, followed closely behind by Farid Zamet, he noticed a tent pitched between two oil derricks.

The tent was lighted from the inside by what looked like a lantern hanging on a pole in the center of the tent.

Kuchkool pointed with the barrel of his Kalashnikov. "Look there, Farid, there is a radio antenna on top of the tent. Perhaps this is the enemy's communications headquarters."

Zamet nodded. "Maybe they left some important papers behind that will give us some insight into the strength of their forces in the city," he suggested.

"Let us go look," Kuchkool said, smiling at the thought of the praise he would receive from El Farrar if he found something important.

As he moved toward the tent, a tremendous explosion came from fifty yards away, followed immediately by screams of pain and terror as a giant fireball roared into the sky.

Kuchkool and Zamet both hit the dirt, landing on their faces in the gravel and sand as hundreds of pieces of molten shrapnel tore over their heads and shredded the walls of the tent in front of them.

Once he was certain there were going to be no more explosions, Kuchkool got slowly to his feet, dusting himself off as he glared toward the source of the explosion.

"What happened?" he asked a soldier who was walking toward him, a dazed expression on his face.

"The enemy soldiers left a box full of grenades behind, Commander," the young man said, sleeving soot and dirt off his face. "It must have been mined, for it went off and killed almost a dozen men who were nearby."

Kuchkool glanced at Zamet, and then at the tent in front of them, a speculative expression on his face.

Zamet, catching the meaning of his stare, backed slowly away from the tent, his eyes wide with fear.

"Soldier," Kuchkool said, "there are some papers in that tent over there. Go and get them for me."

The soldier, still dazed from his close call of moments before, nodded and moved toward the tent.

Kuchkool, following Zamet's lead, also backed away from the tent and moved over behind a nearby oil derrick.

Just as he got to the tent, the soldier stumbled over the wire Harley had left, and had time to look down before the plastique bricks attached to the wire exploded.

The soldier was blown into several pieces, and both Kuchkool and Zamet were knocked off their feet by the force of the blast.

"Allah be merciful," Zamet groaned from his position flat on his back. A small trickle of blood ran down his forehead and onto his cheek from where a small pebble had ricocheted off a beam and into his skin.

Once again, Kuchkool got to his feet and brushed himself off. Several soldiers ran up to him and asked him if he was all right.

"Yes, yes, of course," he answered impatiently. He looked at Zamet as he was climbing to his feet. "Perhaps we should hold off searching the oil field until dawn. It will be easier to spot the traps that have obviously been left for us in daylight," he said.

Zamet nodded, only too happy to get out of this accursed place before he too was blown apart.

"Gather the troops," Kuchkool ordered a nearby junior officer. "We move against the city."

As he walked toward his HumVee, Kuchkool growled, "I swear by Allah I will destroy the infidel dogs for what they've done to my troops tonight."

Zamet kept his mouth shut. He wasn't about to tell the commander he hadn't done all that well so far.

* * *

Once he was sure the medic had done all he could for Buddy, Harley called a strategy meeting of the squad leaders of the Scout teams holed up in Tehran.

Major Jackson Bean, Willie Running Bear, Samuel Clements, and Sue Waters were all in attendance.

"Major Bean," Harley began, "as ranking officer, you are next in line to Buddy to take command."

"I'm told Buddy asked you to take command, Harley," Bean said, smiling. "Let's hear what you have to say before I decide whether to take command or not."

Harley shook his head. "That order by Buddy was just to get us out of the desert and into the city, Major."

Bean nodded. "All right then, here's how I see our situation. We're outnumbered a hundred to one. The only thing we've got going for us is we're small enough to be extremely mobile, while the larger force will be forced to move at a snail's pace."

Harley grinned, seeing where the major was going with his talk.

"The other thing in our favor is that it is the middle of the night. Scouts are trained to fight in darkness, while most regular troops are not."

He paused. "My idea is to leave half our forces here in the city, spread out among as many buildings as we can so they'll seem like a larger force. When they draw the hostiles' fire, the rest of our men and women, divided up into small two- and three-man groups, will attack from the flanks and rear, hitting hard and fast and then disappearing back into the darkness. Pretty soon, the bastards won't know whether they're coming or going."

Harley laughed. "And with our silencers, half the time they won't even know they've been attacked until they're already dead."

Bean looked at his squad leaders. "Okay, guys and gals, let's get our teams put together and get them out of sight and ready to move."

He glanced at Harley. "I think your team is most used to guerrilla warfare, so we'll have your guys be some of our mobile troops, if you agree."

"Absolutely," Harley said, glad he hadn't been consigned to sit on a rooftop waiting for the enemy to come to him. He knew the rest of the team felt the same way: They'd all rather take the fight to the enemy than the opposite.

Back in the room where the rest of the team waited with Buddy, Harley told them the good news. "Coop, you and Jersey team up; Anna, you come with me; Hammer, you and Beth take Corrie with you and you'll be in charge of communications with Major Bean and the other mobile teams. He'll let us know through you if any of the stationary troops come under too much fire so you can send a mobile team to take the heat off them."

"What about Buddy?" Jersey asked, looking over at his sleeping body on a cot against a far wall.

"Major Bean is going to leave some men here with him. He'll be a lot safer than any of us, Jersey."

Everyone nodded, and began to move off together in their teams, discussing among themselves how they were going to work the attack.

As they went down the stairs, Coop leaning heavily on the handrail and still limping, Jersey glanced at him out of the corner of her eye.

"Maybe you'd better ask Jackson if you can take a position in one of the buildings, Coop. That ankle still looks pretty bad," she said.

Coop pressed his lips together and shook his head.

"Not on your life, Jersey." He paused and looked at her. "But it might be better for you to ask Harley to assign you another teammate. I'll probably just slow you down."

She stopped and turned to look square at him. "You say anything like that again and it won't only be your ankle that's swollen . . . it'll be your jaw too."

"But . . . but I just . . ." Coop began as she turned and walked away down the stairs.

"Shut up, Coop," she growled over her shoulder. "For once in your life, shut up!"

"Uh, yes, ma'am," Coop said, grinning at the back of her head.

"Wait right here," she ordered when they got to the door. "I'll be right back."

Five minutes later, she returned, driving up in an old U.S. Army jeep that looked as if it'd spent the last fifty years in the desert. The tires were worn almost flat and the paint had faded to the color of rusted metal, but the engine still sounded good.

"Jesus," Coop said. "What museum did you find that in?"

"I saw it on our way in to town earlier," she answered. "Remember the history of World War II?"

"Yeah, what of it?" Coop asked as he climbed into the passenger seat.

"In the deserts of North Africa, there were squads of men driving these jeeps against the Germans. They called themselves The Desert Rats, if I remember correctly."

Coop laughed and grabbed the windshield as Jersey took off in a cloud of smoking exhaust. "Well, fellow rat," he yelled over the sound of the engine, "let's go get us some cheese!"

THIRTY-FIVE

As the battle over Tehran began to rage, the silver space ship flashed into the upper reaches of the earth's atmosphere, leveling off at a distance of some two hundred miles.

Since all of the satellites monitored by the U.N. and by the Intel officers at the SUSA were turned to observe the goings on in the Middle East, the ship was unobserved by anyone in authority on the planet.

The navigator of the ship, still flushed and breathing heavily from his encounter with his new female friend, punched a button on the console in front of him. Moments later, his captain's voice came out of a nearby speaker.

"Yes, Garthul, what is it?"

"We have reached the planet where the radio-frequency emissions originated, Captain."

"Have you set up a synchronous orbit?"

"Of course, sir."

"Then I shall be there momentarily. Call the science officer and have him begin his measurements of atmosphere and surface temperatures."

"Yes, sir," the navigator replied, and hastily buzzed the cubicle of the science officer. He would be glad to have someone else on the bridge when the captain arrived. It was nerve-wracking being alone with someone who might decide you would be more useful as food than as a navigator.

As the navigator circled the planet, the science officer was busily peering through the various instruments on the bridge and making copious notes on his handheld computer board.

Suddenly, he stiffened and pulled his head away from the viewing screen to stare at the navigator. "Garthul, stop the ship and hold it steady over this position for a while," he ordered.

"Yes, sir," the navigator answered, twisting dials to slow the ship. Sometimes it seemed to him that everyone on this blasted ship outranked him, even though it was his skill that kept them all from flying into the nearby sun and being incinerated.

"What is it you see, Science Officer," Garthul asked, making sure to keep the tone of his voice subservient.

"There seems to be an armed conflict occurring in that area of what looks like desert below us."

"Are the radiation levels climbing?" Garthul asked, since armed conflict on civilized worlds usually meant the use of atomic weapons.

"No, and that is somewhat strange. Perhaps this world has not progressed to the level necessary to produce atomic weapons yet."

Garthul smiled. That would indeed be good news. Pre-atomic civilizations were always easy to overthrow, whereas some of the post-atomic ones had given them trouble in the past.

At that moment, the captain strolled into the control room. Garthul noticed the captain's chest and genital area were as flushed as his were. Perhaps the captain too had missed feminine companionship in the fifty years of their sleep.

"Science Officer, what do you have to report on the status of this planet?" he asked.

The science officer snapped to attention, carefully keeping his eyes off the flushed, swollen genitals of the captain.

"It looks well so far, sir," he replied. "The ambient temperature, while a little low for optimum levels, is certainly within our parameters, as is the atmosphere."

While his officer was reporting, the captain bent and peered through one of the telescopic screens at the surface of the planet below. "What are those flashes I see?" he asked, looking up from the screen at the science officer.

"There appears to be a war going on, sir."

"No increase in radiation levels?"

"None."

The captain gave a rare smile. "Good. Then we shall send a message back home that we've found a planet that looks suitable for colonization. That will make the supreme commander very happy, as I'm sure the population pressure is getting stronger by the day."

The science officer snapped off a salute. "I'll ready the subspace probe immediately, sir."

"Garthul," the captain said as he lowered his head to the screen again, "make a circle of this planet. I'd like to see what this misbegotten hunk of rock looks like from all sides."

He grinned out of the side of his mouth. "After all, if it is to be named after me, perhaps I should know what I'm getting as a namesake."

"Yes, sir," Garthul answered, and he began to change the dials on the console.

"Uh, one thing, sir," the science officer said hesitantly.

"Yes?"

"From what I've seen, almost two thirds of the planet is covered with water and will be totally useless to colonization."

"No matter," the captain replied, his grin fading. "A few thermonuclear charges should take care of that. Within a few kronons, the areas will be as dry as a tritonare's tongue."

Both the navigator and the science officer laughed at the slightly off-color joke.

THIRTY-SIX

Major Jackson Bean elected to stay with the soldiers guarding the building where Buddy Raines was sleeping. He did send his squad leaders out with the mobile patrols to harass and bedevil the invading terrorist troops, and hopefully slow them down until help from Ben Raines could arrive.

Willie Running Bear and Samuel Clements couldn't wait to get a chance at the invaders, but Sue Waters hesitated as she left the room. She turned in the doorway, her hand on the jamb, and asked, "You sure you don't want me to stay here with you, Chief?"

Bean shook his head. "Naw, I wouldn't dare try and keep you from sending a few of our visiting friends to see Allah, Sue. Go ahead on, these boys here will keep Buddy and me safe."

Sue gave the Scouts in the room with Bean a somber stare. "They'd better, or they'll have someone a lot worse than those ragheads to worry about!"

She whirled around and ran from the room to join her friends as they rounded up some transportation to carry them out into the desert and away from the city.

* * *

As Jersey drove out into the desert in the jeep she'd commandeered for her and Coop to use, she saw the lights of the huge convoy of troops and vehicles as it turned from its assault on the oil fields and headed back toward Tehran.

"Jesus, look at that," she said, loudly enough to be heard over the engine. "There's a lot men who're gonna be awfully pissed at the surprises Harley left for them."

Coop smiled as he checked the loads in the magazine of his Heckler and Koch MP-10 machine gun. "Yep, I reckon so," he drawled in a very bad Gary Cooper imitation.

Jersey glanced at him and shook her head. "What? Now you're pretending to be John Wayne?"

"John Wayne?" Coop protested. "Are you deaf? That was Gary Cooper."

"Gary Cooper never played in any war movies," Jersey said, grimacing as the jeep bounced into the air as it ran over a boulder in the middle of the camel track that was supposed to be a road.

"Oh, no?" Coop jeered. "What about *Gunga Din?*"

Jersey nodded, conceding the point. "Okay, I'll give you that one. Of course, I'm not old enough to remember those old movies you love so much."

"You think it's about time we turned the headlights off, dear, or do you want them to see us coming?" Coop asked, pointing at the line of lights on the main road off to the side that the terrorists were using.

Jersey leaned forward and snapped off the headlights, letting the jeep slow so she wouldn't run too far off their trail in the sudden darkness.

As the jeep slowed to a stop, she looked over at him. "Okay, Gary or Gunga, or whatever you want me to call you . . . what's your pleasure? Do we sit back and stay on the edges of the troops and snipe them a few at a time, or do we charge in like the Light Brigade and do a little maximum damage before turning tail and running back out into the night?"

"Well, since our only purpose is to slow them down and confuse the hell out of 'em, it won't do much good to kill a few at a time," Coop said, his eyes glued on the enormous amount of men and machines slowly passing a couple of kilometers away.

"My thoughts exactly, Coop old boy. You may be a chauvinistic pain in the ass, but we do speak the same language when it comes to wasting enemies," Jersey said as she fiddled with the gearshift.

"Well, thank you, Jersey," Coop replied, his lips curling in a half smile. "And even though you are a ball-breaking, dyed-in-the-wool feminist man-hating asshole, there's no one I'd rather be in a firefight with than you."

Jersey laughed. "Thanks, Coop, I think," she said. "But seriously, Coop, I don't hate men . . . just jerks."

As the last of the vehicles in the convoy rolled past, leaving nothing but darkness in their wakes, Coop got up on the backrest of his seat with his feet on the seat itself. He jerked back on the loading lever of his MP-10, clicking a shell into the firing chamber. "Hand me that gym bag on the floor there, will ya?" he said.

Jersey finished getting her Uzi ready and then handed Coop the gym bag. She'd picked a Mini-Uzi so she could fire it one-handed while steering the jeep with the other hand. That would have been impossible with the MP-10 she preferred for normal combat.

Coop opened the gym bag he'd brought with them and took out four fragmentation grenades. He hung them on his belt by their trigger-levers, settled himself back with his MP-10 held in both hands, and looked at Jersey. "Ready to rock and roll?" he asked.

"Let's boogie!" Jersey growled, and she jammed the jeep into gear and popped the clutch.

The rear wheels spun and the rear of the jeep veered around until they were headed toward the road the terrorists were using to approach Tehran.

The rear of the terrorist column was about a hundred yards ahead of them on the road when Jersey got to it and swerved onto the potholed tarmac after them.

She quickly ran through the gears until she was in high, and then she took her Uzi and held it out over the door with her left hand, flicking the safety off with her thumb.

As they drew closer to the last vehicle in line, a deuce-and-a-half with a canvas top that was full of foot soldiers, she and Coop both began to fire, sending a stream of 9mm slugs into the mass of soldiers in the rear of the truck.

Swerving again at the last moment, she swung off the road and sped past the truck while Coop emptied his magazine into the driver's compartment.

When the driver's head disintegrated into a mass of bone and hair and brains, the truck veered to the side and overturned. It rolled twice before its gas tank exploded, sending pieces of soldiers and metal and canvas flying through the air.

The next truck in line slowed, and the soldiers inside began to aim their rifles and open fire. The jeep's windshield shattered, a dozen bullet holes in it, as Coop pulled the ring out of one of his grenades with his teeth and pitched it into the back of the truck.

Jersey yanked hard on the steering wheel, almost throwing Coop out of his seat as she turned hard to the left.

The grenade went off and blew the canvas top off the truck, and most of the soldiers out onto the road behind the truck. The rear wheels, flattened by the force of the blast, sent out a stream of glowing sparks as the tire rims skidded on the road's surface. The driver of the truck, killed by a piece of shrapnel through the back of his skull, leaned forward on the steering wheel and the truck slowly turned out into the desert away from Jersey and Coop's jeep.

Jersey kept the jeep headed out into the desert at right angles to the road, heading away from the convoy so she and Coop could reload.

Behind them, they could see the lights of several vehicles turning toward them as the terrorists began to give chase.

Coop looked up from fumbling with his spare magazine, and grimaced as Jersey raced blindly into the darkness with her lights still off.

"Jesus," he yelled, "I hope there aren't any trees out here!"

"When's the last time you saw a tree in the desert?" Jersey yelled back at him without taking her eyes off the front of the jeep, even though she couldn't see much past the hood.

The jeep hit a rise in the ground that was invisible in the night, and all four tires left the ground as the jeep became airborne.

Jersey had time to yell, "Oh shit!" before the jeep hit the ground again, bouncing and jigging from side to side as she slammed on the brakes. Luckily, the jeep was barely moving when the left front tire exploded and the jeep jerked hard left and overturned, throwing both Jersey and Coop out onto the sand and gravel.

Jersey shook her head and scrambled around on her

hands and knees until she found her Uzi. She looked around and saw Coop lying on his side with his leg bent under him and his arms bent around his abdomen.

She took a quick look, and saw the vehicles from the convoy a couple of hundred yards away, but headed right for them.

She crawled over to Coop and shook his shoulder. "Coop, Coop, are you okay?" she asked anxiously.

He opened one eye and stared at her as if she were crazy. "Are you kidding?" he asked. "Of course I'm not okay. I was just in a car wreck!"

Jersey laughed, glad to see he hadn't lost his sense of humor. "Well, you'd better get off your ass and on your feet, 'cause we're about to have some company."

He craned his neck to the side and saw the headlights of several vehicles headed their way.

"Come on," she urged, pulling on his arm. "Let's get over behind the jeep. At least we'll have some cover."

Coop moaned as he tried to straighten his leg. "A lot of good that'll do us," he groaned, but he managed to get up on hands and knees, and crawled after Jersey back to where their jeep lay on its side, its rear wheels still slowly turning.

As he scrambled behind it, he saw Jersey crawling inside and fumbling with the seats.

"What the hell are you doing?" he asked.

"Looking to see if that bag of grenades is still here," she answered.

Coop felt his belt. Only one grenade was still there. He figured the others must've fallen off when he'd been ejected from the jeep.

"I've got one," he called, taking it off his belt and laying it in the sand next to him as he got up on his knees and sighted his MP-10 over the rear part of the jeep.

Suddenly, Jersey was kneeling next to him. "I found the bag," she said, rummaging inside it. "It looks like there's four more grenades in here."

"Good," Coop said, staring at his sights as four pairs of headlights bore down on them. "I'm gonna try and put their lights out with the MP-10. Maybe that'll slow 'em down enough for you to put a grenade in their laps."

"Go for it!" she said, taking a grenade in her right hand and putting her left index finger through the ring.

Coop took dead aim and slowly squeezed the trigger on the MP-10. His first burst took out both headlights on a large HumVee, drawing return fire from the fifty-caliber machine gun in the rear.

Jersey didn't duck as the slugs pinged and screamed off the metal of the jeep. She jerked the pin, laid her arm back, and lobbed the grenade toward the oncoming Hummer.

It missed to the side, but exploded in the air above the HumVee, and killed the driver and machine-gunner in the rear. The passenger jumped out of the big truck just before it ran full tilt into the jeep.

Jersey and Coop barely managed to get out from behind the jeep before the collision. Somehow, the HumVee didn't flip over, but just ground to a halt up on top of the jeep, its front wheels still spinning.

The other three vehicles behind veered off to the sides and ran by the jeep, their drivers trying to see what had happened.

Jersey wasted no time. She grabbed Coop by the arm and pulled him up into the HumVee. She managed to push the dead driver out of the door and took his place.

"Coop, see if the fifty's still working," she yelled.

Coop, sensing what she had in mind, climbed in the back seat, ignoring the bleeding body of the gunner. He felt around the machine gun, and thought everything was in good working order. "I think it's okay," he said. "Let me give it a try."

He aimed the gun off to the side and jerked the trigger once. The gun burped and chattered out fifteen bullets before he could let go.

"She's fine," he hollered. "Now, see if you can get us outta here!"

Jersey put the HumVee in reverse and floored the accelerator pedal. The rear wheels spun for a moment and then took hold, and the big truck backed itself off the jeep.

As Jersey was about to shift gears, a pistol shot sounded from off to the side and she felt a burning in her right shoulder. "Goddamn!" she cursed, thinking, *Not again.*

Coop whipped the barrel of the big fifty around and let off a burst in the direction the sound had come from, though he was able to see nothing.

He stopped firing when he heard an earsplitting scream of pain and anguish from in front of him.

"Got the bastard," he said.

"Not before he got me," Jersey said, her voice growing weaker from the front seat.

"Shit!" Coop said, and climbed over the seat next to Jersey.

"You all right, babe?" he asked gently, his eyes narrowing at the dark stain on her shirtsleeve barely visible in the starlight.

"Don't call me babe . . ." Jersey said, and fainted.

"Sorry about that, darlin'," Coop said as he grabbed her under the arms and pulled her into the passenger seat. He took off his belt and hurriedly tied a tourniquet around her upper arm.

Turning back to the steering wheel, he put the HumVee

into gear, and began to drive off away from the jeep. He could see several sets of lights in the distance as their pursuers turned around to come back after them.

Making sure not to touch the brakes and give their position away with brake lights, Coop gunned the engine and raced away into the darkness and safety.

THIRTY-SEVEN

As Coop drove the HumVee as fast as he could through the darkness, his attention was divided between checking Jersey to make sure her bleeding had stopped, and following the progress of the three remaining vehicles that were still on his trail.

Since they were able to use their headlights, they were slowly gaining on him, even though he drove a zigzag course through the desert.

His heart almost jumped into his throat as he passed a dark object coming toward him out of the darkness, until he saw it was one of the jeeps from Tehran. He caught a quick glimpse of a woman driving and a huge bear of a man in the passenger seat that could only be Harley Reno.

When they passed, Coop raised a fist in salute, and thought he saw the gleam of Harley's teeth as they flashed past, also running without headlights.

Moments later, Coop heard the rapid chatter of an MP-10, and saw in his mirror one of the pair of headlights following him veer sharply to the side and overturn, the headlights now vertical instead of side by side.

He chuckled to himself, thinking, good ol' Harley.

After another minute, a large fireball erupted into the

night sky as another of the chasing vehicles felt the sting of Harley's wrath.

Coop slowed and turned in his seat to see the final pair of headlights change direction and head back toward the road and the convoy of troops heading toward Tehran.

As dawn sunlight began to tinge the eastern horizon with shades of orange and gold, Coop stopped the Hum-Vee and got out of the car. He ran around to the passenger door and flung it open, slipping inside to check on Jersey.

Still unconscious, she moaned as he gently removed his belt from around her arm to check on her wound. Slipping his K-Bar assault knife from its scabbard, he sliced through her shirt and peeled it down over her chest.

There was a small hold in the front of her right biceps, and a slightly larger hole in the rear part of her arm where the slug had exited after plowing through the muscles of the upper arm.

"Thank God they're using steel-jacketed bullets," Coop mumbled to himself, thinking the wound would've been much worse with lead-tipped bullets.

He squeezed around the edges of the wound, checking for any signs of arterial bleeding, which would mean he'd have to reapply the tourniquet. There was only a slow oozing of dark blood—a good sign.

Jersey's head rolled to the side and her eyes blinked open. She stared down at her exposed breasts and then glanced up at Coop, whose eyes were firmly fixed on her shoulder wound.

"Hey, partner," she croaked through dry, chapped lips. "You trying to get a free look?"

He glanced down at her breasts once, and then shifted his attention back to her wound. "What?" he asked scornfully. "You think I'd waste my time scoping out those little things?"

He shook his head, a slight smile on his lips. "Hell, I've seen better breasts on a chicken, my dear."

Jersey managed a low chuckle. "In your dreams, mister."

And then she groaned as he wrapped a piece of her shirt tightly around the wound, pulling it tight to stop the oozing of blood.

"How bad is it?" she asked, not able to see in the early dawn light.

"You won't be shooting any assault rifles for a few weeks," he answered, "but you should be able to play the piano again."

"That's good," she said, her voice growing weaker as she began to feel faint again. "I've always wanted to play the piano."

As she slipped back into unconsciousness, Coop slipped his own shirt off and began to put it on Jersey.

When his eyes drifted downward, he smiled to himself. "Coop, ol' boy, you're a damn liar," he mumbled. "Those are really nice breasts!"

Just as Coop finished buttoning his shirt around Jersey, the jeep containing Anna and Harley drove up. Harley and Anna jumped from the vehicle and ran to the side of Coop's captured HumVee.

"Hey, thanks for the rescue, guys," Coop said.

Anna moved to Jersey's side. "How's Jersey?" she asked as she noticed the dressing on Jersey's arm.

"She got hit in the arm, looks like a through and through wound that missed the bone," Coop answered.

They all looked up as another series of explosions from the direction of the road into town occurred, accompanied by the sound of automatic-weapons fire that carried a good distance in the thin desert air.

Harley grinned. "Looks like the mobile troops are doing a pretty good job of slowing the convoy down," he said, rubbing his jaw.

Coop glanced skyward. "Yeah, an' dawn's just about here. The reinforcements oughta be landing soon."

"Why don't you take Jersey on back to the city where one of the medics can take a look at her?" Anna said. She looked over at the road and the long line of terrorist trucks in the distance. "Harley and I have some unfinished business over there."

"Will do," Coop said, and he got back in the driver's seat.

"Take it easy on your approach to town," Harley advised. "Remember, you're driving an enemy vehicle. We wouldn't want our boys to take you out without knowing you're one of us."

"Don't worry," Coop said, holding up the tattered remains of Jersey's BDU shirt. "I'll wave this like a flag as soon as I get close enough."

Ben was standing in the cockpit door as the big C-141 StarLifter followed the three Apache helicopter gunships toward the Tehran Airport. He was relieved to see columns of green smoke wafting into the dawn sky around the runways.

"Good," he said, "our men still have control of the airport."

The pilot nodded. "You want me to radio the Apaches to fly in a circle around the runways to make sure we get down okay?" he asked.

"Yeah," Ben answered, "if they've got enough fuel left."

The pilot got on the radio, and Ben moved back into

the cargo compartment where the rest of the Scout paratroopers were waiting.

"Shuck your chutes, men," he said, slipping out of his parachute. "Looks like we're gonna get the red-carpet treatment on this landing."

As the men began to get out of their parachute gear, Ben added, "But keep your weapons ready. I don't know how long we're going to have before the hostiles arrive, so we're going to deploy immediately in a line of defense around the runways until the rest of the big birds get down."

By the time all of the six C-14s had landed and the troops had disembarked and the Apaches had been refueled, Ben could hear heavy fighting going on in the city a few miles away.

He got on a SOHFRAD and got in touch with Major Jackson Bean, who was leading the forces in the city.

"Jackson," Ben said, "how are you holding up?"

"It's pretty heavy going, Ben," Bean replied, and Ben could hear the chatter of automatic fire and numerous explosions in the background.

"Okay," Ben replied. "Tell your men to hold on a while longer. I'm gonna send in the Apaches first, but it'll take a little while for me to get my troops there."

"Tell the 'Paches to take out the tanks first, Ben. They're blowing hell out of the buildings we're holed up in," Bean said, evident relief in his voice.

"Roger that," Ben said, and switched his frequency on the SOHFRAD to the one used by the chopper pilots.

"This is Lieutenant Commander Dooley," the leader of the chopper squad answered.

"Hey, Tom, this is General Raines," Ben said. "Our

boys need a little help with some enemy tanks in the city. Think you can oblige?"

"Tell your men to give us five minutes and we'll be in their faces," Dooley answered.

Ben saw the three helicopters take off and make a beeline for the city, flying at high speed no more than a hundred feet off the ground.

Ben almost felt sorry for the tanks . . . almost.

As he sped toward the city, Lieutenant Commander Dooley flipped a switch that locked his Hellfire missiles into the ship's targeting radar, and got ready to make life miserable for some tank jockeys.

On the way into the city, Dooley triggered off his chain gun as he passed hordes of enemy ground troops, grinning as the saw hundreds of bodies torn asunder by the thousands of shells from the gun.

He didn't slow or change his course until he saw an old Army-surplus Abrams tank in the middle of a wide boulevard firing at a six-story building.

He put the tank in the middle of his targeting screen, locked it on, and pressed a button. He felt a jolt as one of his six Hellfire missiles launched from the pod on his right side. The missile streaked downward almost faster than the eye could follow.

The tank exploded in a huge fireball, and Dooley had to jerk the stick to the side to miss the ball of flame that shot into the air.

As he circled around, looking for another target, his Plexiglas windshield was pocked and starred by bullet holes as he came under fire from a fifty-caliber machine gun in the back of a HumVee on the street next to the burning tank.

Dooley triggered his chain gun and tore up the street

on all sides of the HumVee, but somehow managed to miss the vehicle.

As he dove toward the rattling machine gun, Dooley felt as if someone had kicked him in the leg, and he looked down and saw a hole in his thigh he could put a fist in.

As his vision began to blur, Dooley shifted his aim slightly and saw with satisfaction the HumVee disintegrating beneath the onslaught of his chain gun.

Sweat pouring from his forehead and dripping down into his eyes, Dooley knew he had only seconds before he blacked out completely. Blood was pumping from his ruined leg at an alarming rate.

He looked around, but saw no place to land. "The hell with it," he gasped, and wrenched the stick to the side. Another tank came into view, surrounded by enemy troops who were using it as a shield while they attacked a building that had several Scouts on the roof.

Dooley couldn't see well enough to target the tank with a Hellfire missile, so he just lowered the nose, pushed the throttle to full speed, and watched as the troops below scattered trying to get out of his way.

They failed. The Apache hit the tank at almost two hundred miles an hour, and all five of the remaining Hellfire missiles exploded on impact, blowing a crater twenty feet deep and killing almost three hundred troops in the explosion.

The blast was so intense it knocked the Scouts on the building rooftop off their feet, but saved their lives.

By this time, Ben and the rest of the troops had begun to arrive in the city, catching the enemy troops between them, the defenders of the city, and the two remaining

Apache helicopters that were wreaking havoc on the armored vehicles below.

Ben, unlike most generals before him, didn't command the troops from the rear ranks. He was right at the forefront of the arriving troops, carrying his own Thunder Lizard, an ancient M-14 that he preferred in combat.

Since this was practically hand-to-hand combat, Ben had told his squad leaders to do whatever they thought necessary to save the men defending the city. He knew he wouldn't have time to personally direct the battle.

The SUSA troops attacked in a wide line, spread out enough so that they wouldn't make a concentrated target. They attacked with a ferocity never seen by the terrorist troops, screaming and running right into intense enemy fire. There was absolutely no back down in the Scouts commanded by General Ben Raines.

Within a half hour, the terrified terrorists, though they outnumbered the attackers five to one, began to retreat under the vicious onslaught of the Scouts.

When some of the terrorists tried to surrender, they were summarily mowed down by the advancing SUSA troops, who didn't have the time or the manpower to deal with prisoners of war.

THIRTY-EIGHT

Coop, driving like a bat out of hell, made it though the checkpoints at the city limits ahead of the enemy troops, but just barely.

The Scouts positioned there as advance guards grinned as he waved Jersey's bloody BDU shirt and raced through their positions.

He pulled the HumVee to a stop outside the headquarters building and opened Jersey's door. He was shocked at the paleness of her face when she opened her eyes and asked, "Where are we?"

"We're home, baby," he said gently, and reached in and picked her up in his arms.

She shook her head. "Put me down, Coop. I can walk," she protested weakly.

"Bullshit," he said quickly, and proceeded to carry her up the four flights of stairs to the room where the medic was attending to wounded troops.

He laid her gently down on a cot next to Buddy, who was now awake. Buddy grimaced as he rolled on his side to look at Jersey.

"Hey, Jerse," he said. "You catch one too?"

"Yes, sir, I guess so," Jersey answered as the medic bent over her and began to remove the dressing Coop had put there.

As the medic unbuttoned her shirt, he glanced up at Coop. "You'd better leave, Coop," he said.

Coop grinned, staring into Jersey's eyes. "Don't worry, Doc," he said. "I've seen 'em before."

Jersey's eyes narrowed and she scowled. "Coop, so help me, if you breathe a word . . ."

He held up his hands, palms out. "Don't worry, darlin'," he drawled with a smirk on his face, "my lips are sealed."

Jersey laid her head back and moaned, "Oh, God, why did you cause me to have to put up with this?"

Major Bean stuck his head in the door. "Coop, if you've got a minute, could you give me an idea of what we're facing?"

Coop bent down and patted Jersey on her good shoulder, the one with only a bullet crease in it. "I'll see you later, Jerse. Duty calls." As he walked toward the door, he added over his shoulder, "Now you mind the doc, you hear?"

"Get out!" Jersey commanded, though her eyes held the hint of a smile.

As the attack on the terrorist troops was pushed forward by Ben Raines and his Scouts, the mobile units sent out by Major Jackson Bean joined them in the fight, moving in and out of the fracas in their jeeps and HumVees and the other assorted vehicles they'd used to harass the enemy troops on the road into the city.

In the headquarters building, while Coop and Major Bean and a few other Scouts were firing from windows and the roof down on the advancing terrorists, Jersey had to be physically restrained from joining in the battle.

"Hell," she groused as the medic ordered her back to her cot, "I can still fire with my left hand!"

"You pull those stitches out, soldier," the medic said in frustration, "and I'll put them back in without anesthetic!"

Haji Kuchkool, seeing his troops in near rout after the arrival of Ben Raines and the reinforcements, yelled in rage at his troops to regroup and fight back, but it was no use.

Demoralized by the constant attacks of the Apache helicopters and the ferocity of Raines's troops, the terrorists began to run out into the desert and deeper into the city, trying to escape being slaughtered by the oncoming SUSA men and women.

Kuchkool's driver, seeing the desertions of his fellow troops, looked across the seat at Kuchkool. "Perhaps we should leave and try and make our way back to our ships in port, sir," he said.

Kuchkool, knowing that to escape would also mean certain death at the hands of El Farrar for his failure, shook his head. "No, we fight to the death here!"

Farid Zamet, realizing the fight was already lost, disagreed, though he didn't dare voice this opinion to Kuchkool.

As Kuchkool ordered his driver to drive toward the thick of the battle, Zamet, in the backseat, quietly opened the door and dove out of the HumVee as it careened down the street toward a group of soldiers in hand-to-hand combat.

Seconds after he hit the street and rolled into the gutter, he heard a loud roaring overhead and saw one of the Apache helicopters rushing downward at the HumVee.

He ducked and covered his head just as the rattling chain gun shredded the vehicle and its two occupants into confetti-sized bits and pieces.

Zamet got to his feet and dusted himself off, his hands shaking at the closeness of the call. He was still dressed in civilian clothes instead of the terrorist uniform favored by the troops, and hoped he would be able to melt into the Muslim community of Tehran and disappear from sight. With luck, someday he could make his way back home and take up life with his family again. His days of revolution were over.

By mid-afternoon, the battle was all but over. Of the ten thousand terrorist troops that had come to Iran, less than a few hundred were left alive, and most of them were on the run in the desert trying to escape.

While his squad leaders rooted out isolated groups of terrorists that were still fighting, Ben entered the headquarters building occupied by Major Jackson Bean.

Harley Reno, Anna, Hammer Hammerick, and Beth and Corrie joined him. He'd run into them in the streets outside the building, and asked them to accompany him to see Major Bean.

Bean met him at the top of the stairs. "Hello, Ben. Glad to see you," Bean said, shaking Ben's hand.

Ben laughed. "Glad to see you too, Jackson."

Bean waved a hand at a nearby doorway. "Buddy's in here."

Ben nodded and walked into the room. Buddy was lying on a cot next to Jersey, who was being fussed over by Coop. He was trying to get her to drink some juice.

"Jerse, the doc says you lost a lot of blood. He wants you to drink this."

"I told you once, Coop, I'm *not* thirsty," Jersey replied, clamping her lips tight.

"You want me to make you drink it?" Coop asked, scowling.

"You and what army?" Jersey asked, her voice low and dangerous. "Even with one arm I can still kick your butt, Cooper!"

Ben laughed out loud. "Jesus, I'm glad to see things haven't changed."

Buddy looked over at him and smiled. "They've been going at it like this for hours. Thank God you're here to make them stop."

"Sir," Coop said in exasperation, "would you order Jersey to drink this? The doc says she needs it."

Ben held out his hands. "Uh-uh, Coop. I'm just an adviser here. Buddy is still in charge."

Buddy shook his head. "No, Ben. The medic says I'm gonna need some major surgery when we get back home. It looks like you've got your old job back."

Ben smiled, and even though he tried to hide it, it was clear he'd missed leading his team into combat.

"So, General," Major Bean said from behind Ben. "What do we do now?"

Ben turned, his face grim. "Now we go after the bastard who started all this . . . Abdullah El Farrar!"

THIRTY-NINE

Lieutenant Sohail Shaeen couldn't believe the infidel commander, and it was a woman no less, trusted him with a jeep. As he drove toward the oil fields in the distance, he reflected that it wasn't all that much of an opportunity after all. If he tried to escape by driving out into the desert, all she had to do was to send one of those devilish helicopters after him.

On the way to meet his comrades and try to talk them into surrendering, he thought about the infidels and their strange ways. Imagine, letting a woman fight in the army, and even more strange, putting one in a command position where men would have to take orders from her! And to make matters worse, she hadn't even had her head or face covered.

He shook his head. That would never work with Muslim troops. In the Muslim world, women were kept in the place God intended: in the home, cooking and cleaning and obeying their man's orders. In fact, in most of the countries Shaeen had been in, women weren't even allowed education. That would only put unrealistic ideas in their heads. He'd heard that in the infidels' world, women considered themselves equal to men—an absurd notion on the face of it.

Still, he had to admit, the woman's army had defeated

his, and rather handily too. He made a face and spat out the side of the jeep. No, it couldn't be. She must have had a man telling her what to do the entire time. That was the only thing that made any sense to him.

Now, putting these crazy ideas out of his head, he had to decide what to do when he came to the oil fields. Should he instruct the men to fight to the death and to destroy as many of the oil rigs as they could before they were killed? That was surely what the Desert Fox, Abdullah El Farrar, would want.

On the other hand, Shaeen thought, it was one thing to be a martyr when you had at least some small hope of changing things for the betterment of the Muslim world. It was quite another to die when the war was already lost and to accomplish nothing by dying.

Surely Allah did not want his servants to die needlessly. Perhaps *he* would rather have his faithful men surrender and live to fight the infidels another day. After all, the Westerners were known for their softness when it came to prisoners. They didn't have the sense to destroy their enemies, but would in most cases let them live to come back and fight against them in years to come.

Shaeen smiled to himself. That was it! He would convince his soldiers to give themselves up, telling them that that way they could survive and reform another army in the future to kill the devil infidels.

As the jeep approached the first of the oil derricks, some overanxious soldier began to shoot at Shaeen, as if he were an enemy soldier.

Two slugs shattered the windshield of the jeep, causing Shaeen to swerve to the side and hurriedly jump out onto the sand so the soldiers could see his uniform.

When there were no further shots, Shaeen stood up and waved his arms in the air, shouting in Arabic that he was a friend.

After a few moments, a man in a corporal's uniform stepped out from behind the oil derrick and waved Shaeen forward.

Shaeen approached him and tried to remember the man's name, but it wouldn't come to him.

When the man saluted, Shaeen returned the salute and said, "I am Lieutenant Sohail Shaeen."

The man gave a slight bow of his head. "I am Corporal Hekmatullah, sir."

"Are you in charge of the forces guarding the oil rigs, Hekmatullah?" Shaeen asked, glancing around, thinking there should be someone here of higher rank.

"Yes, sir, I guess so," Hekmatullah answered, looking a bit uncomfortable. "There was a lieutenant here last night, but he was supervising the placing of the mines on the oil rigs and there was an accident. One of the mines went off prematurely," Hekmatullah finished, glancing off to the north.

Shaeen followed his gaze and saw the still-smoking ruin of a distant oil rig. Its derrick was collapsed and the girders were bent and twisted as if some giant had stepped on the steel and crushed it underfoot.

"I see," Shaeen said.

"Do you have news of the fight in the city?" Hekmatullah asked. "How goes it?"

Shaeen hung his head. "I am sorry to say we have lost the battle, Corporal. Haji Kuchkool fought a glorious fight, but we were severely outnumbered," Shaeen lied, thinking the men would feel better if they thought that was the case, rather than know the truth, which was that the Muslim soldiers had been outfought.

"Then, we must martyr ourselves and blow up the oil rigs," Hekmatullah said vigorously. "That was Commander Kuchkool's final order to us when he sent us here to mine the rigs."

"No, that is no longer the case," Shaeen said. "I spoke with Commander Kuchkool just before he was killed in the battle."

"Commander Kuchkool is dead?" Hekmatullah asked, his face a mask of disbelief that such a thing was possible.

"Yes, I am afraid so," Shaeen said. "However, just before he was killed, he told me that I had to tell the men to save themselves and to not blow up the oil field."

"But . . . why?" Hekmatullah asked.

"He told me that Allah needed all of his faithful soldiers to stay alive so they could come back and fight another day against the infidel pigs," Shaeen said, casting his eyes heavenward as if Allah had told Kuchkool this himself.

"But if we surrender, the infidel soldiers will kill us," Hekmatullah said.

"No, that is not true," Shaeen said. "The infidels are much too soft to do that. They will hold us here for a while, and then we will be returned home to our families, where El Farrar will find us when he is again ready to do battle with the foreign devils."

Hekmatullah looked doubtful. "Are you sure that is what Commander Kuchkool ordered?"

Shaeen raised his hand toward the sky. "As Allah is my witness," he said, mentally hoping Allah would forgive him this small lie since it was in *his* service he said it.

"Do you want us to remove the mines from the wells?" Hekmatullah asked.

Shaeen thought for a moment, and then he shook his head. "No, we are not here to do the infidels' work for them. We will surrender, but if they want the mines removed, they can do it themselves."

It was less than an hour and a half after Jackie Malone had sent Lieutenant Sohail Shaeen into the desert that her sentries reported he was on the way back. His jeep was leading a long column of men who were on foot as they headed toward Riyadh.

Jackie glanced out of her headquarters window. She leaned out and hollered down at one of her squad leaders. "Make sure they're unarmed and then put them somewhere where we can keep an eye on them."

"Yes, ma'am," the soldier said.

Jackie turned back to Bartholomew Wiley-Smeyth, with whom she'd been talking. "Bart, what do you think we ought to do with the prisoners?"

Bart shrugged. "I don't know, Jackie. As far as my government is concerned, about all they could tell us of any interest is where they obtained the plutonium they used in their initial oil rig mines."

She nodded. "Yeah, and I'll bet you dollars to donuts none of these lower-level guys know dick about that."

"I agree. For that kind of information, we're going to have to go to the original source, this El Farrar or one of his top lieutenants."

She frowned. "I just hope the bastard isn't in Afghanistan or some such godforsaken place. It'd be hell trying to roust him out of there."

"Why don't you check in with General Raines? Maybe he has some intel on El Farrar's current location."

"Good idea. I need to call him and tell him we're all clear here anyway."

Jackie went into the communications room and had the radio officer put in a call to the SUSA headquarters in Tehran. After a few moments, Ben Raines was on the line.

"Hello, Jackie," Ben said. "What's your situation?"

"A-1, Ben. We've taken the city of Riyadh and we've cleared the terrorists out of the oil fields. There are still some conventional mines and booby traps hooked up to the rigs, but I'll have my explosives guys go over the field with a fine-tooth comb tomorrow at first light and clean them out."

"Excellent, Jackie. We're in about the same situation here, but at least the major threat to the world's oil supply has been averted."

"Ben, I do have a couple of questions for you."

"Shoot."

"First of all, what do you want us to do with our prisoners? We've got a few thousand men here who are too dangerous to just release into the country."

She heard a low chuckle come over the air. "My first thought would be to turn them over to the Saudi royal family. They're not gonna be too happy with a group of men who tried to take their oil revenues away."

"But Ben, you know what they'll do. They'll have a mass beheading and kill every one of the poor sons of bitches."

"I know, and that's probably what needs to be done. These men came a long way to impose their will on the rest of the world, and I don't think if we show mercy and let them go home, they're gonna go back to herding sheep and goats and be good little boys."

"You're right, Ben, but it still goes against my grain to kill prisoners."

"Mine too, Jackie, but we can't be responsible for what other sovereign nations do with their prisoners."

"Okay. I was just talking with Commander Bartholomew Wiley-Smeyth, and he said his government would very much like to find out where this El Farrar got the plutonium he used."

"That will be the first question I ask him when I see him," Ben said in a low, dangerous voice.

"You have any idea where he is?" Jackie asked.

"Not at the present, but I've got Mike Post in Intel working on it."

"Okay, Ben. I'll check back after I've gotten the prisoners taken care of."

"Roger, Jackie."

"And Ben."

"Yeah?"

"I'd very much appreciate being in on the op when you go after El Farrar."

"I wouldn't have it any other way, Jackie."

Jackie told Bart what Ben had said, and then went to see to the disposition of the prisoners. After placing a call to the royal palace and being assured that the Saudi royal family would indeed take possession of the prisoners the first thing in the morning, Jackie went to take a look at them for herself.

The prisoners had been placed in a huge arena that Jackie was told had been used for sheep and goat auctions.

She and Bart stood in the stands, looking at the prisoners as they milled around the dirt floor of the arena.

"A pretty dangerous-looking lot," Bart observed.

"Yeah, but I still wish there were something else we could do other than turn them over to be executed," Jackie said.

As she spoke, her eyes fell on a soldier dressed in an officer's uniform. He looked a cut above the others, both in intelligence and demeanor.

"Isn't that the men who arranged for the men in the oil field to surrender?" Jackie asked, pointing Sohail Shaeen out to Bart.

"Why, yes, I think it is," Bart replied.

She glanced at Bart. "You know, he did us an enormous favor by getting those men to give themselves up without destroying the oil rigs," she said.

Bart smiled down at her. "You want to save him, don't you?" he asked.

"I think it'd be the right thing to do," Jackie replied.

"Then, by all means," Bart said, waving his hand in front of her, "be my guest."

Jackie told a nearby guard to have Shaeen brought to her office in the headquarters building.

Sohail Shaeen stood at attention in front of Jackie's desk, his eyes averted from the infidel woman.

"Your name?" Jackie asked.

"Lieutenant Sohail Shaeen," he replied, keeping his eyes straight ahead.

"Do you know what is going to happen to your fellow soldiers, Lieutenant Shaeen?"

He shrugged. "We will be held a while and then you

will send us home. That is the way it has always been with you infidels."

Jackie shook her head. "Not this time, Lieutenant."

The tone of her voice finally made him look at her.

"This time, we're turning you over to the imperial guards of the Saudi royal family here in Saudi. The men in Iran will be turned over to the government troops there."

"But they will surely execute us," Shaeen said, his eyes wide.

"That'd be my guess, Lieutenant."

Shaeen straightened his back and firmed his lips. "Is that all?" he asked, ready to return to join his men.

"Lieutenant, you did us a good deed when you got your men to surrender without a fight. If you will make me a promise never to take up arms again, I will see to it that you are given a chance to return to your home."

"Hah!" he said, a look of derision on his face. "Why would you believe me even if I agreed to say that?"

"Are you a religious man, Lieutenant?"

"I am a devout Muslim!" he answered.

"And doesn't Islam teach that it is a sin to lie?" she asked.

"Yes, certainly."

"Then, if you give me your word, I will let you go free."

As Shaeen thought about her offer, a vision of his wife and two young children back in Pakistan flashed into his mind.

"Then I give you my word," he said.

FORTY

Abdullah El Farrar was furious, and he was making no effort to conceal the fact from the men with him in Dhahran. Muhammad Atwa was in his office, a fine sheen of sweat on his face, worrying that El Farrar would take out his anger on him.

El Farrar had the radioman in front of his desk, and he was grilling him unmercifully.

"Do you mean to tell me that you cannot establish contact with either Jamal Ahmed or Haji Kuchkool?" he asked, his face a mask of anger and disbelief.

"Yes, sir," Omar Othman, the unfortunate man in charge of communications, replied. "I was in contact with both of them last evening, and they were about to proceed with attacks on Tehran and Riyadh. They informed me they would be back in touch once they had managed to retake the cities back from the infidel soldiers."

"And you have heard nothing since last night?"

"No, sir. The last message from each of them indicated they had control of the oil fields and were about to attack the cities. In fact, Commander Ahmed indicated his men were already in the oil fields and were in the process of mining the oil rigs with explosives."

"What about Commander Kuchkool?"

"He said that his men had driven the infidels out of

the oil fields, but because they'd left the fields mined with traps, he was going to take the city and then return to the oil fields at first light to remove the infidels' mines and then replace them with his own."

"Then why haven't we heard from them?" El Farrar asked, slamming his hand down on his desk.

Othman shrugged. "I do not know, sir. I have been at the radio continuously since the last messages were received, and I have tried to call them both several times. I have gotten no answers to any of my calls."

El Farrar turned his attention to Atwa. "What do you think, Muhammad?"

Atwa hesitated. He hated to tell El Farrar what he really thought, but he had to say something. "There can be several explanations for the lapse in communications, my leader," he answered diplomatically. "The battles for the city might still be going on and the commanders could be too busy to use the radio, or their radios may have been damaged in the battle and they have no way to fix them until the battles are over and the cities are secured."

"Do you think that is a possibility, Omar?" El Farrar asked.

Omar Othman hesitated. "I do not think so, sir. Each of the armies had several backup radios with them. It would be extremely unlikely that all would be so damaged they could not place a call."

El Farrar waved a hand at Othman. "That is all, Omar. Stay by your radio and notify me immediately if there is any word."

"Yes, sir," Othman replied, and he hurriedly left the room to return to his post.

El Farrar turned to stare at Atwa. "There is one other possibility you neglected to mention, Muhammad."

"Oh?"

"Perhaps both of my commanders have failed in their attempts to take the cities."

"But sir," Atwa said, "surely that is not possible. Our information was that the infidels had very minimal forces in the regions. How could they possibly defeat over twenty thousand men armed with the latest weapons and equipment?"

"You forget, Muhammad. We are up against the devil himself, Ben Raines. I would put nothing past him, even the seemingly impossible."

"But just for the sake of argument," Atwa said, rubbing his beard with his right hand as he thought, "if we have lost this war and our armies have been defeated, what are we going to do?"

"One thing is for sure," El Farrar said. "We do not dare to return to Afghanistan or even to our previous homes. The men and families who backed us in this endeavor will not be happy to see us if we have lost the war."

"What about the United States?" Atwa asked. "Do you think President Osterman would give us sanctuary?"

El Farrar laughed bitterly. "If we lose this war, the president will pretend she has never heard of us, Muhammad." He shook his head. "No, I think we had better think of someplace else to retire to if the news is as bad as we fear."

"But who would take us in with the entire world searching for us?" Atwa asked.

El Farrar didn't answer. He was already trying to figure out if the money he'd held back out of the funds his backers had provided was going to be enough to bribe some country's leaders into giving him shelter. He looked at Atwa out of the corner of his eyes. One thing was certain.

It was not nearly enough for two men, so Atwa was going to be left behind if he decided to make a run for it.

Ben was in the process of arranging for the wounded, including Jersey and Buddy, to be airlifted to Kuwait City in one of the C-14s when he was notified that Mike Post was on the radio wishing to speak to him.

He went into the communications room and took the microphone from Corrie.

"Ben Raines here," he said.

"Hello, Ben," Mike replied. "I've finally got some information on the whereabouts of Abdullah El Farrar and his top men for you."

"Good," Ben answered, anxious to find out where the leader of the terrorists was so he could finish his campaign against the terrorists.

"The last word we have on him is that he went to the port city of Dhahran in Saudi Arabia in his Lear jet a few days ago. Evidently, he wanted to personally supervise the retaking of Riyadh and Tehran."

"Do you think he's still there, now that his army has been so thoroughly defeated?"

"My contact in Dhahran says the Lear jet is still on the runway, but he can't confirm just where El Farrar is staying in the city or even if he is in fact still present."

"Thanks, Mike," Ben said. "Maybe I'll just take a little trip to Dhahran and find out for myself."

Ben signed off the radio, and then asked Corrie to get him in touch with Jean-François Chapelle at the United Nations.

Chapelle was on the line in minutes. "Hello, Ben," Chapelle said.

"Hello, Jean-François," Ben replied. "We have good

news for you. The terrorist armies have been defeated and the oil facilities are in safe hands once again."

Ben could almost hear the sigh of relief from Chapelle. "That is excellent news, Ben. The world owes you a great debt of gratitude."

"I will leave my soldiers here until they can be replaced by United Nations troops, Jean-François," Ben said.

"I will make arrangements immediately to have your troops relieved, Ben."

"That's good, Jean-François," Ben said. "I've still got a little mopping up to do, and then we can put this behind us."

"Oh?"

"Yes. Abdullah El Farrar is still at large, and I will need to see to it that he causes no more mischief before I'll consider the episode finished," Ben said.

"Good luck and good hunting, Ben," Chapelle said before signing off.

"Corrie," Ben said after she'd disconnected from Chapelle. "You have one more call to make. Get me Jackie Malone on the horn. I want to make a date with her to call on El Farrar as soon as possible."

Ben gathered his team together in the ready room of his headquarters building. Everyone was present except for Buddy and Jersey, who'd had to be sedated when she was told she wouldn't be able to accompany them on this next mission.

"Get your gear together, men and ladies," Ben said. "We're gonna make a call on the man who started this mess and make sure he pays for his deeds."

"Full parachute gear, Ben?" Harley asked, his teeth bared in a savage grin.

"Yeah. The quickest way to get to him is to make a drop outside the city of Dhahran just before dusk. I'm sure he's got the airport guarded, so we'll just drop in unannounced and surprise him.

"Oh, and Jackie Malone and Commander Bartholomew Wiley-Smeyth have asked to join us, so they'll be coming in from Riyadh at the same time. We're to rendezvous five miles west of the Dhahran Airport."

"Sounds like a great party," Coop said. "Too bad Jerse and Buddy won't get to attend."

"They'll be with us in spirit," Ben said, and he got to his feet and led the team from the room.

FORTY-ONE

Jackie Malone checked her GPS instrument, and saw that she was at the exact coordinates Ben had given her when they made arrangements to meet in the desert outside Dhahran.

It was just after dark, and she could see nothing in the scant starlight. Bartholomew Wiley-Smeyth, his aide, Sergeant Major Alphonse Green, and the Davidson brothers were with her.

She gave a low whistle, and was relieved when it was answered from a dozen yards away.

Soon, Ben and his team, along with Major Jackson Bean, Willie Running Bear, Samuel Clements, and Sue Waters, appeared out of the darkness.

Jackie grinned and shook hands with Ben. "Boy," she said, looking around at the men and women in the group. "This is like old-home week."

"Do you think we have enough men, Ben?" Bart asked.

Ben nodded. "Yeah. Our Intel says there's no sign of a significant number of men here with El Farrar in Dhahran. My guess is he kept just his personal guards and enough men and equipment to hold the airport and protect his jet."

"Any idea where he's holed up?" Jackie asked.

"No, but it's got to be near the airport," Ben answered.

"He wouldn't want to get too far away from his jet in case things went bad for him."

Ben turned and looked toward the airport lights, a few miles away. They appeared closer in the thin desert air. "Let's spread out in a line and move toward the airport. Be careful. We don't know where the sentries he'll have posted are."

Harley and Anna moved off together, as did Hammer and Beth. Coop moved next to Corrie. "Mind if I tag along with you?" he asked.

She glanced down at his leg, noticing he was still limping on it. "How's the ankle?" she asked, adjusting the straps on the portable SOHFRAD on her back.

"The medic double-taped it for the jump, so it ought to be okay," he replied, not mentioning the pain that stabbed up his leg with every step.

The rest of the group moved off in teams of two, and made their way toward the airport lights. Dressed all in black with black greasepaint on their faces, they were almost invisible from only a few yards away.

Since they had to move slowly and be on the lookout for sentries, it took them almost an hour to walk the three or so miles to the outskirts of the airport.

As they crouched just outside the light cast by the runway spotlights, they could see teams of men patrolling the runways, and several armed men in the control tower across the way.

Ben pointed to each of the sentries one at a time, and then to a team that he wanted to take them out. All of the Scouts' guns were silenced, so there wouldn't be any noise, but when the men went down, the guards in the control tower were sure to notice.

"We hit the runway guards in five minutes from . . . *now*," Ben said. He pointed to Harley and Anna. "You two take out the control tower thirty seconds later. Make sure you get the radio antenna so they can't warn anyone of the attack."

Harley Reno and Anna moved over until they were directly across from the control tower, and squatted as close to the runway as they could get without being in the light.

When the other teams began to take out the guards, Harley and Reno jumped up and sprinted as fast as they could across the two runways between them and the control tower.

Abu Sayyaf, the lieutenant in charge of the night-shift guards, was in the corner of the control tower pouring himself a cup of coffee when one of the guards in the tower yelled, "Abu, come here!"

Sayyaf cursed when the man's yell caused him to pour hot coffee on his hand.

"What is it, Essar?" he exclaimed irritably, wiping his hand on his pants and moving to the window overlooking the airfield.

"Look there!" Essar cried, pointing at the men patrolling the runways.

The men were grabbing themselves and falling to the ground as limp as rag dolls.

"What the . . . ?" Sayyaf said. The men appeared to have been shot, but he heard no sounds of gunfire.

His attention was caught by two figures running across the runways toward the control tower. They were dressed all in black and looked to be carrying rifles.

"In the name of Allah, we're being attacked!" Sayyaf yelled, turning to the radio to call and warn El Farrar.

The two running figures suddenly dropped, kneeling

on one knee as they pointed their weapons at the control tower windows.

Though no sound came from their weapons, the tower windows shattered under the onslaught of hundreds of bullets.

Essar, standing by the window, was riddled with slugs and whirled around, his uniform covered with blood.

Sayyaf frantically keyed the microphone, but heard only static as the desk the radio was on suddenly exploded into splinters as steel-jacketed slugs tore into it.

Sayyaf threw the microphone down and reached for his Kalashnikov, standing in a corner.

He stumbled, feeling as if he'd been kicked in the back by a mule, and fell to the floor. He glanced down and saw red stains appearing on his tunic, and then the pain came, like molten lead being poured on his skin.

He had time to scream once, before blackness opened up in front of him and he dived in.

Once the airport was secure, Ben gathered his team and had a conference. "Now, we've got to find which of the buildings near the airport El Farrar is using as his headquarters."

Jackie nodded. "Spread out and each of you teams take a different building. Report back on your headsets to the others if you find a building with sentries."

Muhammad Atwa, unable to sleep, was standing on the balcony outside his bedroom, sipping a scotch whiskey and smoking a cigar. Both activities were considered sins in the Muslim religion, but Atwa didn't care. His meeting with El Farrar earlier had left him with lots of things to worry about, and the smoke and the scotch helped to calm his nerves.

He almost dropped his whiskey when he happened to glance toward the control tower of the airport, a few hundred yards away, and saw the windows disintegrating and the flash of what could only be small-arms fire from the runways.

He heard no gunshots, but he knew what was happening. Their base was under attack.

He ran back into the bedroom and threw on his robes and clothes as fast as he could. He knew there was precious little time before the attackers found their headquarters building.

As soon as he was dressed, he ran down the hall and banged on El Farrar's door.

"Abdullah, wake up!" he screamed.

The door opened and a sleepy El Farrar glared out at him. "What is it, Muhammad? Bad dreams?" El Farrar asked sarcastically as he rubbed his eyes.

"The airport! We're under attack!" Atwa yelled, pushing past El Farrar into his bedroom. "Wake up the guards!"

El Farrar came instantly awake. He moved quickly to the phone on a desk in the middle of the room and dialed a number. Speaking rapidly, he alerted the guards of the situation and ordered them to take up defensive positions in the building at once.

He hung up the phone and moved without speaking to his closet. Instead of El Farrar putting on his uniform, Atwa noticed he dressed in civilian clothes—the robes and headdress of a typical Saudi citizen.

Once he was dressed, El Farrar took a suitcase from the back of his closet and threw it on the bed.

"What are you doing?" Atwa asked. "We don't have time to pack."

El Farrar smiled grimly. "The suitcase is already packed, my friend. It has bearer bonds in it worth five million dollars."

"But, what . . ." Atwa started to ask, until he saw the pistol suddenly appear in El Farrar's hand.

"I'm sorry, Muhammad," El Farrar said. "You've been a good and loyal friend, but I only have enough for one."

Atwa whirled and dove for the door just as El Farrar fired. The bullet entered Atwa's back just to the right of his spine and threw him facedown on the floor.

El Farrar picked up the suitcase and hurried down the hall toward a back stairway. He had no intention of staying and fighting. Much better to run away and live to fight another day, he thought to himself as he made his way down the stairs and out a side door of the building into the darkness.

Coop, who was walking toward the building when the lights came on and a shot rang out, immediately notified the other teams of the building's location.

Within minutes, the building was surrounded and the teams were trading fire with the guards that seemed to be at every window.

A lone figure scurried from the side of the building and ran up a dark street just as the first shots began.

Coop saw the man escape, and made his way down the line of Scouts until he came to Ben.

After he quickly explained what he'd seen, Ben grinned, his teeth gleaming in the starlight. "I think the head rat is abandoning his ship," he growled.

"Jackie," he said to Malone, who was lying next to him firing into the second-story windows. "Take over here," he ordered, and he ran off into the darkness after the fleeing figure.

It didn't take too long for the Scouts under Jackie's leadership to take out most of the guards in the building. Once the murderous fire of the Scouts' automatic weapons had pinned down the guards, Willie Running Bear and Sue Waters ran to the main door.

Running Bear kicked the door in, and Sue lobbed a couple of fragmentation grenades into the first floor. When they went off, killing the guards there and filling the stairway with billowing smoke, it was only a matter of a few minutes before the guards that were left alive on the upper floors threw down their weapons and surrendered.

As the defeated men filed out of the building, Coop and Harley and Hammer Hammerick rushed up the stairs to make sure the building was cleared.

Coop entered the room that El Farrar had used as his office, and found Muhammad Atwa laying in a pool of blood. Since he was the only wounded man in the building who wasn't in uniform, Coop called down to Jackie that she should come up.

Jackie kneeled next to the wounded man and rolled him over. Atwa coughed and spewed blood from his lips, indicating he had a lung wound.

"We need to save this one," she said. "He might know something useful."

Samuel Clements, who doubled as a medic, took his medical pack and began to apply field dressings to the wound in Atwa's back, then gave him a shot of morphine to help ward off shock and some antibiotics to prevent infection.

After a few moments, Atwa's eyes opened and he glanced around at the Scouts standing over him.

"Am I going to live?" he asked, his voice slurring from the morphine.

Jackie glanced at Clements, who shrugged and nodded. "I think so," she said.

"Then, perhaps a glass of scotch would be in order," Atwa groaned. "It's in the next room."

Jackie laughed. The man had balls. She glanced up at Coop. "Get him his scotch," she said. "It's the least we can do."

FORTY-TWO

Ben jogged down the dark street, carrying his H&P MP-10 cradled in his arms. Up ahead, he could see a man wearing the flowing white robes of a Saudi citizen walking at a fast pace and carrying a suitcase in his right hand.

Ben slowed and moved in behind the man, making sure he made no sounds as he trailed the man. Waiting until there were no other people around, Ben called softly, "Abdullah El Farrar."

The man jerked as if he'd received an electric shock, and then he stood stock still, not looking behind him.

"I am afraid you're mistaken," the man said as he slowly turned around. "My name is Ahmed Ressam and I am a citizen of Saudi Arabia."

Ben laughed out loud, letting the barrel of his MP-10 drop toward the ground. "Bullshit!" he said. "Your name is Abdullah El Farrar, and you are not only a scoundrel, you are a coward who deserted the men who'd followed him into battle."

El Farrar's eyes narrowed, and Ben saw his hand move toward a fold in his robes.

Ben raised the barrel of the MP-10 and clicked the safety off with a metallic sound. "If that's a gun in your robes, you'd better not pull it or I'll cut you to pieces."

El Farrar slowly let his hand fall to his side. Ben moved

in close, reached into his robes, and pulled out the automatic pistol El Farrar had hidden there.

"You must be the infamous Ben Raines," El Farrar said scornfully.

"One and the same," Ben replied, stepping back a few paces.

"I assume I am under arrest?" El Farrar asked, setting the suitcase down on the street.

Ben pursed his lips. "No, not tonight, El Farrar. You are much too dangerous a man to leave alive, even in captivity."

"So, you plan to shoot me down in cold blood?" El Farrar asked, his eyes wide.

Ben shook his head. "Nope, not my style," he replied, laying the MP-10 down on the ground.

El Farrar nodded and smiled evilly, his hand going to the curved knife on his belt that all male Saudis wore with their robes.

Ben grinned back and pulled his K-Bar assault knife from his scabbard. "I'm going to give you a chance, El Farrar," he said. "Defeat me, and you go free."

"You are a fool, Ben Raines," El Farrar said, "To try and best an Arab in a knife fight is to lose your life."

Ben crouched, holding his K-Bar in the underhanded manner of the experienced knife-fighter.

"We'll see," he said, and moved from side to side as he closed the space between them.

El Farrar also crouched, waving his curved stiletto back and forth, its blade gleaming in the starlight.

Suddenly he lunged forward, the knife flashing toward Ben in a sweeping arc.

Ben leaned back just enough so the knife missed him by inches, and slashed horizontally with his own blade. The K-Bar slashed through muscles and tendons of El

Farrar's right arm, opening a deep gash and causing him to drop his knife.

He grabbed his arm and doubled over, groaning in pain.

"Pick it up," Ben growled. "I'm not through with you yet."

Tucking his right arm tight against his side, El Farrar bent and retrieved his knife.

He bared his teeth in a savage grimace and lunged at Ben once again, slashing back and forth with his knife held in front of him.

Ben leaned to the side, kicked sideways with his combat boot, and caught El Farrar in the right knee, caving it in and snapping the cartilage in two.

El Farrar went down on one knee, hissing between his teeth at the searing pain in his leg. He held the knife out before him. "I give up, Raines. You are too much for me."

Ben shook his head. "Like I said, El Farrar, a coward to the end."

As Ben moved to take the knife, El Farrar jumped to his feet and stabbed overhand at Ben's chest.

Ben blocked the movement with his left arm and swung upward with his right hand, burying the K-Bar to its hilt in El Farrar's abdomen.

El Farrar grunted and sagged, all of his weight on Ben's knife hand. With a grunt of effort, Ben jerked the knife upward, severing all of El Farrar's abdominal muscles and slicing up to his rib cage.

El Farrar opened his mouth in a gasp of pain and fell against Ben, who whispered in his ear, "I'm going to leave your body here, El Farrar, to be buried in a pauper's grave, unknown to your family and followers."

El Farrar's eyes stared up at Ben, full of hatred and fear, until the pupils finally dilated in the long stare of eternity.

FORTY-THREE

Ben decided to take the wounded Muhammad Atwa back to Kuwait City with him and his troops in hopes the man might have some useful information about El Farrar's organization.

After his surgery to remove the bullet from his right lung, Ben visited him in the hospital ward where he was being held under tight security.

"Hello, sir," Ben said, standing next to the bed. "My name is Ben Raines."

"Ah," Atwa said, "the leader of the Great Satan's troops in person."

Ben smiled. "And what is your name?"

"Muhammad Atwa."

"You know why I'm here, Mr. Atwa?" Ben asked.

Atwa sighed. "I suppose you want me to give you information about Abdullah El Farrar." He hesitated. "He is dead, is he not?"

Ben nodded.

"I thought so," Atwa said. He glanced at a nurse standing in the corner, and then lowered his voice to a whisper. "I don't suppose you could arrange for some cigars, or a bottle of scotch whiskey, could you?"

Ben laughed. "I'm afraid the cigars are out of the question. You've just had a significant portion of your right lung removed."

When Atwa's face fell, Ben leaned down and also whispered, "But I think a small bottle of scotch could be arranged."

Atwa smiled. "You are a scholar and a gentleman, sir."

Ben looked puzzled. "Mr. Atwa, you seem to be an educated man, and since you asked for whiskey and tobacco, you aren't exactly a Muslim fundamentalist. Why on earth did you elect to follow and work with a man such as El Farrar?"

Atwa turned his head to stare out of the window. "You probably won't believe this, but it was to help my people."

"Oh?"

He turned back to look into Ben's eyes. "The people in my region in, Pakistan live in the most dreadful poverty, without even the most basic of human needs; there is little food and even less potable water. I thought that if El Farrar succeeded, perhaps some of the money and power he achieved would be used to better the lives of our people back home."

Ben thought for a moment. "Mr. Atwa, where did El Farrar obtain the plutonium he used to blackmail the entire world by threatening its oil supply?"

"That was my doing, I'm afraid," Atwa answered. "I traveled to the United States and asked President Osterman for it."

Ben wasn't all that surprised. "And what was President Osterman to get for giving you the plutonium?"

Atwa smiled. "Actually, she was to get nothing, according to El Farrar, but she thought she would get a larger supply of oil than she presently is allowed."

"I see," Ben said. "Mr. Atwa, did you know that El

Farrar had in his possession a suitcase with over five million dollars in it?"

"No, but I suspected as much. El Farrar was not above lining his own pockets at the expense of his people."

"And you were not a partner in this theft of funds meant to be used to help the Middle East's poorer peoples?"

Atwa looked offended. "Of course not."

"Could much good be done with five million dollars in your country?" Ben asked.

"An enormous amount of good, sir."

"Then, I'm going to take a chance on you, Mr. Atwa. As soon as you've recovered from your wounds, I'm going to see to it that you are released and sent back to Pakistan, with the five million dollars in El Farrar's suitcase."

Atwa looked astounded.

"But," Ben added, pointing his finger at him, "I will be checking up on you to see that you spend the money wisely, to help your people. If you don't, you will wake up one night and I will be at your bedside, and it won't be a happy reunion."

Atwa's face sobered. He stuck out his hand. "Thank you, sir, I will not disappoint you."

Two weeks later, Ben Raines got on a long-range transport helicopter and flew north. Harley Reno, Jackie Malone, Coop, and Jersey, who had refused to be left behind, accompanied him.

President Claire Osterman finished her dinner, which she'd had served in her quarters, and looked across the table at her personal bodyguard, Herb Knoff. "I hope you didn't eat too much, Herb," she said, her eyes bright and shining.

"Oh?" he asked. "Why?"

"I've heard it's not good to exert yourself too much after a heavy meal."

He smiled. "And am I going to be exerting myself tonight?"

She stood up and began unbuttoning her blouse. "I certainly hope so."

Two hours later, they were sound asleep, both exhausted after some vigorous post-dinner activities.

Claire blinked and opened her eyes. Something had awakened her from a deep sleep. As her eyes became accustomed to the darkness, she saw a dark shape leaning over her and felt a sudden stinging in her left ear.

"Ouch!" she exclaimed, sitting up abruptly in bed. "Goddamnit, that hurt."

"What'd you say, dear?" Herb asked sleepily from next to her in the bed.

Suddenly, the lights came on and Claire saw a group of men and women standing around her bed. They were dressed all in black and had black greasepaint on their faces.

She punched Herb in the shoulder, waking him up. As he scooted up in bed and sat up, Claire said, "I'm really getting tired of waking up and having strange people in my bedroom."

Herb glanced at her, noticing blood was running out from between the fingers of her left hand, which was cupping her left ear.

"Claire," he said, "You've been hurt!"

She took her hand away and saw the blood on it, and then her eyes went to a female face next to her bed. She recognized Jackie Malone from their previous meeting when Jackie had cut a notch in her right ear.

"Shit! Not again?" Claire said.

Jackie nodded. "Yes, now your left ear matches your right, Madame President."

A male voice spoke from the other side of the bed. "Good evening, Claire."

Claire looked over at him. It was Ben Raines.

"Ben, you son of a bitch!" she almost yelled. "You'll pay for this!"

Herb cast his eyes toward the bedside table, where he kept a 9mm automatic pistol.

Ben held out a Beretta. "Are you looking for this, son?"

Herb relaxed back against the headboard.

"What are you doing here and why did you let that crazy woman assault me?" Claire asked in her most imperious voice.

Ben smiled. "Just a reminder, Sugar Babe," he said, using his pet nickname for Claire.

"A reminder?"

"Yes. A reminder that no matter where you are and no matter how tight your security is, I can get to you any time I want and do to you whatever I want."

"But why are you here?" Claire asked, sitting up in bed.

When she sat up, the sheets covering her fell to her lap, exposing her breasts.

Ben looked away. "Cover yourself, Claire," he said.

She jerked the sheets up under her neck and glared at him.

"To answer your question, I'm a little put out with you for giving a madman fifty pounds of plutonium."

Claire looked shocked. "I don't know what you . . ."

"Come off it, Claire," Ben said. "The man you gave it to has given us a full confession, which I've naturally forwarded on to the United Nations."

"But . . . but . . ."

Ben held up a finger. "This visit is just a little warning, Claire. People who play with fire often get their fingers burned."

"I don't know what you mean."

"Jean-François Chapelle has assured me that the next time the Oil Allocation Committee of the U.N. meets, they will almost certainly lower the amount of oil allocated to the United States." He grinned. "We'll leave it up to you to explain to the people who elected you just why that happened."

"You bastard!" she screamed, stretching out her hands toward him, her fingers curled into claws.

Jackie stepped forward, jammed a hypodermic needle into Claire's left shoulder, and then watched as Claire's eyes shut and she collapsed in the bed.

As Herb's face reddened and his muscles bunched for retaliation, Ben held up a hand. "Easy, son. It's just a tranquilizer to put her out long enough for us to get away."

Herb relaxed back against his pillows and held out his arm, an expression of resignation on his face while Jackie gave him the same shot.

In the helicopter headed back to SUSA headquarters in Louisiana, Jackie asked Ben, "Do you think she learned her lesson this time?"

Ben shook his head. "People like her never learn, Jackie. They just keep on making the same mistakes over and over again."

"Then, why didn't we just take her out permanently?"

"Because the people of the United States elected her, and people usually get the kind of leaders they deserve."

For a sneak preview of
William W. Johnstone's
new action adventure novel,
CODE NAME: QUICKSTRIKE,
coming in May 2003
from Pinnacle Books,

just turn the page . . .

ONE

Knoxville, TN:

It was half-time in the game between the University of Tennessee and Auburn University, and because both schools have orange as one of their school colors, the stadium was ablaze with the pumpkin hue. The bands had just left the field, and with the score tied at seventeen-all, 92,315 fans were waiting for play to resume.

Although Auburn is known as the "Tigers," for some reason lost in the mists of legend and lore, their loyal supporters often refer to their team as the "War Eagles." Therefore, when a U.S. Air force A-10 approached the field, an Auburn fan pointed to it and shouted the Auburn war cry.

"War Eagle!"

His cry was repeated by thousands of throats and they watched as the airplane banked, then made a low fly-by over the stadium. The Auburn fans stood and cheered. But the Tennessee fans, not willing to concede that the airplane was making a flyby in support of Auburn, stood and cheered as well. After all, this was a visual representation of the United States military, and the U.S. military was an all volunteer force. The Tennessee team is known as the "Volunteers," thus, the plane could just as easily be representing them.

The airplane pulled up at the end of its pass, then made a long, lazy, one-hundred-eighty-degree turn and started back. The cheering was loud and boisterous. In this time of war against terrorism, the fans of both Tennessee and Auburn were united by a spirit of patriotism, and they waved school pennants and national colors as the A-10 tilted down toward the stadium.

Suddenly a ring of fire appeared on the nose of the fighter-bomber. For just an instant the crowed thought it was some sort of salute. A portion of the crowd realized very soon, however, that it wasn't a salute, for explosive cannon shells and machine-gun bullets made of depleted uranium slammed into the stands at the Auburn end zone.

When the A-10 pulled up after its first pass, there were some in the crowd who were still cheering, not yet aware that the plane had just launched an attack against them. Turning sharply, the plane came back for a second pass, once again firing cannon and machine guns at the crowd. But by now word was spreading quickly throughout the stadium that this was a deadly attack. The crowd panicked and tried to get out of the way. The machine-gun bullets and cannon shells caused terrible carnage, but the panicked crowd did even more. Hundreds of spectators were crushed in the mad rush as the crowd stampeded toward the exits.

Although the airplane belonged to the U.S. Air Force, the pilot, Abdullah Afif Akil, was a lieutenant in the Sitrarkistan Air Force, in the U.S. as part of a military exchange program. No one on the ground yet knew this, but Akil didn't mind. Soon, the entire world would know of his martyrdom. "Allah Akbar," he said, as he continued his strafing runs, delivering a deadly cargo with grim efficiency. Finally, with the last round expended, the pilot turned away from the stadium.

Washington, D.C.

Andy Garrison, the assistant director of Homeland Security, was watching the Illinois-Ohio State game when suddenly the picture on the screen switched to the game in Tennessee.

"Come on," Garrison grumbled. "What's the use of paying for the sports package if I can't watch the game I want?"

Suddenly, on the screen, he saw explosions ripple through the stands. Confused, he leaned forward. "What is this, a movie?" he asked. But, even as he asked the question, he knew he wasn't watching a movie. There was something about the texture of the picture that told him what he was watching was real.

"We don't any more about this than you do, ladies and gentlemen," the sportscaster was saying in a breathless voice. "You are seeing it happen, just as we are. What? What?" the sportscaster asked, just off mike, though loudly enough for his question to be picked up. Then he cleared his throat. "All right, I'm being told now that we have a nation wide feed. Ladies and gentlemen, this is Charley Keith. Normally I would be bringing you the play-by-play commentary of the Tennessee-Auburn football game but all that seems terribly insignificant now. To update those of you who are just tuning in, moments ago a United States Air Force plane began strafing Neyland Stadium. We don't know why, nor do we know yet, how many casualties have been sustained, but we can report that there are many injured, and probably killed. Wait a minute folks, we thought the plane had left, but here it comes again!"

Andy Garrison called his liaison in the FBI. "Peter, turn on the TV," he said.

"I'm watching it," Peter Simmons said.

"Has POTUS been informed?"

"The President of the United States has been informed," Peter answered.

"Are we doing anything?"

"The Air Force is scrambling fighter jets," Peter replied. Thought that's a little like shutting the barn door after the horse is gone."

"Yes, well, we can't undo what has been done. But maybe we can shoot this bastard down, whoever the hell he is," Andy said.

"Wait, are you watching this? He's coming back," Peter said in alarm.

On screen, the A-10 was heading straight for the camera.

"He doesn't seem to be shooting this time," Charley Keith, the sports-caster was saying. "Hopefully, he's run out of ammunition."

"Charley, he's coming straight for us," the color commentator said.

"Bobby's right, folks," Charley said. "He's coming right at us. We should be able to get a really good look this time."

"My God, Charley! He's not turning away!" Bobby shouted.

On screen the airplane got bigger and bigger until it filled the screen. Then there was nothing but a few lines across the screen, followed by snow, then black. Almost instantly thereafter, the picture returned to the studio where, normally, a sports news reporter would be updating the nation on the latest scores of all college games in progress. But now the reporter was sitting behind the familiar curved desk in front of a large board filled with team names and scores, holding his finger to his earpiece. He nodded, then looked at the camera. As the camera moved in, the patina of sweat that covered his face was clearly visible. He licked his lips.

"Uh, ladies and gentlemen there has obviously been some sort of major malfunction in our feed from Knoxville. We'll get that taken care of as quickly as we can. In the meantime, we're," he halted in mid-sentence, obviously listening to instructions in his earphone, then he nodded. "Yes, we're going to our news central desk."

Langley AFB, Virginia:

As the F-15 Colonel Bob Jackson was flying, roared into the sky on twin pillars of fire, he felt his weight increase many times by the effects of acceleration. Working hard to overcome the G forces, Jackson lifted his hand to the radio-control panel and changed frequencies from tower to command.

"Charley-Charley, this is Gunslinger One with flight of two, requesting a vector and clearance."

Because of the readiness plan that had been put into effect after the terrorist attacks of September 11th, 2001, there were jet fighters on standby at various bases all across the country. This Saturday afternoon Colonel Jackson and his wingman, Captain Hugh Taylor had drawn the alert duty, and it was they who were scrambled in response to the attack in Knoxville.

"Gunslinger One, take a heading of two-six-zero. You are cleared at any altitude, proceed at maximum possible speed. Squawk your parrot and scramble, please, sir."

"Roger, squawking," Colonel Jackson replied. He "squawked his parrot" by pushing a button on his IFF that would emit a coded signal, thus identifying him as friendly. He also turned a switch on his radio that would make it impossible for anyone listening in to understand what was being said. "Scrambled," he reported.

The voice of Charley-Charley came over the headset once more.

"Gunslinger One, my authenticator is mad dog. I say again, my authenticator is mad dog. Respond, please."

"Sea Biscuit," Colonel Jackson replied, responding with the correct code to authorize the reception of top-secret information.

"You are cleared to engage."

"Roger," Jackson replied.

"Colonel, I can see smoke ahead," Captain Taylor said after several minutes.

"Light up the afterburner, Captain," Jackson replied. "If that son of a bitch is anywhere in the area, I don't intend to let him get away."

"Roger, lighting the burner."

The afterburners of both F-15s kicked in with a boom, increasing the speed so dramatically that, once again, the pilots could feel themselves bring pressed back into their seats. A three-minute burn took them to the site of the billowing smoke; then both aircraft throttled down as they orbited the stadium to check out the scene.

"Charley-Charley, this is Gunslinger One. We're on station," Colonel Jackson called.

"Your target is an A-10," Sector Control replied.

"Negative, there is no target," Jackson said as he banked sharply around the burning press box.

"Has the target departed the area?"

"I think he crashed into the press box."

"Please confirm."

"Roger."

Colonel Jackson and Captain Taylor made a very low fly-by to examine the press box. A large percentage of the crowd were still in the stands, and not understanding that the two fighters had been sent to help them, they dived under the seats to avoid them.

"Did you see anything definite, Captain?" Colonel Jackson asked, as they pulled up from their first pass.

"Negative."

"Give me a covering orbit. I'm going back for another look," Colonel Jackson said.

"I have you covered, sir."

Captain Taylor flew a wide orbit, high above the stadium, while Colonel Jackson dropped gear and flaps and made another low pass, this time coming down even below the top level of the bleachers. There were some in the crowd who thought he was actually going to land on the football field, but in truth, he had just made his airplane "dirty" so he could perform the very low, and very slow, fly-by.

Although the activities of the two F-15s were cause for concern and curiosity in the stands, there was no reaction at from the press box. That was because Charley Keith, Bobby Sawyer, and every other occupant of the press box lay dead in the twisted and burning wreckage.

"Book 'em!"
Legal Thrillers from Kensington

___Character Witness** by R.A. Forster $5.99US/$7.50CAN
   0-7860-0378-2

___Keeping Counsel** by R. A. Forster $5.99US/$6.99CAN
   0-8217-5281-2

___The Mentor** by R.A. Forster $5.99US/$7.50CAN
   0-7860-0488-6

___Presumption of Guilt** by Leila Kelly $5.99US/$7.50CAN
   0-7860-0584-X

Call toll free **1-888-345-BOOK** to order by phone or use this coupon to order by mail.
Name_____
Address_____
City_____ State_____ Zip_____
Please send me the books I have checked above.
I am enclosing $_____
Plus postage and handling* $_____
Sales tax (in New York and Tennessee only) $_____
Total amount enclosed $_____
*Add $2.50 for the first book and $.50 for each additional book.
Send check or money order (no cash or CODs) to:
Kensington Publishing Corp., 850 Third Avenue, New York, NY 10022
Prices and Numbers subject to change without notice.
All orders subject to availability.
Check out our website at **www.kensingtonbooks.com**